The Green
Glass Sea

The Green Glass Sea

ELLEN KLAGES

SCHOLASTIC INC.
New York Toronto London Auckland Sydney
Mexico City New Delhi Hong Kong Buenos Aires

The last chapter appeared in slightly different form as the short story "The Green Glass Sea" in the online magazine *Strange Horizons* (www.strangehorizons.com) in 2005.

Although this is a work of fiction, the historical events portrayed are quite real, as are the scientists and personnel of Los Alamos. The author has used history as a stage setting for fictitious characters, and any resemblance of those characters to actual people is unintentional.

ISBN-13: 978-0-545-03613-9
ISBN-10: 0-545-03613-5

12 11 10 9 8 7 6 5 4 3 2   7 8 9 10 11 12/0

Printed in the U.S.A.   40

First Scholastic printing, October 2007

Set in Sabon
Book design by Jim Hoover

To Jane Heller, for childhood talks
on the shelf and pearls in the creek.

To Delia Sherman, my writing sister, who
knows when it's time to send the Goon.

And to my dad, Jack Klages, who lived
through the war I've only read about.

The Green
Glass Sea

1943

November 15
TRAVELING

DEWEY KERRIGAN SITS on the concrete front steps of Mrs. Kovack's house in St. Louis, waiting for her father. He is in Chicago—war work—and she has not seen him since the Fourth of July. It's almost Thanksgiving now. She looks toward the corner every few seconds.

She is small for her age, thin and wiry, with dark, unruly hair and big front teeth that she has not quite grown into. Her eyes are large and gray-green behind a pair of steel-framed glasses. Her right foot is in a brown shoe that laces up one side, her left in an ordinary saddle shoe.

"Oh, for the love of Pete, will you just come inside?" says Mrs. Kovack. She has opened the front door and stands holding a red-striped dishtowel in one hand and a glass mixing bowl in the other. "You're going to catch your death out here."

Dewey sighs and looks longingly at the wide wooden porch of her Nana's house, next door, where she lived until last Friday. "I'm fine," she says. Mrs. Kovack's house smells like sour pickles and sick-sweet perfume, and she would rather be a little cold. But she doesn't say this, doesn't want to be rude to Mrs. Kovack, who has been doing her good Christian duty by taking Dewey in. Or so she tells Dewey, every chance she gets.

"Well suit yourself," Mrs. Kovack says with a little huff. Then, under her breath, as if Dewey can't hear her from five feet away, she adds, "No wonder poor old Mrs. Gallucci had a stroke, with sass from the likes of you." She closes the door with more force than necessary, to show Dewey that she does not approve. But Dewey already knows.

Dewey turns to make sure her suitcase is still there. No one else has been on the porch, but it is all she has. One brown suitcase and a Marshall Field's shopping bag. She moves the bag a fraction of an inch, so its corners line up square with the edge of the top step, and pulls her good wool coat tighter around her. She looks down Hollis Street, toward the newsstand on the corner, hoping for a glimpse of Papa's big green Studebaker.

Five minutes later a car turns the corner. Not a green Studebaker, just a black Ford. She expects it to drive by, but it pulls up at the curb in front of Nana's house. A woman in a green army uniform, a WAC, gets out, looks at a piece of paper in her hand, then up at the house number. She sees Dewey and strides quickly up the walk, tugging at her skirt to straighten it.

"Is this the Gallucci house?" she asks.

Dewey shakes her head. "Next door."

"Oh. Well, I'm looking for a Du—" She looks down at her paper again. "Miss Kerrigan?"

"I'm Dewey," Dewey says, and a little wave of fear makes her stomach flutter and then knot. Why would an army person be here, unless something has happened to Papa?

"Is Papa okay?" she asks in a voice that trembles, just a little.

"What? Oh, no, it's not that, honey." The WAC smiles. "He's fine. Just a little busy right now. The war, you know. So they sent me to pick you up. I'm Corporal Beckwith. Margaret." She smiles again. "Is that all your things?"

Dewey looks at her suitcase and nods.

"Okey-dokey, then. You go say good-bye to your grandmother while I put your gear in the trunk."

"Nana had to go to the Home," says Dewey quietly. "This is just the neighbor's house."

"Oh." Margaret seems startled by this news. "Oh. I'm sorry. Do you want to say good-bye to your neighbor then?"

"Not really," says Dewey. "But I guess I should." She turns and walks up to the front door, opening it a few inches. "Mrs. Kovack? I'm leaving now. Thank you for letting me stay here," she calls down the dim hallway.

There is silence, then a muffled response from the kitchen. Dewey waits for a moment, but when Mrs. Kovack does not appear, she closes the door quietly, and walks down the steps to the big black Ford.

Her suitcase is already in the trunk, and Margaret has come back for the shopping bag. She looks down into it in surprise. "What's all this?"

"Just my radio set and some experiments. And a few books."

Margaret pulls a stuffed yellow duck from the top of the bag and smiles. "And who's this?"

Dewey shrugs. "Einstein. He was a present from Papa, when I came from Boston on the bus to live with Nana. I was only seven then."

Margaret puts the bag in the trunk and closes it with a solid thunk. "How old are you now?" She walks around and opens the passenger door for Dewey.

"Eleven next month." Dewey gets in and presses her face to the window to look at Nana Gallucci's house one last time. Her coat still smells like Nana, like face powder and cocoa. She wonders how long that will last. "Goodbye, Nana," she whispers to the vacant house.

Margaret pulls the car out and they drive away.

"What time will we get to Chicago?" Dewey asks after about a mile. It is already the middle of the afternoon, and that's a long, long drive. She wonders if she will have to nap in the car, if Papa will be awake when they arrive.

Margaret frowns. She turns, still watching the road, and talks in Dewey's direction. "No one's told you?"

"Told me what?" Dewey feels the fear creep back into her stomach like a trickle of ice water.

"Well, there's been a little change in plans," Margaret says slowly. "Your father's not *in* Chicago anymore. He's working out west."

"Out west where?"

"Somewhere in New Mexico. I don't know any more, actually. It's top secret. My clearance is only high enough to pick you up and drop you off."

"War stuff?"

"Exactly. Your father must be pretty important, to have the army send an escort for you."

"I guess so," Dewey says. She doesn't like this. Everything is changing, and it is all changing too fast. She takes a deep breath. "If you don't know where Papa is, how are you going to drive me there?"

"I'm not, honey. My orders are to get you to Union Station in time to catch the four o'clock Chief. Your ticket's in my pocket."

Dewey says nothing. She feels like a package that is being delivered. Her excitement about seeing Papa again has gone away and in its place is a growing dread of what will happen next. She does not like surprises, and there have been too many this week. She sits and looks out the window, numbly watching the houses of St. Louis turn into businesses as they near downtown.

The train station is a huge stone structure that looks like a castle with a tower. Margaret pulls the car up in a line of twenty others. There are people everywhere, hundreds of them, all walking very fast in every direction. Most of them are men, and half of those are in uniform. Dewey stands on the curb and feels very small and alone.

"Well, here we are," says Margaret. She takes Dewey's things from the trunk and waves a finger in the air. A Negro man in a gray uniform hurries over. He tips the shiny black brim of his red cap.

"Yes, ma'am. Where to this afternoon?"

"Checking one bag through to Lamy, New Mexico," Margaret says. She hands the man a white envelope. "This is her ticket, and three meal vouchers. Will you see to it that the porter keeps an eye out for her?"

Dewey feels even more like a package.

"I will surely do that," the man says, smiling. He squats down so that he is at Dewey's eye level. "If I'm gonna introduce you, I better do it proper. What's your name, little miss?"

"Dewey," says Dewey.

"Ain't that a pretty name. Now, lemme see. The train for Lamy leaves from Track Seventeen in 'bout half an hour. I'll take you and your valise there directly." He stands up again. "Is you ready?"

I'm not ready for any of this, thinks Dewey, but she says nothing out loud.

Margaret hands the man a dollar bill and looks down at Dewey. "The porter will take good care of you. I'm sure your parents will be waiting in Lamy tomorrow afternoon." She pats Dewey on the shoulder. "Have a good trip."

"Well, well, well," says the man, picking up her suitcase and the shopping bag. "All the way to New Mexico, all by yourself? You off on an adventure."

"I guess so," says Dewey. But she is not very sure at all.

The train is long, shiny, and silver. There are so many people, all taller than Dewey, and the only thing she can see is the back of the man in the red cap. The air is filled with the sounds of shouting and talking, of machines and engines roaring, of the metal wheels of trains and luggage carts rolling over rails and cement. If the redcap disappeared right now, Dewey thinks, she would be as lost as if she were in a dark forest.

"Here we is," says the redcap. He hands her ticket to an older man in a fancier uniform, blue with brass buttons. He is also a Negro. All the passengers are white. "Eddie, this here is Miss Dewey. She's gonna be ridin' with you all the way out to *New* Mexico." He tips his cap to Dewey and walks away with her suitcase.

"You want me to take that bag, miss?" says the new man, Eddie.

"Am I allowed to keep it with me?"

"Sure thing. There's a rack you can put it up on. I'll just show you where your seat is."

He helps Dewey up the steep metal steps and into the train car. A narrow aisle separates two pairs of gray fabric seats, each with a wide white napkin across its back. A dozen people are scattered through the car, most of them men reading newspapers. Dewey's seat is at the far end, next to the glass-and-metal doors that open with a hiss.

"Nobody's next to you, least not until morning. You 'bout as small as a bug in a rug, so you can stretch out and have a nice sleep," says Eddie.

"Sleep?" In all the confusion, it hasn't occurred to Dewey that the train will involve bedtime. She has never slept without a bed, or in the middle of a whole room full of strangers. It doesn't feel safe.

"Yes, miss. Right after we leaves Kansas City, I'll come by with a pillow and a blanket for you, make this seat up into a nice comfy bed. Then it's lights out and off to dreamland for everybody. Scoot right in here, make yourself to home."

Dewey climbs into the seat. The fabric is scratchy on the backs of her bare legs, under her plaid dress. Her feet do not reach the floor, not by many, many inches.

"We pull out at four o'clock sharp," Eddie says, putting her shopping bag on the empty seat next to her. "Dinner service starts at six. You want me to come take you down to the dining car?"

"Okay," says Dewey softly. "Is there anything about the train I can read?" She will feel better if she knows some things without having to ask.

Eddie furrows his brow and thinks. "Best I can do is a timetable. It tells where we're goin', when we get there, and a few other things besides."

Dewey nods. Eddie tips his cap and is three steps away when she remembers something very important. "Mister?" she says, and he turns and leans over her seat.

"Yes, miss?"

In a voice that is just barely above a whisper, Dewey asks, "Is there a bathroom?"

"Why, yes, miss. Up by the front there, where we came in. Commode and a sink."

"Thanks. I can—" Dewey stops in mid-sentence in a small panic. "I don't have a toothbrush."

"Didn't nobody pack one for you?"

"Nobody packed me except me," Dewey says. "I have

a toothbrush in my suitcase, to take to Chicago, but now I'm not going there because the war moved my papa again." She *always* brushes her teeth before bedtime. Now there is no order, no routine, nothing familiar at all.

Eddie makes a clucking sound with his tongue. "That's a shame," he says. "This war shakin' up families all over. I see it every day." He smiles down at Dewey. "But least I can find you a toothbrush. You just sit tight." He tips his cap again, then hurries to help a woman with two large hat boxes.

When the train pulls out of the station, the car is about half full. Dewey can't see any faces, just hair and hats over the seat tops. She watches out the window as the backs of downtown buildings roll past, dirty brick and stone with ashcans and piles of wooden crates stacked up on loading docks.

When the buildings turn into farmland, she takes a book out of her bag and begins to read. It is called *The Boy Mechanic*, and she is reading a chapter about building radios. Her fingers itch with the urge to have all the parts in front of her, to pick them up and put them together the way the book shows. They're in her bag, but there is no place to spread them out, except on the seat next to her, and she is afraid the tiny pieces will get lost. Instead she reads about *how* they will work, and soon she is absorbed in the world of facts and diagrams, a world with very few surprises.

At 6:00, Eddie comes back. He hands her a timetable and a red plastic toothbrush, still wrapped in crinkly cellophane. "You ready for some supper?" he asks. Dewey nods, her stomach growling. The cheese sandwich Mrs. Kovack made her for lunch seems like it was years ago, in another life.

The dining car is very fancy, with real silverware and white tablecloths. It is noisy with people laughing and talking, the clatter of knives and forks, and the tinkling sound of ice cubes in glasses. The table is too tall, but the waiter brings her a thick cushion to sit on. She orders the pork chop. At home, Nana mostly made red-sauce spaghetti, because their meat ration coupons only allowed for chicken on Sunday. The waiter brings her a basket of hot rolls and a Shirley Temple cocktail, pink and bubbly with ginger ale and lots of cherries.

She is sorry that she didn't bring her book, because she's bored eating all alone. She reads the timetable, twice. At least it is words. The pork chop is very big, and she can only eat half. But the waiter brings her a chocolate sundae anyway, with nuts and a cherry. It has been a long time since anyone has given her a treat, and she lingers over it, smiling down to the last spoonful.

When she is through, the clock says 7:00, too early to

go to sleep. Dewey is tired of just sitting. She decides to explore, just a little.

It is strange to walk through rooms that are moving. The train sways and rolls from side to side, and she has to concentrate to keep her balance. In between cars, the noise of the wheels and the wind is much louder. The first two cars look like her own, with different people. Not very interesting. If the next car is just more people, she will go back to her seat and read.

But the next car *is* different. A sign on the door says OBSERVATION CAR. Maybe she will be able to see the stars. She opens the door and walks into a long, smoke-filled room. Twenty or thirty people, men and some women, are sitting in armchairs around the edge of the car, not in rows and aisles. They are smoking cigarettes and drinking cocktails and talking very loud. In the middle of the car, a fat man with a yellow tie suddenly bursts into laughter and slaps his pin-striped thigh.

Dewey stands near the doorway, pressed against the wall where she won't be in the way. Round tables with ashtrays in their centers are scattered among the chairs, their shiny chrome surfaces covered with glasses and packs of Camel cigarettes and the bull's-eyes of Lucky Strikes. Large windows line both sides of the car. It is dark outside, so all she can see are the reflections of the talking people. The end of the car is a curve of windows from floor to ceiling. Dewey wants to go and look out, but it is too crowded.

She turns to leave just as the fat man gets up. He has been sitting next to a radio, a big wooden cabinet radio with black knobs and a glowing yellow dial. Dance music is coming out of it, which means that it works, even on a moving train.

Dewey smiles. Maybe she will come back and try out her own radio in the morning, when it is too early for cocktails. It is almost finished, and she has been wanting to test it for a week, but Mrs. Kovack didn't approve of girls building things and was always watching. The timetable says the train will stop at a place called La Junta at 6:50. She isn't sure where that is, even what state, but if it has a train station, it might have a radio station too.

Dewey whistles softly under her breath as she walks to her car. She feels better having a plan.

Back in her own seat, she reads the timetable again to make sure about La Junta, then returns to her book. When they pull into Kansas City, at 9:30, it is snowing. A gust of cold air blows through the car when the doors open. She watches the flakes fall through the cones of yellow light cast by the lampposts of the station.

The train stays in this station for an hour, so Dewey brushes her teeth in the little steel sink in the bathroom and gets ready for bed. She takes off her shoes, leaving her socks on, in case her feet get cold in the night, and hopes her dress will not be too wrinkled in the morning. She doesn't want Papa to think that she is sloppy. He will probably understand because of the train and the war.

When she returns, Eddie has tipped both seats back into reclining positions, and laid out a bed with a white pillow and two cream-colored blankets that say SANTA FE on them in red letters. The blankets are a little scratchy, but warm. Dewey takes her glasses off and tucks them inside her saddle shoe, sliding it under the seat. The train pulls out of the station, and five minutes later all the lights go out, except a line of dim blue bulbs near the floor.

In the darkness, Dewey reaches down and pulls Einstein from her shopping bag, uncovering a packet of letters from Papa. She strokes one envelope with a fingertip, then cuddles the soft yellow duck tightly under one arm and burrows under the blankets. The wheels of the train make a steady, soothing chukka-chukka-chukka sound and soon she is fast asleep, rolling west across the dark prairie.

The sound of a man's loud snoring wakes Dewey up. She lifts the corner of the window shade. It is not quite morning, but light enough to see shapes outside—low hills and a few scattered trees. She puts on her glasses and lopes to the bathroom in her bare feet. Men are sleeping sitting up, their ties loosened, their hats tilted down over their faces. A few are awake, rubbing their eyes and grumbling in their blankets, but the car is quiet.

Dewey doesn't know how long people are allowed to sleep on a train, if there will be a bell to start the day, like school. Now is a good time to go to the observation car to test her radio, if she wants any time alone. She puts on her shoes and then, as quietly as she can, picks up her shopping bag by its twisted paper handles. The bag crinkles and she freezes, holding her breath for a minute, then walks very cautiously, heel-to-toe, out of the car of sleeping people, holding the bag out from her body so it will not make noise. She is used to being quiet in the morning because Nana is always cranky until she's had her coffee.

The observation car is completely empty. Dewey smiles and opens the blue curtains covering the long windows at the end. They are traveling west, so the back of the train faces east, where they have been. The tracks seem to emerge in two unending lines from underneath the train. The sun is just peeking over the horizon, and the light in the car is reddish gold. Everything is quiet and still, except for the sound of the train wheels, which she is getting used to.

She sits on the carpeted floor of the car, between a half circle of armchairs and the windows, and carefully arranges the pieces of her radio around her. The chrome tables are big enough for cocktails, but not for setting up an experiment. She opens *The Boy Mechanic* and weights the book flat with the edge of the bag so that she can read with both hands free.

The radio is inside a wooden cigar box so its delicate parts won't get wrecked inside the shopping bag. She lifts it out and sets its wooden base, the lid from another cigar box, flat on the carpet. A round blue paper Morton's Salt container, wrapped around and around and around with copper wire, is screwed onto the base. The wire is wrapped so tight and close together that it looks like the bottom of the cylinder has been corrugated with melted pennies.

Wires dangle from the top and bottom of the cylinder, and bolts and screws dot its wooden base. A metal arm, canted out from a slender post like a tiny fishing pole, ends in a minuscule whisker of wire suspended over a lump of a dark gray mineral.

Dewey stares at the diagram in the book, then winds the bottom end of the copper wire tightly around the bolt holding the metal arm. She looks back and forth between the book and the radio on the floor and tests a few connections with her fingers. Then she pulls a single black Bakelite earphone out of her bag and winds the last inch of bare wire from its brown fabric-wrapped cord around another bolt.

She holds the earphone up to one ear and listens. Nothing. She peers intently at the picture in the book, then back at the radio. It *looks* right. She wishes she knew what time it was, how close they are to La Junta. She looks out the window. The landscape shows no sign of civilization, just flat brown plains with mountains in the near distance. She sighs, loudly.

"Oh!" says a voice from behind her. "Sorry. I thought I had the place all to myself. I didn't see you down there."

Startled, Dewey drops the earphone, and turns around.

Sitting in one of the armchairs along the wall is a slender young man in brown pants and a very wrinkled white shirt. He is reading a copy of *LIFE* magazine with a general on the cover. A lock of curly dark hair hangs over one eye. He is smiling, a kind of silly grin, and needs a shave. He stands up and looks over the chairs to see what Dewey is doing.

"Ah, *The Boy Mechanic*," he says. "One of my favorite books. A little dry, but very instructive. I built my first radio from it, except I used an oatmeal box. Can I take a look?"

Dewey nods, and the man moves one of the chairs out of the semicircle and steps carefully into the make-shift laboratory that Dewey has created on the carpet. He squats back on his heels and examines the radio.

"Nice work," he says after a minute. "That's a beautifully wrapped inductor coil."

"Thank you," says Dewey. She feels pleased by the compliment, because he knows what he's talking about, even if he looks like a bum. "Except it doesn't work."

The man looks at the radio again, and snaps his fingers. "Ah! I see your problem. You haven't hooked the coil up to the aerial wire."

"So I'm not getting any signal," Dewey says slowly. "Or any power."

"None at all." He looks out at the desolate landscape. "No guarantee there's anything out there to get, but we can try. Do you have more hookup wire?"

Dewey reaches into a crumpled brown paper bag and pulls out a metal reel of thin, cotton-covered wire. She hands it to him.

"Perfect. We'll need about twenty feet." He takes out his pocketknife, unrolls a length of wire, cuts it, and hands the reel back to Dewey. "Do you know how to strip the ends?"

"Yes."

"Great. Here." He turns the knife around in his hand and gives it to her, handle first.

Dewey scrapes the black cotton off each end, leaving an inch of bare silver wire. "It wraps around here, right?" she says, pointing to the dangling bit of copper wire at the top of the coil.

The man nods, and she wraps the silver and copper wires together like two tightly entwined snakes.

"Excellent," he says. He looks around. "Now, if we were in a house, our best bet would be to run the aerial out a second-story window. But I don't think these open." He taps on the glass. "Still, reception is better through window glass than metal train sides." He stands up and pushes the loose end of the long wire through a curtain loop. The silver metal rests against the glass a few inches from the ceiling of the car.

"Give it another listen."

Dewey holds the earphone up to her head. "I hear static!" she says excitedly.

"Good. Something's working." He looks down at the radio. "You don't have a slider on this one, so you can't really tune it. But try moving the cat whisker around on the crystal, see if you can pick up anything else."

Dewey extends a finger and gently moves the little fishing pole around, a tiny fraction of an inch at a time. After a few minutes, she shakes her head. "Just fuzz," she says. She looks out the window again. "Do you know if there's a radio station in La Junta?" She pronounces the hard J.

He smiles. "La *Hoon*-tah. It's Spanish. But no, I don't know for sure." He looks at his watch. "We're only ten minutes out from the station. You'd think if they were broadcasting we'd pick *some*thing up. Maybe it's just too early."

"Maybe," Dewey says slowly, thinking. "I know how we can find out."

"How?"

She points to the cabinet radio in the center of the car. "*That* one has a tuner. If we can find a station, then we know there's a signal. And we'll know what to listen for."

"Brilliant," says the man. "Let's do it."

"Are we allowed to turn it on?"

"I see no signs or armed guards."

They grin at each other like co-conspirators and approach the big radio. He turns a large black knob and the set begins to hum. The yellow dial in the center glows faintly, then brighter as the tubes warm up.

"Start at the high end and work down," he says. He slouches into the chair next to the radio and cocks his head, listening.

Dewey turns the dial. The cloth-covered speaker of the big radio pops and hisses with static, and once they hear a faint hint of what might be voices, but they won't come in any better than a faraway whisper. She gets all the way to the other end of the dial without finding a clear station.

"Nothing out there," she says, turning off the radio with a sigh. "I'll have to test mine some other time. Thanks for helping me."

"Sure thing. Let me unhook you." He gets up and removes the long wire from the curtain, wrapping it in a neat coil around his fist before handing it to Dewey. She tucks it between the salt canister and some bolts, then puts the radio back into the cigar box as the train begins to slow down.

"La Junta, Colorado, right on schedule. It's six forty-nine, Mountain War Time," the man says, looking at his watch again. "I'd guess you'd better scoot on back. Your folks are probably up and ready for breakfast by now."

"I don't have any folks," says Dewey. "Not on the train." She closes *The Boy Mechanic* and slips it sideways into the shopping bag.

"You're by yourself?" The man sounds surprised. "How far are you going?"

Dewey puts the wire back in the paper sack. "The next station. Lamy, New Mexico."

"Really?" The man smiles. "Me too. Is that where you're from?"

"No, my papa just moved someplace around there. I don't know where yet."

"What kind of work does he do?"

"He used to teach math at Harvard, before the war. Now he's doing some kind of secret stuff. I don't know exactly what." Dewey shakes her head.

"Well, well, well," says the man. "I did my undergrad work in Cambridge, at MIT. Small world. What's your dad's name?"

"Jimmy Kerrigan." Dewey looks up and is puzzled to see that the man is grinning as if he just won a prize. "What?" she asks.

"I know Jimmy. I met him at a party last month. We got to talking about codes and puzzles, and he gave me a dandy." He puts out his hand. "Looks like you and I are going to be neighbors at a place we call 'the Hill.' I'm Dick Feynman."

"I'm Dewey," says Dewey, shaking it. "Dewey Kerrigan. Where is the Hill?"

"Up in the mountains a bit." Dick waves his hand at the landscape beyond the window. "You'll see in a few hours. But hey, now that we're properly introduced, do you want to have breakfast with me? I'm dying for a cup of coffee."

"Will there be pancakes?" Dewey loves pancakes with syrup. Nana mostly made her oatmeal.

"They were on the menu last time I took the Chief."

Dewey looks around to make sure that there aren't any radio pieces left on the carpet and thinks about breakfast. Nana said never to eat food from strangers. But since yesterday there have been nothing *but* strangers. And Dick has introduced himself, and knows Papa, so it is probably fine. She hopes so, because she would like to talk more about radios.

"Okay," she says. They walk back through the train,

toward the dining car. "So what do you do? Do you teach math too?" she asks when he pauses to open the door between two cars.

Dick looks around, then shakes his head. "No. Physics," he says in a low voice. There is no one else around. "But I can't talk about what I'm doing now, either."

"It's secret, right?" she sighs. She is tired of the war. Everything interesting is a secret.

"Yeah, 'fraid so," he says. "It has to be." He opens the door and motions her to go through.

Dewey nods silently and wonders just what Papa has gotten himself into.

After breakfast, she goes back to the observation car, but it's crowded again, so she returns to her seat, back in its daytime position. There is not much to see out the window, but she pretends that it's the scrubby bushes that are moving, moving backward, and that's interesting to watch. For a while. Then she gets *The Boy Mechanic* out of her bag.

Dick said that she should read another section about making a radio do more things. Some of it she doesn't quite understand. She is glad when Eddie comes and gets her at lunchtime. She has grilled cheese in the dining car and reads while she eats. The chapter makes a little more sense the second time, but she hopes she will see Dick again to ask him some questions.

The train pulls into Lamy one minute after 2:00 in the afternoon. Eddie brings Dewey and her bags to the front of the station, a little one-room building. No green Studebaker. She sits on a wooden bench and pulls her good coat around her. It is cold, even colder than in St. Louis. There are only a few straggly trees, and not much of a town: a diner with a buzzing neon sign, a few houses that need paint and repairs. Dewey is amazed to see a goat wandering down the middle of the dusty street. It stops and nibbles at something she can't see. She does not want to live here.

Dick comes out of the station carrying a brown duffel bag and his *LIFE* magazine. "Hey," he says. He looks around. "Your dad's not here yet? Want me to wait with you until he comes?"

"You don't have to," says Dewey in a small voice, but she doesn't really mean it. Half a dozen other people are hugging and carrying luggage off to cars, and she can feel her heart racing with the thought that Papa will not come.

"My pleasure," Dick says. He drops his bag and leans against the wall of the station. "I've got a little time."

They wait for what seems like forever to Dewey. She asks him some radio questions, and he is in the middle of a very interesting answer about antennas when a black car pulls up. A sandy-haired man in an army uniform gets out. He looks at Dewey, then at Dick, and wrinkles his forehead in confusion.

"Afternoon, Mr. Feynman. You're not on my list today."

"I borrowed a car this time," says Dick. "I'm just keeping this young lady company."

"Kerrigan?" asks the soldier.

Dewey nods.

"I'm your ride, ma'am. I'll take your things to the car."

Dewey is relieved that someone has finally come to get her, and disappointed, again, that it is not Papa.

Dick looks at her and says, "It's okay. That's Sergeant Prager's job. The army's answer to the Fresh Air Taxi Company."

"I could just ride with you," Dewey suggests. Dick is much better than another stranger, and she wants to hear more about antennas.

"Sorry, not this time. You need to go to Santa Fe and get a pass from Dorothy first. But I'll see you up on the Hill. We can talk more then." He pats Dewey on the shoulder, then salutes the soldier with two fingers and walks over to a battered beige Chevy.

"Ma'am?" says the soldier.

"Okay," Dewey says with a sigh.

The car jumps and jolts over the uneven pavement for almost an hour. Sgt. Prager doesn't say much, which is fine with Dewey. She does not feel like talking. She is more tired than she can ever remember being. Not sleepy, but weary. Tired of strangers and "ma'am" and being in the same clothes. Tired of having no idea where she is or where she's going.

She expects Santa Fe to look like St. Louis. A city. It is the state capital of New Mexico, and she expects trees and tall brick-and-stone offices and a highway. But it is just a village, with low, beige buildings, shrubs and cactuses, and narrow, cobblestoned streets. Most of the buildings have rounded corners with logs sticking out of the sides, like Abe Lincoln's cabin.

"I've got your bags, ma'am," Sgt. Prager says after he parks. "You just follow me."

He leads her through an archway and into a sunny plaza, a city block–size square of winter-dead grass surrounded by buildings that look like they have grown right up out of the muddy ground. In one corner, though, there is a Woolworth's, and Dewey smiles at its familiar red-and-gold sign. They turn down a small alley and through a wrought-iron gate into a courtyard dominated by a large, leafless tree.

"Where are we?" asks Dewey.

"109 East Palace Avenue, ma'am." He opens a door

marked U.S. ARMY CORPS OF ENGINEERS, and gestures for Dewey to go in.

It does not look like an official army place. Boxes and crates and paper shopping bags are piled everywhere around two desks and a few wooden chairs, kitchen-looking chairs, painted yellow and blue. A middle-aged woman stands behind one of the desks, talking on the phone. She is not in uniform, just a sweater and a tweed skirt. Her face is round, with rosy cheeks, and her eyes crinkle with a smile when she looks up and sees Dewey. She holds up one finger; she'll be just a minute.

A small white dog is sleeping next to a stone fireplace. Dewey doesn't think it looks much like an army *dog*, either.

Behind her, Sgt. Prager clears his throat. The woman on the phone waves her hand at him, dismissing him.

"Sit, sit," mouths the woman, motioning to a chair by the fire.

Dewey sits. It is warm, and the smoke smells like pine trees. She takes off her coat and wonders what a place like this has to do with the war.

"Sorry about the wait," says the woman after she hangs up the phone. "There are more and more people to get settled every day, it seems." She smiles and walks around the desk, holding out her hand. "I'm Dorothy McKibbin. Think of me as the welcoming committee. Everyone does."

Dewey shakes her hand. "I'm Dewey Kerrigan," she says. She is also getting very tired of introducing herself.

"Oh, good. I've been expecting you. Your father called a little while ago. He was just leaving, so I imagine it'll be another half an hour or so."

"He's really coming?" Dewey asks.

"Yes, why?" Mrs. McKibbin looks puzzled.

"He was supposed to come to St. Louis too," Dewey sighs. "But I had to take a train to New Mexico. And he wasn't at that station either. Just an army man."

"St. Louis! Gracious. You poor lamb. You must be exhausted, traveling all that way by yourself. Would you like a cup of hot cocoa?"

"Yes, please," says Dewey. "I'd like that very much."

"Good. I think I'll have a cup too. It's awfully chilly today." Mrs. McKibbin uncorks a large green metal thermos and pours steaming brown cocoa into two china mugs.

"Why don't you pull your chair up to the desk, so you've got someplace to put your cup," she says, putting one of the mugs down. "Don't worry about the wood. Nothing can hurt an army desk."

Dewey moves her chair over to the desk and inhales the chocolate steam.

"While we're waiting for it to cool, I can make out your pass and tell you some of the rules—there are a lot of rules, the army, you know." Mrs. McKibbin shakes her head, but Dewey is glad there are rules here. Rules are like the directions in *The Boy Mechanic*. You know what to expect.

"And I'll try to answer any questions you might have. Of course, your mother and father will be able to show you the ropes once you get settled, but—"

"Just Papa," says Dewey.

"Oh, your mother isn't here yet?"

"I don't know where she is. She left when I was a baby."

"Oh, dear. I am so sorry. I had no idea." Mrs. McKibbin bites her lip and clucks to herself under her breath.

"It's okay," Dewey says. "It was a long time ago. I don't really remember." There is an awkward silence. Dewey takes a sip of her cocoa. The milk skin sticks to her lip and she licks it off. "Will you tell me about the rules now?" she asks.

"Of course." Mrs. McKibbin looks down at the wood of her desk, as if there is something in the grain that will tell her what to say next, then looks back at Dewey and smiles. "Well, the main thing is that everything about your new home has to be a secret. Off the Hill, you can't tell anyone where you live, or who you live with, or what you see or hear. I know that sounds hard, but it's important," she says in a gentle voice.

Dewey nods. "*Every*thing is secret." She makes a

gesture that Nana used to do, running her thumb and forefinger across her lips as if she is zipping them shut. "Because of the war, right?"

"Yes. Your father and the other men are working to win the war. And we don't want anything to get in the way of that, do we?"

"No ma'am." Dewey pauses for a moment. "But what is he *doing*?"

Mrs. McKibbin shrugs. "I honestly don't know. And I don't need to. I just do my part. And, Dewey? That's one question I'm afraid you aren't allowed to ask anywhere, even up on the Hill. Okay?"

"Okay," says Dewey, even though she *really* wants to know.

"Good."

"What else am I not allowed to do?" The rules here sound very strict. Worse than Mrs. Kovack.

"It's not as bad as all that," says Mrs. McKibbin. "It's really a lovely place to live. And most of these rules only apply in the outside world, like not using anyone's title."

"What?" Dewey is confused.

"I'm sorry. That wasn't very clear, was it?" Mrs. McKibbin shakes her head. "Let's see. Even though your father has a Ph.D., I don't call him *Doctor* Kerrigan. Just Mister."

"How come?"

"Because if the people in Santa Fe notice that there

are an awful lot of doctors living up on the Hill, they might start to wonder."

"Like spies," says Dewey. "Loose lips sink ships."

"Ex-actly." Mrs. McKibbin beams at Dewey, a smile so warm and friendly that for the first time since she left Mrs. Kovack's house, Dewey starts to feel like everything might just turn out okay.

"Finish up your cocoa and I'll make out your pass." Mrs. McKibbin rummages in a drawer and comes up with a small printed rectangle of stiff paper. "Don't lose this," she says. "You can't get in—or out—of the project without one. You'll get a permanent one next week, with a photo, but this will get you through the gate today." She uncaps a fountain pen and begins to write.

"But I'll be with Papa, right?"

"Doesn't matter. *Every*one has their own pass. Think of it as a membership in a *very* exclusive club," she says, winking. "Now, can you spell your name for me, dear?"

"Does it have to be my whole name? That's kind of long. Everyone just calls me Dewey."

"For today, I'm sure Dewey is just fine. D-E-W-E-Y, like the admiral?"

Dewey nods.

"And you're what, seven, eight?"

"Ten," Dewey sighs. "I'm just little. I'll be eleven next month."

"Ten it is." She fills in the last blank, signs the bottom

of the card, and passes it across the desk.

Dewey starts to put it into her pocket, but she is wearing a dress, which is inconvenient. She tucks the card into the top of her right kneesock.

"I think that's about it," says Mrs. McKibbin. "We can just—" She stops in mid-sentence when the heavy outside door opens with a loud click, and a cold breeze ruffles the papers on her desk.

Dewey turns around. "Papa!" She jumps out of her chair and throws herself into his arms.

"Hey, Dews," Jimmy Kerrigan says, returning the hug with equal enthusiasm. He is a trim man in his middle thirties, with wavy dark hair and blue eyes behind tortoiseshell glasses. He is wearing a heavy blue turtleneck sweater over a pair of chinos, a gray felt hat tipped back on his head.

He closes the door with one foot and they stand in the warm, piñon-scented air and hug. He kisses the top of her head, then holds her at arm's length. "You've gone and grown again, haven't you?"

"A little," Dewey giggles.

"A lot. Half a centimeter, at least." He puts an arm around her shoulder, and she leans into him. He smells like cold wool and aftershave. "Thanks for taking care of her, Dorothy. I don't know what we'd do without you."

"We had a lovely time," says Mrs. McKibbin.

"You ready to go, Dews? You have your pass?"

Dewey nods into her father's arm. "I am *very* ready."

"Thought so." He gives her a squeeze and reaches down to get her bags.

Dewey and Papa walk out through the iron gate into the plaza. "I'm parked behind Woolworth's," he says. "Are you hungry? Do you want a Coke or something?"

"Not really. The lady gave me cocoa."

"Dorothy's aces. Her office is pretty much Grand Central when any of us are down in Santa Fe." They walk through a narrow passageway and out onto a side street where the green Studebaker is parked. Its wheels are caked with reddish mud, the bottoms of both doors splattered up several inches.

"Climb in. I'll put your things in the trunk." He stows the suitcase, then gets into the driver's side. She keeps the shopping bag.

"I'm sorry about Nana," he says as he pulls onto the highway heading north. "You've been really brave. I'm proud of you."

Dewey feels her whole body get warm as she flushes with pleasure. She looks over at him, studying his profile, not quite believing that he's actually here, sitting next to her. The tight little knot of faith that has been holding her together for the last twenty-four hours lets go, and a tear trickles down her cheek. "I missed you," she says.

"I know. I missed you too." He reaches over and squeezes her hand. "I wanted to come to St. Louis, take care of you. But I couldn't get away. There's just so much work." He looks over at her for a moment. "I'm so glad you're here."

"How long will we stay here?"

"Hard to say. A year, maybe two. I hope to god the war doesn't go on longer than that."

"Me too," says Dewey. She sits back in her seat, relaxed for the first time since she left Nana's house. She is with Papa, and they won't have to move again for a very long time. Until she's old. Until she's *twelve*. She watches the desert land go by the window, brown and foreign-looking, with distant mountains on either side of the road. It is a late autumn afternoon, and the fence posts cast long shadows as the sun drops in the west.

"How much farther is it?"

"Well, in about five miles we'll turn off the highway onto the Powakuh road, and it's a little more than half an hour from there. You can help me watch for the sign."

"Okay." Dewey is pleased to have something specific to do. She peers out the window intently until she sees a wooden sign that says POJOAQUE. "I see a sign," she says. "But it doesn't look like what you said. It says Po-jo—something."

He glances out the window and chuckles. "That's it. It's pronounced Po-*wah*-kuh. It's Spanish."

Dewey thinks about La Junta and shakes her head. "Spanish people spell funny."

"It takes some getting used to. I bet you'll pick it up pretty fast." He turns left onto a dirt road that makes the car bounce like it's driving over a washboard. But only for about a mile. Then the road turns muddy, thick slippery mud that makes the car skid and slide from side to side. Papa slows the car down until they are crawling along. In front of a cluster of small mud-colored houses with strings of bright red peppers hanging by their front doors, he gets out to wipe the slurry from the windshield with an old towel.

"Is it like this the whole way?" Dewey is beginning to wonder about what kind of place they are going to, at the end of a muddy, bumpy road. It isn't looking good.

"Used to be like this all the way up. Except steeper. No fun to drive. But the army engineers have just about finished paving the really tricky part. It'll be smoother once we cross the Rio Grande. The bridge isn't too much farther."

It takes them twenty minutes to get there, but then the road *is* smoother, with brand-new black asphalt, so new there are still yellow bulldozers parked off to the side. The road begins to wind and twist, looping around on itself in tight switchbacks, so that Dewey is looking down at where they were a minute before. It climbs very uphill very quickly, and her ears feel too tight, then make a popping sound and are fine.

Dewey stares out the window with her mouth open. She has never seen anything like this, not even in pictures. One side of the road drops off into a deep canyon scattered with scrubby dark bushes. The walls on the other side of the canyon look like a layer cake that some giant has cut cleanly with a knife. Sheer vertical cliffs are striped in horizontal bands of color, layer after layer of crumbly-looking rock, red and pink and brown, with the green valley below, and the distant mountains turning lavender in the twilight.

The farther they climb, the more the land seems to fall away below them, until Dewey feels as if the rest of the world, everything she has known before, has become a distant memory.

Ten minutes later, the road levels off again and she feels the car slow down. "Okay, we're here," says Papa.

Dewey turns from the window, from the rocks and the sky that seems to stretch forever. In front of the car is a long chain-link fence, topped with many strands of barbed wire. A small green wooden building stands to the left, with a large sign that says: DANGER! PELIGRO! KEEP OUT!

Three uniformed men, wearing battle helmets and holding rifles, surround the car.

"Passes?" says one of them, holding out his hand.

Papa hands over a laminated card with his picture on it. The man writes his name on a clipboard. "Ma'am?" he asks.

Dewey reaches into the top of her sock and pulls out the little card. She scoots over on the seat until she is sitting right next to Papa, his body between her and the men with guns and the danger signs and the barbed wire. What if they find something wrong with her pass and take her away, away from Papa again?

Her hand shakes as she gives the card to the guard. The man looks at it carefully, looks at her, then hands it back. He waves them through the gate.

They drive around a curving dirt road flanked with pine trees. "Welcome home, Dews," he says as they pass an open area with a lot of partly finished buildings. He puts one arm around her shoulders and kisses the top of her head. "Welcome to Los Alamos."

1944

August 25
JUMPING ROPE

TERRY GORDON SAT at the kitchen table staring at the cards in her hand. She took a puff of her cigarette, then discarded the seven of clubs. Her daughter Suze looked at it, shook her head and drew a card from the pile. A queen. She needed an eight. She made a face and tossed the queen onto the discard pile.

"Hah!" said her mother. "Gin!" She tossed her cards onto the table in groups of three and four and smiled triumphantly.

Suze laid her cards down with a sigh. So close. She'd only needed one card to go out herself. She counted up her unmatched cards. "Six, eleven, twenty," she said.

Her mother picked up the pencil and scribbled the total onto their score pad. "Okay, that gives me 25,658 to your—" She looked at the other column of numbers. "22,485." She glanced at the clock, then stubbed her

Chesterfield out in the glass ashtray. "That's it for today, sweetie," she said. "I've got to run. Remember to tell Daddy that I'll try and meet you in the Lodge for dinner."

She put her coffee cup in the sink, blew a kiss from her fingertips, opened the screen door, and ran lightly down the outside staircase that led from their second-floor apartment to the road below. Her moccasins made soft thuds on each riser, and then she was gone.

As usual.

Suze looked at the ivory plastic clock on the kitchen wall. Five minutes to one. She put her fingers in her ears and waited.

A few seconds later, at exactly 12:55, a shrill siren sounded its warning blast, signaling the end of lunch hour. Suze counted to ten, then took her fingers out of her ears. It would go off again in another five minutes, and by then her mother would be through the Tech Area gate and back in her lab, doing whatever she did with her chemicals, six days a week. Daddy too, in his own lab. He hadn't come home for lunch, the third time this week. She hoped he'd remember to stop for dinner.

Suze sighed and pushed her blonde hair back behind her ears. It was getting to be an annoying length, too long to be short, and its blunt bowl cut meant that the sides were always falling in her face. Her mother had trimmed the bangs with nail scissors last week, but she needed a real haircut, and that meant a trip to Santa Fe. Or to the army barber, which was starting to feel like a reasonable solution to Suze. She could walk there by herself.

She pushed the score pad and pencil to the corner of the table. The numbers were written in pencil, pen, all different colors of ink, because the game had started more than a year ago. They used to play every night, after dinner, but lately her mother had been too busy. This was their first game in two weeks.

Both her parents had always worked. Back in Berkeley, though, where they'd been professors at the university, they'd had regular hours. Here on the Hill, she was never sure when she would see them. Especially Mom. Suze missed having her around, which was unpatriotic, because whatever the scientists were working on was going to end the war, and she knew that was more important than playing cards.

Most days.

The second siren went off, startling her. She'd forgotten.

"Do you ever miss our old life?" she asked her cat, Rutherford, who was lounging by the kitchen door. He was a big orange-striped tom who didn't seem to notice any difference between one sunny floor and another. California sun, New Mexico sun. It didn't much matter to Rutherford.

But it did to Suze. She had spent her entire life, up until last fall, in a rambling old house on Russell Street, half a mile from the UC campus, and only a block from College Avenue, with a movie theater and *two* drugstores. There were never any sirens, unless there was a fire, and they had had a yard with grass and trees with leaves.

Not like here. Here they lived upstairs in a tiny apartment with only four rooms. In the summer it was hot outside, and dust blew in, making the wooden floors gritty. In the winter, it was too hot *in*side, and soot from the coal furnace coated the walls and tabletops with a greasy black film. The walls were so thin that she could hear the family next door talking in their living room when she was trying to fall asleep.

She had her own room, but it was just barely big enough to hold her bed and desk and dresser. If she stuck her head way, way out the window, she could see mountains and pine trees and the rocky slopes of the canyon, and about a million stars at night. That part was okay. Mostly though, when she looked out the window normally, all she saw was laundry and dirt and army-green everything. Green houses, green trucks, green uniforms.

Suze liked colors. She liked crayons and paints and Oz books full of pictures of the Emerald City. But she was getting very tired of the army's kind of green.

She put her plate and milk glass in the sink, and

thought about writing a letter to her grandmother. She'd gotten one last week, a late birthday card, so she ought to write back. Except she wasn't allowed to say anything interesting. She wasn't allowed to talk about the people here, or what happened last week, or even where she *was*. She had to leave the envelope open too, so the censors could read her letter before it left the Hill. Suze hated having some old army man read her private thoughts.

Once she had drawn a picture for Gramma Weiss, the view from her bedroom, the stick-your-head-out view, which had been very hard to draw. But the stupid old censor sent it back and said it wasn't allowed. If she couldn't talk about where she lived or anything, what was the point of writing a letter?

Through the open kitchen window, she heard voices from the road below, so she walked out onto the tiny porch they shared with the neighbors, letting the screen door bang behind her. A small knot of kids was down by the garbage cans at the bottom of the stairs. Back home, the street was at the fronts of the houses, but here it was at the backs. The army built it that way, her father said, because making deliveries would be easier. Her mother said it made the place look like a slum.

"What're you doing?" Suze called down.

"Nothin' much," a boy named Tom answered. He tossed a stone a few feet, raising a tiny mushroom of dust in the dirt road. They always played in the street. There weren't any lawns or yards or sidewalks, and no traffic during the day, except for an occasional army truck. And you could hear those coming from a long way away, bouncing and clattering over the rutted dirt roads that crisscrossed the site.

She thought for a moment. Doing nothing with the other kids might be more fun than doing it by herself. She pounded down the back steps, two at a time.

Suze Gordon was a stocky child with cinnamon-brown eyes, dressed in a striped shirt and cut-off khaki pants, the edges of the legs jagged and raveling. She had just turned eleven, and was as tall as most of the boys in her class, taller than some of them. She hoped she could talk the other kids into playing Red Rover. She was a good runner, and strong, and could almost always break through.

A blonde girl named Judy sat on the concrete stoop at the bottom of the stairs. She moved over to let Suze pass, but not enough to make room for her to sit. Judy was in her class at school, but she and Barbara and Betty and Joyce always hung out together, or with the other Girl Scouts. "Thick as thieves," her mother said.

Suze had been a Brownie in second grade, back in Berkeley. They'd gone on field trips to the zoo and made plaster casts of animal tracks up in Tilden Park and even rode horses once. So when they moved to the Hill and her mother suggested that she join the troop because it would be a good way to get to know the other girls and give her something to do after school, Suze had agreed.

She lasted two meetings. There weren't going to be any field trips, because of security. And the first meeting, two whole hours, was Joyce's mother lecturing about rules and uniforms and requirements for badges. More rules? More green uniforms? Suze had enough of that with the army.

The next week, Joyce's mother's idea of "fun" turned out to be making plaques with the Girl Scout motto spelled out in macaroni letters—the kind that were supposed to become alphabet soup. And when Suze showed her mother the two-page typed list of "Girl Scout DOs and DON'Ts," even Mrs. Gordon made a face, and said that life was too short.

But Suze wondered sometimes if the other girls would ask her to play jacks or jump rope more if she'd stayed a Girl Scout. Finished her plaque, learned the pledge, wore a white blouse. Or would she just be in a uniform and still outside their special circle? Because it wasn't just Girl Scouts. It was movie magazines and paper dolls of Deanna Durbin in frothy pink dresses, and the lipstick Betty had gotten the last time she went to Santa Fe, the one that her mother could *never* find out about, but wasn't it a *dreamy* color?

Suze had gotten herself invited over to Judy's or Joyce's apartment a few times, and had tried to pretend she was interested in all that, but mostly she was bored. Did they really *like* that stuff? Suze just didn't get it.

She leaned against the stair railing and listened as Joyce and Barbara twirled the jump rope and chanted the rhyme for Betty:

"V is for Victory, dot, dot, dash!
Hitler lost his little mustache!
If you find it, let him know,
And he'll give you a bag of dough!
How much money is in that bag?
One dollar, two dollars, three dollars . . ."

Betty got all the way up to twenty-seven before she missed, which Suze thought was pretty good. Suze wasn't good at jump rope. Her feet got tangled too fast.

"I'm hot," said Betty, who was red in the face from jumping. "Let's take a break." The other girls nodded and went and sat down on the other stoop, fanning themselves.

"So, what're you doin'?" Suze asked a crewcut boy named Jack. He was leaning on the side of the stair rail, whittling pieces of wood into splinters with his pocket-knife. She tried to sound casual, but it came out sounding like a line from a play.

"Waiting for my brother Charlie. We're going to go work on our fort," he said, throwing away the last bit of wood. He folded his knife and put it in his pocket. "No girls allowed."

Suze made a face. She tried to think of something snappy to say back, but came up blank. Then she got an idea. "*I'm* going to the PX for a Coke," she said in a loud voice, and looked across at the other stoop. "The Tech PX." She held her breath, waiting for someone to say what a swell idea that was, and maybe they'd come along. But they almost never did anything she said.

Joyce looked up at her for a long second, long enough to make Suze feel uncomfortable, as if she was being judged, or Joyce was trying to figure out if there would be a better offer.

"It is hot," Joyce said finally. "Barbara? Bets? You wanna get Cokes?" She made it sound like it was her idea, but Suze didn't say anything.

"A cold Coke sounds nifty-keen," said Betty, sounding like one of her movie magazines. "But the Tech PX is awfully far."

"We can stop at the Pond," said Suze, and just then she got another idea that was even better. "Besides, I know a shortcut. Lemme get my shoes." She turned and ran back up the stairs and grabbed her sneakers from where she'd dropped them on the porch the night before.

Hardly any kids on the Hill wore shoes in the summer, unless a grown-up said they had to, but her plan wasn't a barefoot idea. She looped the laces together, strung her shoes around her neck, and clattered down the stairs, quick, so they wouldn't leave without her.

Joyce always wore shoes, and Betty had put hers on for jumping. "We have to stop so I can get mine," Barbara said. She lived in one of the houses over on Bathtub Row, because her father was a big shot. He was a captain, in the navy, not the army. Suze wasn't sure why he was here, since there wasn't any water for about a thousand miles.

The four girls walked down the middle of the road, with Betty and Joyce a little behind, giggling to each other. They headed south, the pine-studded canyon far over on their right. The road didn't have a name, none of them did. Suze thought this made it really hard to give anyone directions, but the army didn't want people knowing much about the Hill. Even if you lived there. She had learned to navigate by landmarks, like Fuller Lodge, or the tall wooden water tower to the west of it, which was visible from almost everywhere.

"Hi, Sergeant Walter," Barbara said to the military policeman who stood guard outside her house. He wore a black armband with the white letters MP. Barbara pointed to the pass safety-pinned to her blouse. "I'm just going in to get my shoes."

The MP glanced at the pass. "Your mother's having a tea party. Mrs. Oppie and some of the other ladies," he said. "You might want to go in the back way."

Barbara nodded. "Thanks. I could get stuck in there all afternoon." She made a face. "You have to wait here," she said to the other girls. "I'll be right back."

Betty and Joyce sat down under a pine tree. Suze stood in the shade. They watched Sgt. Walter on his patrol, walking up to Oppie's house, then back again. These five houses were sturdy, built of logs and stone, remnants of the old boys' school that used to be on the Hill, before the army. The most important people on the Hill lived here. Sgt. Walter walked up and back, up and back. He didn't pay any attention to them.

"I'm glad my dad's not a big shot," said Suze, sucking on a pine needle. It tasted faintly like turpentine. "What a pain to have to show your pass just to go *home*." Hers was in the top drawer of her dresser. She didn't need it unless she left the Hill, to go down to Santa Fe, and that had only happened three times since they'd moved here.

"Oh, but it would be *so* nice to live in a real house. With a bathtub," Joyce said, sighing. "But the guards are a little creepy. I guess it's okay my daddy's just a fizzler." Her father was a physicist, but no one was supposed to talk about that, so people called them "fizzlers." Chemists were "stinkers." Suze's mother was a stinker.

It was cooler under the tree, and they stayed there for a little while, even after Barbara came out of her house wearing her loafers. They watched Sgt. Walter make three trips up and down Bathtub Row.

"I'm thirsty," said Betty, standing up after the MP had turned to go back up the road again. "And if we wait too long, the PX will be full of soldiers and they'll ditch us out of line."

They continued down the road.

TREASURE
AT THE DUMP

DEWEY TOOK A FINAL bite of her apple and, without taking her eyes off her book, put the core into the brown paper sack on the ground next to her. She was reading a biography, the life of Faraday, and she was just coming to the exciting part where he figured out about electricity and magnetism. She leaned contentedly against Papa's shoulder and turned the page.

Today they had chosen to sit against the west wall of the Commissary for their picnic lunch. It offered a little bit of shade, they could look out at the Pond, and it was three minutes from Papa's office, which meant they could spend almost the whole hour reading together.

"Dews?" Papa said a few minutes later. "Remember the other night when we were talking about how much math and music are related?"

Dewey nodded.

"Well, there was a quote I couldn't quite recall, and I just found it. Listen." He began to read, very slowly. "'Music is the hidden arithmetic of the soul, which does not know that it deals with numbers. Music is the pleasure the human mind experiences from counting without being aware that it is counting.' That's *exactly* what I was talking about."

"Who said it?" Dewey asked.

"Leibniz. Gottfried Wilhelm Leibniz. He was an interesting guy, a mathematician and a philosopher and a musician to boot. You'd like him."

"Can I borrow that book when you're done?"

"I don't think you'd get far," he laughed. He turned and showed her his book, bound in very old brown leather that was flaking off in places. The page it was open to was covered in an odd, heavy black type.

"It's in German," Dewey said, surprised. That explained why he had read so slowly. He'd been translating. "So is Leibniz a Nazi?"

"Hardly. He died more than two hundred years ago, long before there were any Nazis." He shook his head. "Don't make the mistake of throwing out a whole culture just because some madmen speak the same language. Remember, Beethoven was German. And Bach, and—"

The rest of his sentence was interrupted by the shrill siren from the Tech Area. He sighed. "Time to go back to my own numbers." He closed his book, then leaned over and kissed Dewey on the top of her head. "What're you up to this afternoon?" He stood up, brushed the crumbs from his sandwich off his lap into the dirt, then brushed the dirt itself off the back of his pants.

Dewey squinted up at him. "I think I'll sit here and read for a while. A couple more chapters anyway. Then I'm going to the dump. Some of the labs are moving into the Gamma Building, now that it's done, and people always throw out good stuff when they move."

He smiled. "Looking for anything in particular?"

"I don't know yet. I need some bigger gears and some knobs and dials. And some ball bearings," she added after a short pause. "I'll show you at dinner if I find anything really special."

"Deal. We're just analyzing data this afternoon, so I may actually get out at five thirty. If you get home before me, put the casserole in the oven and we can eat around seven." He tucked his book under his arm.

"Okay." Dewey watched him walk around the corner of the building, then turned back to her book.

Twenty minutes later she came to the end of a chapter, and was tired of sitting on the hard-packed ground. She stood up and stretched, put her book into the red wagon parked a few feet away, and picked up its wooden handle.

She had found the wagon at the dump at the beginning of the summer, a rusted former toy that was missing one wheel. Their neighbor, Mr. Sandoval, was a machinist, and had made her a replacement. It was the right size, but metal instead of rubber, and now the wagon rolled along with an odd, lopsided syncopation on the rutted dirt roads. Still, it meant that she could bring home heavier things, and carry them all in one trip.

She walked down to the road that bordered the Tech Area, pulling the wagon behind her, leaving parallel trails in the dust. It was hot, and the wagon made walking a little awkward, but she was looking forward to seeing what might be in the dump. You never knew. Sometimes it was just lumber and wire-studded chunks of concrete—construction stuff. But other times there were machines with lots of wonderful tiny parts, or tools like the drill she'd found whose wooden handle was cracked a little, but worked just fine.

Dewey whistled under her breath. She still marveled at the freedom she had on the Hill. In St. Louis, Nana had only allowed her to walk to school and back—four blocks—and no dawdling, because Nana knew just how long it took, so there was no chance for Dewey to go off exploring by herself. It wasn't safe, Nana said. But it was safe here. There were guards, so inside the fence, she could go anywhere she wanted, anytime. Even at night.

She and Papa knew just about everyone who lived here, and no strangers could get in from outside.

Her favorite thing was that no one ever told her she asked too many questions. In the nine months that she'd lived here, Dewey had explored almost every inch of the project, except for the parts that were secret and had extra guards. And everywhere she went, there were men just as smart as Papa—or just as clever—who would help her figure out how to fix a busted clock or radio or motor, take it apart, and explain how it worked.

It was wrong to think, but sometimes she hoped the war would go on and on and on, so she and Papa could stay here forever.

As she rounded the corner of the fence near the dump, she heard voices and stopped. The dump wasn't guarded. Anyone could come and take whatever they wanted. But she just wanted to rummage, and didn't want to talk to anyone official.

She peered around the corner of the fence and saw that it was just her friend Charlie and his little brother Jack. She'd been in Charlie's algebra class all spring, even though he was thirteen. Her fifth-grade class had been doing fractions, and she'd been bored. She was used to that. But this time, the teacher had noticed, and after giving Dewey a little test to see what she knew, had asked her if she'd like to take math with the eighth grade, because it would be more of a challenge. So she knew Charlie.

Both brothers had reddish blond crewcuts and freckles. Charlie was half a head taller, and was wearing dungarees that ended two inches above his black high-tops. Jack wore cutoffs ragged at the knees. Both boys had T-shirts that had started out white. They carried a long piece of lumber, dropping it onto a pile by their bikes with a loud *crack*. As they turned to go back for another, Dewey pushed her wagon forward and waved.

"Hey, Dewey," said Charlie. He pulled a bandana from his back pocket and mopped his reddening forehead.

"Hey," said Dewey. "More wood for your tree house?" The boys had been building a secret fortress somewhere in the woods all summer. Everyone knew about it, all the kids at least, but Dewey had never seen it.

"Yeah, great stuff today. Look, shingles!" Charlie pointed to a stack of sand-encrusted rectangular plates, the size and shape of books but as thin as records, that lay in his wire bike basket. "It's the last of Morganville, and there's enough to cover our whole roof. Maybe now it won't leak when it rains."

"That'll be good," agreed Dewey. She looked over at the wood bins, which were divided into pine, hardwood, and painted wood, each of them full to overflowing. "Is it just lumber today?"

"Heck no," said Jack. "They musta moved a bunch of

labs, 'cause there's about a ton of that busted-up machine junk you like. Over there." He pointed at the far fence, where a spiky jumble of steel and chrome glinted in the summer sun.

Dewey grinned and took a pair of brown leather gloves from the wagon and put them in her pocket. The gloves were way too big for her hands and made sorting clumsy, but sometimes the machines were really busted and their edges were sharp, or there was broken glass.

"What're you looking for?" asked Charlie, walking along beside her as they made their way to the scrap pile.

"Something interesting. I don't know yet."

The first thing she saw was two pieces of copper tubing, one as wide as a cigar, the other smaller. She tugged on them and they came free easily. Each was about two feet long, which meant that she'd have to cut them down with her hacksaw, when she figured out what they were for. She laid them off to one side in the dirt.

Her pile grew over the next few minutes as she added some polished metal discs as big around as coffee cups, an alarm clock with a broken-off key, and a gray metal box with two nice black Bakelite knobs. Her hands were gray from rummaging through metal parts, and she was sweaty. Just a few more minutes, then she'd call it a day and go home and start to dismantle what she'd found.

She smiled at the alarm clock with anticipation. *That* was going to be fun.

"Hey, look at this," said Charlie, to her right. Dewey went over to look.

"It's a typewriter," she said excitedly. She tugged and pulled and pushed on the black steel frame until it came free and crashed to the ground, a small avalanche of metal cascading around it.

Charlie looked down at it. "The roller thing's missing. It won't work."

"I know. I just want the bell. And the springs. And the keys are neat-looking. I can probably do something with them." Dewey squatted down to pick up the typewriter, and staggered to her feet under its weight.

"Here," said Charlie. "Lemme do that." He took it out of her arms and walked easily over to the wagon, which sounded a hollow metal clang when he dropped the typewriter in.

"Thanks," Dewey said.

"S'okay. Can you get the rest? We gotta load the boards onto our bikes and get going."

"Sure." Dewey pulled the knobs off the gray box and carted the rest of her treasures to the wagon intact. She loaded them one by one, writing each down in her notebook, along with the date.

The boys were still struggling to balance Jack's bike

and tie the lumber to its handlebars. Dewey hesitated for a second, then went over to help.

"I'll hold the bike," she said. "One of you can steady the boards while the other one does the twine." She reached over and took hold of the black leather seat.

"Yeah, that's *much* easier," said Charlie after a minute. He added another board, shifting it until it balanced. "How's your radio coming?"

"I haven't done much with it," Dewey admitted. "During the day the lab generators and the transformers make too much static, and it's not much better at night. You've got one up in your tree house, right? Is the reception any good?"

Charlie made a face. "It was. Until the MPs took it last week. Just a little ham setup, but when we broadcast they tracked down the signal. We weren't saying anything classified. Jeez, we didn't even give a location, just call numbers. But you know how it is with the army. We might be Nazi spies, so they snatched it. Do I look like a Nazi spy to you?" He kicked his sneaker in the dust.

"Well," Dewey said, "you are kind of blond." She smiled, so that he would know she was kidding.

Jack laughed. "Anyway, we found another one." He tied a series of half-hitches, then tucked the last bit of twine under them. "Just a receiver. A big black Zenith. It was a real *bitch* getting it up the ladder, but—" He stopped and his face reddened. "Sorry," he said. "My mom says I'm not supposed to swear in front of girls."

Dewey shrugged. "I don't care." Jack took the handlebars, and she motioned toward her wagon. "I'm going to take this stuff home. Which way are you headed?"

"The tree house is back behind the Sundts," Jack said, grinning. "Way back. Kind of on the other side of the fence." He looked over at his brother. "Maybe we could show her sometime?"

"W-ell," Charlie said, drawing the word out as if he was thinking. "No girls allowed. Usually. But, yeah, maybe." He pointed a semi-stern finger at Dewey. "You can't tell, though."

"It's the Hill," said Dewey. "What *can* you tell?"

The boys laughed. "You wanna stop and get Cokes at the PX?" Jack straddled his bike, but gave up on riding it after a few wobbly feet and began to walk it out toward the road.

Dewey picked up the handle of her wagon and followed him. "The Tech PX?"

"Nah," said Charlie, walking his own bike. "Too far. The Trading Post over by the Lodge. It's right on the way."

THE MOTOR POOL

SUZE AND THE other girls walked slowly along the curving road, green-painted wooden buildings scattered on each side, some so new their nails were still shiny. The air smelled like sawdust and pine resin. Off to the south they could hear the pounding of hammers and the whine of motors. New people moved to the Hill almost every week, and the army was busy building more apartments and bigger labs.

The Hill was a funny place, separate from the outside world, filtered through the army. Suze missed the colors of the neon and the painted signs that had decorated the streets of Berkeley. She missed the comings and goings of a real city—streetcars, milkmen and ice-cream trucks, newsboys and unfamiliar faces. The Hill was always the same, day after day.

They stepped to the side to allow a trio of army trucks

to lumber through, lumpy green tarps obscuring the cargo underneath, and waited until the dust settled before continuing on.

"Which do you think is worse, dust or mud?" asked Joyce.

"Dust," said Barbara.

"Mud," said Betty at the same time. "It never comes all the way off your shoes, and my mother yelled all winter about her kitchen floor."

"Yeah, but dust goes *every*where," said Suze. "In your eyes, up your nose—" She sneezed very dramatically and was pleased that the other girls laughed.

Just before they got to the post office, there was a loud *boom*. They all stopped for a minute, and looked off to the south, toward S-Site, to see if there would be smoke this time. Some explosions were bigger than others. A few made booms loud enough to rattle the glass in the buildings' windows. But this one was just ordinary.

"That wasn't much," said Joyce. "Let's go."

But Betty stood still, her mouth open. "Look," she said, pointing.

Suze followed Betty's finger. Two boys were walking their bikes on either side of a small figure with a red wagon. They had just come around the corner of the post office, and were heading their way.

"Oh great," said Joyce, groaning. "It's Screwy Dewey and her little red wagon."

Dewey Kerrigan was the weirdest girl Suze had ever met. It wasn't just that she was smart and wore glasses. Lots of kids on the Hill, Suze included, had been the smartest kids in their old schools. But Dewey didn't play with the other kids. She spent every recess at one of the picnic tables next to the playground, fiddling with her stupid radio, or some broken garbage with wires and springs, taking notes about it, like it was homework.

"But why's she with Charlie?" asked Betty, frowning. She said Charlie's name in what Suze thought of as her girly-girly voice. She'd had a crush on Jack's brother all summer. Suze rolled her eyes.

"She's not *with* them," Joyce said. "They're just walking on the same road. Why would they be hanging around with that four-eyed gimp?"

Barbara nodded. "If I had to wear that ugly shoe, I'd never leave my house."

Suze didn't know what was wrong with Dewey's leg. She always wore one normal shoe and one brown shoe that laced up the side and had a thick rubber sole, which meant she couldn't run for beans. That was probably why she never played Red Rover or anything. She wouldn't be any good at all.

The boys stopped about ten feet away, and it looked like maybe they *were* with Dewey, because she stopped too. She stood a few feet back, partially hidden by their bikes.

"Hi, *Char*-lie," said Betty. She was trying to sound like a movie star, all smooth and breathy, but Suze thought she just sounded dopey.

"Hey, kids," said Charlie.

Betty frowned.

"Where are *you* going?" Joyce asked.

"None of your beeswax," said Jack.

"*We're* going to the Tech PX for Cokes. You wanna come?" Betty said it as if it had been her idea all along.

"Nah." Charlie shook his head. "We got plans."

"No *girls* allowed," said Jack.

"And Screwy Dewey doesn't need to go to the PX," Joyce said. "Not as long as the *dump's* open." She walked over and poked the alarm clock with one finger. "Why buy anything when you can pick through other people's trash?"

Dewey looked right at Joyce, but said nothing.

"Hey, leave the kid alone," said Charlie. He took a step forward, but the load of boards on his bike began to wobble and slide. He steadied it, then rattled some coins in his pocket. "C'mon, Dewey. Let's go to the Trading Post. I babysat for Teller's kid the other night, so I'm flush. I'll blow you to a Coke." He gestured to the building up ahead on their right.

Betty looked at Charlie, wide-eyed. "You're buying *her* a Coke?"

"*She's* a good egg," he said. He glared at Betty for a moment, then gave his bike a shove and started walking. Jack followed, and after a moment, so did Dewey.

"*Rotten* egg's more like it," said Suze loudly, so the other girls would know she was on their side. She waited for a reaction, and when none came, said, "C'mon, the heck with them. Let's get those Cokes." She gave Joyce's arm a buddy punch, not very hard at all.

"Ow." Joyce frowned, rubbing her arm. She watched the rolling trio disappear around the corner of a building. "Yeah, okay."

To get to the Tech PX, they had to take the road between the post office and the Commissary, then turn down another road that ran along the side of the Tech Area, with its high, barbed-wire fence. The T had its own gate and was off-limits for anyone without a white badge. Both Suze's parents worked inside.

"Hey, how 'bout that shortcut?" she said, as if she'd just remembered it. "The boys told me about it the other day. They said it's *much* faster." She looked at Betty to see if she was impressed.

"What kind of shortcut? You can't get through any-where. It's all fences," said Betty.

"The boys do," said Suze. "C'mon." She stepped off the road and onto the hard-packed dirt beside it. The only real difference between the two surfaces was that the dirt of the road was raked and had tire marks, and the ground was webbed with cracks where the flat plane of mud had dried.

The other girls looked at Betty, who shrugged. "I guess so."

Suze led them down a narrow strip between the white clapboard post office and the long, two-story Gamma Building, which was painted green and had a barbed-wire fence around it.

"That's my dad's new office," said Joyce. "He calls it the Gadget Building, because that's what they're making. He says they had to give it the Greek letter, gamma, because the Tech Area already *had* a G Building." She sounded very important.

"I knew that," said Suze. Everyone's father was working on some part of the gadget, whatever it was. Some kind of big gun, she figured. Building it was going to end the war, which was why they were all here. She hadn't known about the Greek part, though. She didn't even know Greek had a different alphabet. Daddy probably did. She'd ask him at dinner.

She walked along the edge of the fence, trailing her fingers through the lattice of thin wires, feeling the inaudible thrum, like a cheap toy guitar. She picked up some pebbles and tossed them into the Pond, visible again on their right, watching the ripples radiate out from each impact, the edges of the circles sparkling in the sunlight.

A few minutes later, Betty stopped walking. "Now what?" she asked in a smug voice that sounded like she had also said "I told you so."

They all stopped. The Gamma Building and its fence were on their left, and directly ahead of them was the six-foot chain-link fence that surrounded the Motor Pool. It stretched off to the right for more than a hundred feet, then turned a corner. A narrow strip of dirt separated the fence from the end of the Pond.

"This isn't a shortcut," said Joyce. "Walking around the Motor Pool is even longer than taking the road." She glared at Suze.

Suze faltered, then forced a big grin. "But we're not going around." She unlooped her shoes from around her neck and sat down in the dirt to put them on. "We're going through."

The other three girls stared at her.

"Holy Joe, we can't go through *there*," said Barbara. "We're not allowed. It's off-limits."

"It's not really restricted," said Suze. "There's no gadget stuff. It's just trucks." She put on her other sneaker.

"But there are still guards," said Joyce. "MPs. With guns," she added, as if Suze had never seen one.

"They're not going to *shoot* us. We're kids. They only shoot Nazi spies," Suze said, trying to sound confident.

At least that was what Tom had told her. "C'mon."

Suze jumped up onto the chain-link fence, fitting the rubber tips of her sneakers into two diamond-shaped openings about a foot apart. She looked down at the other girls.

"I'm walking around," said Barbara. Suze wasn't surprised. Barbara was a year younger, and her father was Navy.

"Me too," said Betty. "This is stupid." She looked at Joyce.

"Some shortcut," Joyce said. She looked at Suze and shook her head. "Show-off," she muttered. She linked her arm through Betty's, and they walked away.

Suze felt her face grow hot. *Stupid scaredy-cats*, she thought. It was an adventure. Or had sounded like one when the boys talked about it. But she hadn't counted on doing it alone. The rounded wires of the fence cut into her hands as she clung there a few feet off the ground. Maybe she should jump down? No. It *was* a shortcut. They'd have to admit that when she got to the PX first. She'd show *them*.

Suze climbed the fence.

The top wasn't a rounded bar, like the fence at her school in Berkeley. She'd climbed that all the time. This one ended with sharp, stubby Xs of cut wire. She stood for a second with her right sneaker high up on the fence, secure in a foothold, then threw her left leg over. She felt the edge of her shorts catch, but no skin, and freed herself with a small ripping sound. Her left foot found a grip, and she was over. She climbed down quickly and jumped to the ground between two army-green buses.

Suze felt like a commando, a member of the resistance, sneaking through enemy lines. She edged her way along to the front fender of the bus on her left and peered out. No one in sight. She sprinted across an opening, edged along another bus, then moved to her right, under cover of the bulk of a weapons carrier. She leaned up against its side, her heart racing. She could feel the heat of the metal through her shirt. She took a deep breath and tiptoed up to the front of the vehicle, then pulled back abruptly.

An MP with a rifle was walking up the row, only three trucks away. Suze scurried under her truck and lay facedown in the dirt until she saw his black-booted feet pass by. She counted to twenty, then crawled out. The front of her—shirt, shorts, arms, legs—was a solid reddish brown. Probably her face too. She started to brush the dust off, but that made noise. Besides, she was just going to get dirtier.

She looked behind her. It seemed like a long way, almost as far as going forward. And if she went back now, the other girls would really razz her. She peered around the front of the weapons carrier again. The MP was at the end of the row now, facing away from her, watching the other girls as they turned the corner of the fence.

Suze ran across the open lane and crouched beside a jeep. Sweat dripped off her forehead, and her hair was in her eyes. She jammed it behind her ears, looked around, and said a bad word, not quite out loud. The Motor Pool was bigger than she'd thought. Between her and the other fence was about an acre of jeeps. And she'd have to crouch down the whole way. She was taller than a jeep.

She had duck-walked the length of six jeeps when she heard men talking. She froze and tried not to breathe. The enemy was near. If they captured her, she would not talk, would not reveal the names of the others. She waited what seemed like forever, and the voices stopped. There were still a lot of jeeps ahead, but she could see the front door of the PX through the opposite fence now. She didn't see the other girls. If she ran, she could still beat them there.

Now! Suze ran as fast as she could in a crouch, past one jeep, then another. Only three jeeps between her and the fence, and—

"*Halt!*" said a loud, male voice about ten feet behind her. She turned her head for a second and saw a uniformed man in a white helmet, rifle in his arms, walking quickly toward her down the line of jeeps.

Suze stood up and ran as hard as she could. One jeep. Two.

"HALT!" shouted the MP again. She could hear *him* running now, his footsteps pounding on the dirt too close behind her.

Suze lunged for the front bumper of the last jeep and launched herself onto the fence. Her left foot slipped, and she scraped against the metal mesh for a moment, wrenching her arms in their sockets as she fought to hold on. She scrambled, found a foothold, and climbed, fast.

"Got you!" the MP shouted, and grabbed at her foot. Suze jerked her leg, and in a desperate effort, threw herself over the top, just missing the sharp fence ends. She half fell, half jumped the last five feet to the ground and landed on the hard dirt on the other side of the fence with a *whump* that knocked the air out of her for a few seconds.

She got up and looked behind her. The MP stood glaring on the other side of the fence. Then he said something under his breath and shook his head. He turned and walked away.

She'd done it! The MP couldn't touch her. On this side of the fence, the scientists were more important than the army. The MPs were here to protect *them*.

"Later, alligator," she whispered. She was not quite brave enough, or foolish enough, to wave.

By the time the other girls arrived, a minute or two later, Suze was leaning against the wooden sign that said POST EXCHANGE. Her shirt and shorts were ripped and a little rivulet of blood trickled slowly down her dirt-covered leg from the knee she'd skinned coming off the fence. But she'd beaten them there.

"See," she said, triumphantly. "I *told* you it was a shortcut."

IT'S ALL
GREEK TO ME

SUZE GRINNED AND waited for one of the other girls to say something—"Hey, you were right" or "That *was* a good idea." But Betty just stared at Suze for a moment, then sniffed. "Some people will do *any*thing for attention." She brushed by her and held the screen door open for Joyce and Barbara, letting it bang shut just before Suze reached it.

Suze stood there for a moment, stunned. She thought about leaving, but now she was so thirsty she almost didn't care. She opened the door and went in. The PX was full of soldiers and older kids, high-school boys and girls who played the jukebox and giggled too loud. Betty and the other girls stood in line at the counter. When they got their Cokes, Joyce turned and looked at Suze. She wrinkled her nose, as if something smelled bad, and Betty laughed. Suze felt her face flush.

She gave the clerk her nickel and took the green glass bottle, icy cold and beaded with condensation in the hot, dry summer air. She got a paper napkin from the chrome dispenser and used the damp rectangle to wipe some of the dirt and blood off her knee. It would have a good scab.

Suze had felt like a hero, returned from a dangerous mission. But when she got out to the wooden porch and saw the backs of the other girls, just disappearing around the corner of the PX, on the road to the Tech Area, the feeling faded. She barely tasted her Coke, and went back into the PX to console herself with a new comic.

She walked back slowly—around the Motor Pool. In front of the Lodge, she passed a group of dark-haired women chattering in Spanish. One of them was Carmelita Martinez, a woman in her early twenties, with jet-black hair that hung halfway down her back and blunt-cut bangs. She cleaned their house two afternoons a week, and had been teaching Suze a little bit of Spanish.

"*Buenos días*, Carmelita," Suze said.

"Ah, *buenos días*, *Señorita* Suz." Carmelita paused as the rest of the women walked on. "*Hoy, su casa está muy limpia.*"

That was a word Suze didn't know. She held out her hands, palms up. "*¿Qué?*" she asked.

"*Su casa está* clean."

"Oh. *Gracias*." Suze thought for a minute. "Uh, *¿Su camino* to *el pueblo?*"

Carmelita nodded. *"Sí. Sí. Y muy pronto."* She held up her wrist, with its silver and turquoise bracelets, and mimed looking at a watch.

"Oh. Okay. *Adios*," Suze said.

Carmelita nodded and trotted off to catch up with the other women. Every weekday morning, women from the pueblo of San Ildefonso boarded an army bus that brought them to the Hill to clean the apartments of women who worked in the labs. They returned on the same bus each afternoon, the only commuters on the Hill.

Suze got back to the apartment a little after 5:00, *Wonder Woman* in hand. Six days a week, the siren from the Tech Area went off at 5:30, the official end of the work day. That didn't mean much, since many of the scientists stayed in their labs until late at night, if they came home at all. But Suze knew her father wouldn't be home *before* the siren, and that gave her time to clean up. She was too dirty for him not to notice, and she wasn't in the mood to answer any questions.

She tossed her sneakers under her bed and went into the tiny bathroom. In Berkeley they'd had pink-and-gray tiles and a big claw-foot bathtub. This one had wooden walls—green, but a paler green than the outside paint—and linoleum that pulled up at the corners, revealing sticky caramel-brown glue. A stall shower with iron pipes and dull black knobs stood in one corner. The army didn't believe in bathtubs.

The water always came out of the pipes boiling hot, too hot to even touch to test the temperature. So Suze turned on the cold first, and kept one arm in the stream of water while she very slowly turned the hot tap. Thin brown mud dripped off her arm. When the water was just warm, she climbed into the shower and let it sluice most of the dirt off her shirt and shorts, waiting until it ran pretty clear before pulling them off.

They lay in a wet ball in the corner of the stall while she soaped the parts of her she could see. Even Ivory stung the skinned place on her knee, and a couple of other scrapes she hadn't known she had. The shampoo was on top of the medicine cabinet, so she washed her hair with the soap, which left it feeling clean but a little rubbery.

She dried herself off and put a pink Band-Aid on her knee, in case she bumped it. She squeezed as much of the water out of her clothes as she could, and her bare feet made shiny transparent footprints on the hardwood floor when she walked to her bedroom. She draped her wet clothes over the windowsill to dry and put on a clean blue shirt and a pair of seersucker shorts that were on their way to being too small but would last the rest of the summer. She was sitting on the back steps, four pages into *Wonder Woman*, when her father came around the corner of the identical shoebox-shaped building across the curving road, through a clump of pines that shirred and whispered in the late-afternoon breeze.

"Hi, Daddy!" she called, and thudded down the steps to greet him.

Philip Gordon was a tall, square man in his late thirties, with receding sandy-blond hair. He was dressed in his usual work clothes for summer on the Hill—gray twill pants and a short-sleeved white shirt, open at the neck. Two pens and the stem of his briar pipe protruded from his shirt pocket. He was carrying a small sheaf of letters and a newspaper.

"How's my girl?" he said. He reached down and patted Suze's damp hair. "Hey, you're actually clean," he said.

"I took a shower. It was *really* hot outside. How was work?" she asked, changing the subject. She followed him up the white Z of the steps to the second floor.

He frowned. "You know I can't tell you."

"*Daddy*," said Suze, a little annoyed and stung at his tone. "I didn't ask what you were doing. Just how was your day?" Her father was a metallurgist. In Berkeley, he used to bring lumps home for her. Gray lumps, dull lumps, smooth and lustrous lumps. He'd sit down at the kitchen table and drink a beer and tell her how this one cracked when it got too cold, and this one melted too soon, and showed her how this one would snap right in two if he slapped it flat on the table.

Suze was never sure what he *did* with his lumps, and had pretended that gray lumps were interesting presents, because she liked it a lot when he sat and talked to her. But now all his lumps belonged to the government and were classified, which meant he couldn't bring them home, or even talk about them. She sort of missed them.

"Sorry," he said. "I didn't mean to bark." He opened the round-shouldered refrigerator and took out a brown glass bottle of Coors beer. He popped off the cap with the metal opener on a string nailed to the side of the cabinet, and sat down at the table. He took a deep swallow, then put the bottle down on the yellow-and-white-checked oilcloth.

"It was all right," he said. "Frustrating in parts, but we're making progress, I think. Is your mother home yet?"

Suze shook her head. "She's still at *her* lab. She says she'll try to meet us at the Lodge for dinner, but she doesn't know how late she'll be." She sat down in the chair across from him.

"Oh. Okay." This was not unusual. He took another sip of beer and looked at the clock. "Then we should head over in a few minutes. It's steak night, and the Lodge'll be crowded. We don't want to be late."

"How come we get steak every week?" she asked. "At home the butcher sometimes didn't even have hamburger, and we had to have the coupons."

"We're top priority here. The government wants to keep all of us happy, so we'll work hard and win the war." He took another long drink of beer. "Go get your shoes on."

Suze went to her room to find her sneakers, wondering about the war. The war was the reason everyone was on the Hill, but somehow it seemed less real here, like a story she'd seen in a movie. There were soldiers everywhere, but they weren't fighting or going off to die. No one's father was gone, nobody had a blue star hanging in their window.

She tied her shoelace and frowned. If the government really wanted them to be happy, why did they read her mail? Why did they have barbed-wire fences and guards, sirens and passes? Her mother said the front gate was just like the tollbooth on the Golden Gate Bridge. But Suze had never seen a tollbooth man carry a rifle.

War stuff just didn't make any sense.

Suze and her father walked to the Lodge in companionable silence. He had lit his pipe, and the smoke blew over her head, smelling like sweetish-sour burning leaves. The

Daddy smell. She could tell by looking at him that he was thinking about a work problem. He moved his fingers, just a little, when he was calculating.

The sun was beginning to drop behind the mountains to the west, and Suze watched her shadow, long and thin, flow over the ruts and bumps in the road. She loved this time of day, because of the shadows and the light. The light was almost magical, like the Maxfield Parrish pictures in her fairy-tale book. He was her favorite artist. They were passing through the darker shadow of the water tower when her father suddenly snapped his fingers.

"Hold up a sec," he said. He pulled a pen out of his shirt pocket and wrote a few numbers and symbols on the back of his wrist, next to his watchband. Suze had no idea what they meant.

"That's Greek, isn't it?" she said, guessing.

He looked startled. "Yes, as a matter of fact." He pointed to a little blue triangle. "That's the letter *delta*. It means 'change.' How did you know?"

"Oh, some kids and I were talking about Greek this afternoon," Suze said casually. "Because of the Gamma Building. Gamma's like a kind of G, but in Greek, right? What does *it* look like? Do all the letters mean something else? Will you teach me?"

Her father chuckled. "Slow down. One question at a time." They started walking again. "Okay," he said after a moment. "First lesson. Greek letters mean one thing if you're actually talking Greek, and something else if you're talking math."

"Math isn't a language," said Suze.

"Actually, it is. It's the language we use to describe patterns." He stopped and lit his pipe again, which was what he always did when he wanted a little bit of time to think. He exhaled a cloud of bluish smoke. "Take a circle, for example. There's a pattern to circles."

"They're round," Suze agreed. She liked to use a compass to draw circles, because they came out perfect every time.

"More than that. There's a pattern to the relation of their diameters—how big they are across the center—to their circumferences, how big they are around." He looked down at her. "With me?"

"So far." Suze scrunched up her eyes and imagined drawing a circle.

"Okay. If you divide the circumference of a circle by its diameter, the answer is always 3.14159, with a lot more numbers after the nine." He waved his hand off into the air, dismissing the other numbers. "It's the same number, for any circle, no matter how big or how little. 3.14159. So instead of writing that out every time, scientists just use the Greek letter *pi*. Like this." He uncapped his pen and drew what looked like a little blue gate on Suze's wrist. "*Pi*. Elegant, isn't it?"

"I guess so." The circle in Suze's mind had changed into a round apple pie. She could tell by her father's voice that he thought this pie thing was really interesting and exciting. A Greek letter that was also a long number that was really a circle. Maybe it was like a secret science code. But she liked that he was sharing it with her, just the two of them. She slipped her hand into his, and after half a second of hesitation, or surprise, she felt his larger hand close around hers.

They walked the rest of the way to the Lodge without saying anything more out loud.

A CALCULATED MEAL

FULLER LODGE WAS the center of social life on the Hill, and the tallest building, three stories of big pine logs like giant forest columns, with windows in between. Philip Gordon stopped to knock the dead ashes out of his pipe against the big stone steps of the front porch before replacing the briar in his shirt pocket. "Shall we?" he said. He held the left-hand door open for her, and they went inside.

The dining room in the Lodge was one of Suze's favorite inside places on the Hill. It was a long room with log-column walls hung with bright, patterned Navajo rugs. Balconies ran along both sides. At one end stood a big stone fireplace with an elk head mounted over it. On this hot summer night, all the windows were open to catch any breeze. With wooden walls and wooden floors and more than a hundred people all talking and laughing and eating, it was very noisy. Waitresses in white uniforms bustled among the tables, bringing food and clearing away plates.

"Over here, Phil," called a man in a plaid shirt, the sleeves rolled up past his elbows. Her father put his hand on her back and steered her over to a table near the far wall. He sat down across from her.

"Where's Terry?" asked the other man. He had an accent and it sounded like *Vere's*.

"Still in her lab. You know how it is, Hans."

"We all put in our time," the man said, shaking his head. "And you, *liebchen*? How are you tonight?"

"Fine, Mr. Bethe," Suze said. She was pleased that she remembered to pronounce his name the way it *wasn't* spelled—Beh-teh.

He nodded and glanced down at the newspaper folded by his plate. "Still, we're getting there. And maybe we won't need to? The Allies are just outside Paris. It won't be long."

"Good news," agreed her father. "But there's still the Japs. We may need it there."

Suze thought "it" was probably the gadget gun, but knew better than to ask. The waitress came over and her father ordered a steak, medium rare, and coffee. Suze had the same thing, except with milk.

She played with her fork, trying to balance it on the

rim of her glass, while the men talked about things she didn't understand. Mostly work. At the other end of the table, a man and a woman she didn't know were talking in a *language* she didn't understand at all.

Suze was sorry she hadn't brought *Wonder Woman* with her. She had just gotten to the part where Wonder Woman found the hideout of the bad guy, a Nazi mad scientist who was going to blow up the world. You knew he was a scientist because he wore a long white coat and had a pointy beard and thick glasses.

She looked around the room and thought about that. Just about everyone she could see, every man at least, was some kind of scientist in real life. But nobody, not one of them, looked like the one in the comic. No white coats, just T-shirts and plaid shirts and blue jeans. A couple of people had moustaches, but no beards. A lot of them *did* wear glasses, though.

The steaks came, with yellow corn on the cob, glistening with butter, and a baked potato with steam that smelled like edible laundry when she smooshed it open with her fingers. The men kept talking, but Suze didn't mind as much, now that there was food.

Dessert was butterscotch pudding. It was a very satisfying texture to cut, because it made nice clean shapes, and Suze was slicing tawny orange arcs out of its slightly rubbery surface with her spoon when she saw her mother walk into the room. She was with three men, and they were all talking and shaking their heads as if they were arguing, but they were smiling, not mad. When she spotted Suze she waved and threaded her way through the maze of tables.

Dr. Marjorie Gordon—Terry—an athletic-looking woman in gray shorts, had short, honey-brown hair and blue eyes. She was very tan, with crinkly lines at the corners of her eyes when she smiled. A pair of tortoise-shell reading glasses perched just above her forehead. Like most of the women on the Hill, she wore no makeup. Her only jewelry was a gold wedding ring and a Timex watch with a brown leather band.

"Hi, sweetie," she said to Suze. "Coffee, cream," she said to the waitress. She gave Suze a quick kiss on the temple and sat down in the empty chair next to her, then reached across the table and squeezed her husband's hand. "How was your day?" she asked.

"Not bad," he said. "I talked to Cyril about the procurement schedule for forty-nine. I had lunch with some of the X boys. We started looking at the diffusion data. Nothing really new. How was yours?"

She made a face. "Tedious. One of the IBMs broke down again, and we lost half a day's calculations. Dick Feynman got it up and running, thank god, but not until almost four. I managed to get some preliminary results, but they weren't at all what I was hoping." She added a long stream of cream to her coffee and stirred.

"Are you going back tonight?" he asked.

She shook her head. "I'm too tired to think straight. Besides, the computers have gone home for the night. I'll tackle it fresh in the morning."

As far as Suze was concerned, they were both talking in code. Except she knew that the computers were women who ran big adding machines. She thought about asking what they were talking about, but they wouldn't tell her. And it would probably be boring, even if she understood.

"Who were those guys you came in with?" she asked instead. "Do you work with them?"

"Two of them. The bald one is in my singing group. Oh!" She snapped her fingers. "That reminds me. We changed our rehearsal time for the show tomorrow night. I need to find Jimmy, our tenor, and let him know. Glorious Irish voice, and he's *got* to be there, or we're sunk." She looked around the room. "I don't see him," she said after a minute. "Maybe I'll run by his place later, on the way home, and let him know." She shook her head. "Sometimes it's damned inconvenient with no phones up here."

"What are you going to sing?" asked Suze. Around the house, her mother sang along with the radio, and she used to sing her lullabies, when she was little. But neither of them seemed like the kind of songs you'd do for an audience.

"Schubert, mostly. Edward Teller's going to play piano for us," she said. "Imagine that."

"Oh," said Suze. Classical stuff, not real songs.

She sat and ate her pudding in tiny bites, trying to make it last, trying to make circles with secret pies in them, while her mother ate and her father had another cup of coffee. They were talking about grown-up things again. Not work, but groceries and drinks and did they want to have dinner with so-and-so. It was just as boring.

"Oh, say, what do you think of this?" her father asked, showing his wife what he'd written on his wrist.

She squinted, pulled her glasses down onto her nose, and said, "Nice." Then they were both talking in science code again, talking really fast and smiling at each other. They looked like they were having fun. A minute later her mother grabbed a paper napkin, and began scribbling numbers and Greek things on it.

"Okay, but if lambda is the rate of beta decay," she said at one point, and Philip nodded, then said, "Oh! Oh!" He grabbed the mechanical pencil from her hand and scribbled more.

"Is that Greek too?" Suze asked.

He didn't look up. "Yes. Not now," he said, and continued to write.

Suze slumped back in her chair. Right then, it seemed like her parents were from another planet, one that she would never be able to visit. She thought wistfully about *Wonder Woman*, back on the kitchen table.

A few minutes later her father folded up the napkin and put it in his pocket. "This could be good," he said, smiling at his wife. "I'm going to go run it by Cyril." He stood up, patted Suze on the cheek without really looking at her, and walked out of the dining room.

Suze watched him go. "Is Daddy going back to work?"

"Just for an hour or two." Her mother finished her coffee.

"Oh." She would be in bed by then. Suze kicked the rung of the chair.

"What's wrong?"

"Daddy was going to teach me the Greek alphabet after dinner."

"Greek?" Her mother raised one eyebrow. "How come?"

"So I'll be able to talk in math," Suze said. "Like you two do." She bounced her sneaker off the rung of her chair again.

"Oh. I see," said her mother. She tapped her fingers on the table. "Well, tell you what, sweetie. Why don't you come along with me to Jimmy's place. Then when we get home, you and I can sit down and I'll write that whole alphabet out for you." She touched Suze's face with the back of her hand and smiled. "That way if Daddy gets some time, you can surprise him with how much you already know." She winked and stood up. "Deal?"

"Deal," said Suze, and was glad, for once, that her mother was a scientist too.

MORGANVILLE

"YOU KNOW," SAID Suze's mother as they walked out of the Lodge, "I haven't taken my day off this month. What do you say the two of us go down to Santa Fe Wednesday afternoon? School starts the week after, and you'll need supplies."

"Okay," Suze said, smiling. Her grandfather owned a stationery store in Berkeley, and she loved getting new pencils and paper—loved the smell of pencil shavings curling down from the sharpener and the way a needle-sharp new point made black lines as thin as thread on a blank white page.

"We'll make a day of it, you and I. Lunch at the Woolworth's counter, shopping, the whole shebang."

"Okay!" said Suze, with even more enthusiasm. The Woolworth's here served chili over an opened-up bag of Fritos, which she thought was even better than steak.

At the end of Bathtub Row, Suze turned left and started across the road to the row of apartment buildings. Her mother reached out and tapped her on the arm. "This way," she said, pointing off to the right.

"Your friend lives in *Morgan*ville?" Suze asked.

"Unfortunately. He was in the men's dorm when he first got here. Then his daughter came from back east, sometime last winter. He said they spent two months in a trailer while the Morgans were being built. So I guess a duplex is a step up."

"Maybe," Suze said skeptically. Everyone knew which places to live were the best. Bathtub Row, of course, and then the Sundts, the apartments where they lived. There were a lot of Sundts, but not enough, because more people kept moving to the Hill. So the army had built the Morgans, which nobody liked. But even *they* beat living in a trailer.

"Ick," Suze said a minute later. The Sundts had been built among a few trees, against the slope of the hillside, but in Morganville the one-story, barracks-like buildings were lined up in straight rows on the bare, flat ground. And they were just boxes, with no porches or balconies or anything. It looked like a prison camp, she thought.

Her mother made a face. "Yep. Makes our place seem like a palace, doesn't it?" She dropped her cigarette in the dirt and ground it out with the toe of her moccasin. "Third row, second building," she said. They walked over, and she stopped in front of one of the identical boxes. One doorstep was surrounded by cactus plants in colorful clay pots. The door to the other was open, and through the screen Suze could hear a man laugh, and then a child's giggle.

"Jimmy?" her mother called. The laughter continued for a moment, then faded, and half a minute later a dark-haired man came to the door. He was barefoot, in a T-shirt tucked into a pair of khaki shorts with lots of pockets, like Boy Scout shorts. He held a red-striped dishcloth in one hand.

"Hey, Terry," he said with a big smile. "We just finished supper. It's my night for the dishes." He opened the door.

"Your cactus garden?" she asked.

"Nope. The neighbors'. Juanita Sandoval's got a green thumb. Nice to have some color around here too, let me tell you. Come on in."

The kitchen was tiny, barely big enough for them to all stand in at once. The table was a wide counter with a bench, built into the wall, and a corner cupboard displayed bright-colored dishes and white china mugs. At the side of the sink, a wooden dish rack held two plates, two forks, and a glass tumbler, all neatly aligned.

He folded the dishcloth and laid it next to the rack.

"We don't get company very often. Let's go into the living room." He motioned them through a doorway with no door.

The living room was not much bigger. It was less than half the size of theirs, Suze thought, with no fireplace. All the furniture was army-issue, except for some bright watercolor paintings on the wall. Across a low coffee table covered with some papers and a slide rule, two identical wooden chairs with leather seats faced a couch with green-striped cushions. She was glad her parents had shipped their real furniture out here.

The man named Jimmy leaned against the doorframe. "Have a seat. Do you want a Coke? Or a real drink? I heard you had a major snafu with the IBMs today."

Suze's mother smiled. "Maybe just a little one. We can't stay long." She sat down on the couch. "You want a Coke, Suze?"

Suze shrugged. "I guess so."

"*Su*san," her mother said, in her "young lady" tone of voice.

"What?" Suze slumped down on the other end of the couch. "Oh. I mean, yes, please."

"Be right back," said Jimmy. He returned in a minute with a bottle of Coke and two squat glasses with ice and an inch of brown liquid. He handed them their drinks, then perched on the arm of the chair across from them.

Suze thought he looked kind of like an elf.

Her mother took a sip of the drink. "Oh god, Jimmy. It's Bushmills. How heavenly."

"I brought it back from Albuquerque," he said with a grin. "I just can't stand rum, and that's all the Santa Fe store seems to be able to get." He swirled his glass, and the ice cubes rattled. "So what brings you to my neighborhood?"

"Kay had to reschedule tomorrow's rehearsal. An hour earlier, just as soon as the siren sounds," Terry Gordon said.

"No problem. I'll just take my good shirt to the lab in the morning. Saves me the trouble of coming all the way back over here to change."

Suze drank her Coke and tried to read what was on the papers on the coffee table. They were upside down from where she was sitting, covered with drawings and penciled numbers and words, but big, like a kid's writing, so she was pretty sure they weren't top secret. She leaned over a little more and tilted her head.

"Easier to read if you just turn them around," said Jimmy. He reached over and rotated the stack of papers so it faced Suze.

"*Suze,*" said her mother. "It's not polite to—"

"That's okay," Jimmy said, holding up his hand. "The army won't let me keep a diary, and any eyes-only documents are back in my office. It's just a little bit of calculus. My daughter's taking apart a broken clock, and I thought it'd help her understand the gear ratios. She's picking it up pretty fast too." He turned to Suze. "Do you like math?"

Suze shook her head. "Not really," she said. "But I learned about pie tonight. I like drawing circles. They—" She heard a door open down the short hallway to the right of Jimmy's chair.

"Papa!" said an excited voice, coming closer, "I think I figured it out. When the biggest gear—" A small curly-haired girl appeared in the doorway, wearing a sleeveless army-green G.I. undershirt that came down below her knees. She stopped in mid-sentence when she saw there were other people in the room. "Oh. I'm sorry," she said.

"It's okay, Dews." Jimmy Kerrigan reached over and put his arm around his daughter's waist. "This is my friend Terry Gordon, and her daughter Susan. Suze. Terry's in the chorus with me."

"Hello," Dewey said to Suze's mother. A brief pause. "Hi, Suze."

"Hi." A longer pause. "Dewey."

"You girls know each other?" asked Suze's mother.

The two girls exchanged glances. Neither spoke. Finally Dewey said, "Sort of." She stepped in closer to her father.

Suze sat there with her mouth open. This was Dewey Kerrigan's house? She'd been sitting on Screwy *Dewey's* couch? She squirmed and moved her bare legs so that only the fabric of her shorts was actually touching the cushions.

"So what did you figure out, Dews?" asked Jimmy after a few moments, breaking the silence that now seemed to fill the room.

"Just the gears," Dewey said. "I'll show you after your company's gone." She slipped out of his arm. "It was nice to meet you, Mrs. Gordon," she said. She turned and walked the few steps down the hallway and back into an unseen bedroom. Suze heard the door shut with a soft click.

"Oh dear," said Suze's mother. She looked at her watch. "I guess we ought to get going." She drained the last bit of her drink and stood up. "Thanks for the whiskey, Jimmy. I'll see you tomorrow night." She took two steps across the room and rested a hand briefly on his shoulder. "Looks like someone else needs you right now. Gear ratios, huh?" She shook her head, but was smiling.

"You should see her room," he said. "It looks like Rube Goldberg set up an engineering lab in there." He lowered his voice. "I'm getting her an Erector set for her birthday. It'll be fun to see what she does with motors."

"My guess is you'll have your hands full."

"Probably." Jimmy Kerrigan looked fondly toward the

bedroom. "It hasn't been easy, just the two of us. I've been away so much, and she's such a smart kid, a smart *girl* kid to boot. Always asking questions. I'm afraid not many of her teachers could handle that. So this is heaven for her. Everywhere we go, there's one of the best science minds in the world. Nobel Prize winners, just walking down the street. The other night we stopped to chat and she and Fermi spent fifteen minutes talking about why candle flames are blue. Enrico Fermi." He took the glass from Terry's hand. "I've never seen her happier."

"I think a lot of that is having you around too," Suze's mother said with a smile. "And speaking of curious girls, I promised to introduce mine to some Greek, right?" She looked over at Suze and raised an eyebrow.

"I'm coming." Suze put down her Coke bottle and stood up quickly. "Thank you for the Coke, Mr. Kerrigan," she said, without being asked.

"Jimmy, please," he said. "And any time." He opened the screen door, holding it for them as they walked out into the late-summer twilight. The western sky was wiped with wisps of orange and the mountains were dusky gray silhouettes. Suze could smell spices from someone's dinner through an open window.

"Dewey seems like an interesting girl," said her mother as they walked past the houses of Bathtub Row. Lamps in the windows cast rectangles of yellow light onto the dirt at their feet.

Suze couldn't think of anything safe to say, so she nodded to show she was listening.

"Maybe you could ask her to come over and play some afternoon. Or do homework," her mother said. "Once school starts, I mean."

"Maybe I will," Suze said, lying. She kicked a pebble with her foot, skittering it off into some pine needles.

And maybe pigs will learn to fly.

1945

March 24
TIME MACHINE

DEWEY SAT AT the kitchen table, eating a bowl of Kix. She didn't like it much, but it was the only cereal the PX had in stock that week. She was chasing the last little beige ball around in the pool of milk when Papa came in from the hall, knotting his tie.

"Why are you all dressed up?" she asked. When he'd taught at Harvard, when she was a little girl, he'd worn a jacket and tie to class, but except for his singing concerts, she hadn't seen him in anything that fancy since they'd come to the Hill.

"General Groves is here with some committee from Washington. Oppie asked if I'd meet with them, I guess to fill them in on what my section's been doing." He poured a cup of coffee from the glass Chemex carafe on the stove and sat down at the table next to her.

"That sounds important," Dewey said. "More important

than usual, I mean." Everything about the war was important these days.

He made a face. "I'd rather be working. I don't have time to stop and talk to bureaucrats who won't understand half of what I'm saying. But I guess since we're living on government money, they've got a right to ask what we're doing with it."

"Will you be home for dinner?"

"I don't think so, Dews." He shook his head. "This meeting could take up most of the day, and there are a couple of folders on my desk that *have* to get done. I'll probably be pretty late. Do you want to go over to the Sandovals' for dinner?"

Dewey thought about it. The Sandovals lived next door. Mr. Sandoval was a machinist, and his wife Juanita made very good enchiladas. But she shook her head. "No, that's okay. I'll cook macaroni and cheese. There's one more box in the cupboard." She looked out their little window. The late spring snow had melted, except for a few patches in the shadows, and thin, pale sunlight was peeking through the clouds. "If it stays nice, are we still going to Frijoles Canyon tomorrow?"

He smiled. "Absolutely. Sunday with my girl. Not even Washington is going to interfere with that. I used my coupons to gas up the car yesterday, so we're all set. I'll ask the Lodge to make us up a box lunch."

"Okay." Dewey smiled back. Sundays were her favorite day of the week, the only day that Papa didn't go to his lab. No one did. If it rained, people read, or went to the Lodge and talked and played cards. But mostly they went outside and rode horses up into the mountains and fished, or hiked in one of the canyons. Dewey couldn't hike very far, because her leg began to ache after an hour or so. But there were a dozen canyons that Papa could drive to, where they could have a picnic or build a campfire or collect rocks and even arrowheads.

"But," she said, waving a stern finger at him, "you have to promise not to talk to the other men about work the *whole* time." That was usually what happened. The kids ran around, the women sat around the fire and talked, and the men walked a little bit away and spent the afternoon talking science and drawing equations on boulders with charcoal.

"I promise," he said. He pulled out his silver pocket watch and snapped open the case. "Almost eight. I'd better be going." He drained his coffee cup, rinsed it, and put it in the wooden rack. "Are you sure about the Sandovals?"

"I'm sure. I have to do a book report for school, and I want to work on my time machine. It's almost done." She had built a gadget that connected an alarm clock to the radio—not her crystal set radio, but the tabletop model the army had issued them for the house—so that she could wake up to music in the morning. But one of the parts kept sticking, and she wanted to fix it.

"Okay then." He pulled on his jacket. "Wish me luck with the brass."

"Good luck, Dr. Kerrigan," Dewey said, saluting with two fingers, "Give 'em hell."

Jimmy laughed and went out the back door into the crisp morning air.

＝＝＝

For most of the morning, Dewey read *Caddie Woodlawn*, which had won some medal and was about a girl on a farm in olden days. It was kind of boring until the girl started to fix a clock, which Dewey liked. She wrote her book report, two pages, in ink, with Papa's blue fountain pen, starting over twice because she made a mistake, and cross-outs looked messy.

She finally put her homework into her school satchel a little before noon and went back to her bedroom to get the pieces of the time machine. Soon the kitchen table was covered with bits of wire and parts from her new Erector set. She had found a pair of wire clippers at the dump— with just one tip broken off—and that made work much easier. She didn't have to bend a wire back and forth, back and forth until it broke. The cutters bit into the wire with a satisfying *snap*. A few little pieces had flown off onto the kitchen floor, though, and she hadn't found all of them.

She was giving it a final run-through when someone knocked at the door. "Come on in," she said, loud enough to be heard outside. "I've got my hands full."

The door opened, and Papa's friend Terry Gordon peeked around it. "Hi, Dewey. Is your dad around? He's not in his lab."

"Hi, Mrs. Gordon. Papa's not here, either. He's got meetings with Oppie and some brass people today. I don't know where, exactly." Dewey put down her screwdriver.

"Oh. Really. We were supposed to have lunch. Well, another time, I guess." Mrs. Gordon started to leave, then saw the tabletop full of wires and whistled. "Boy, you *did* have your hands full. That's an impressive contraption." She stepped into the kitchen.

Dewey nodded. "It's my time machine."

"Are you planning a trip back before the war? That would be nice." Mrs. Gordon leaned against the counter and smiled, so Dewey knew she was just kidding.

"Sometimes I'd like that," she agreed. "But this is more practical. When I get this last piece fixed, it's going to turn on my radio in the morning. I hate waking up to the alarm bell. Too loud."

"I'm with you there," Mrs. Gordon laughed. She leaned

down to look at the machine, then frowned. "It would help if I could see," she said, and slid her glasses down from the top of her head. "Now how does it work?"

Dewey looked at her in surprise. "You really want to know?"

"Yes, I really do."

"Oh. Okay." Dewey was pleased. She looked down at the machine. "It's pretty simple. First I have to plug in the radio. Papa won't let me take it apart, because it's electric, and that can be dangerous, but as long as I keep the back on, it's okay." She looked up to see if Mrs. Gordon was following, and when the woman nodded, she continued.

"Then I wind up the alarm clock and set it to when I want to wake up, just like a regular one. But when it's time, instead of ringing the bell, the little hammer hits this dowel and pokes it through the tube, and it hits this gate." Dewey pointed to a pivoting piece of wire. "The gate opens, and the ball bearing rolls down the ramp onto the paddle wheel. The weight of the bearing turns the wheel, and that works like a pulley, and winds this string." She touched a piece of kite string with her index finger. "The other end of the string is glued to the radio knob, and when it's wound tight enough around the pulley, it turns the radio on. But not *too* loud."

"That's really ingenious," said Mrs. Gordon. "Did you read about it in a book somewhere?"

"No, I just kind of made it up."

"That's where the best ideas come from." Mrs. Gordon picked up the ball bearing and rolled it around the palm of her hand. "Well, since your dad's not here, would *you* like to have lunch? I'm starving. And I'd love to hear more about your inventions."

Dewey considered this for a moment, then nodded. "My stomach was growling, so I was just about to take a break and make myself a peanut-butter-and-jam sandwich."

"Sounds lovely," said Mrs. Gordon. "If you want, I'll make two of them and you can clear a space on the table. Or we could eat in the living room, if that would be easier."

"No," said Dewey. "We eat in the kitchen." She began to pick up the pieces of her machine. "Will you cut the crusts off mine? I don't like that part, but the ducks in the Pond do."

"Sure. Maybe I'll trim mine too. I always feel bad for those ducks when it's cold. Do you like your sandwich cut into squares or triangles?" she asked.

"Triangles, please," said Dewey.

They ate and talked for almost half an hour. Mrs. Gordon had lit a cigarette and was telling Dewey about teaching chemistry at Berkeley, when she glanced down at her watch. "Oh, good gracious, it's after one. I have to skedaddle." She picked up her plate. "I really liked this. Maybe we could do it again sometime."

"Okay," said Dewey.

"Good. See you soon." Mrs. Gordon let herself out the back door.

Dewey sat in the kitchen for a few minutes, finishing her milk, and thinking about the last half hour. She had never known a real woman scientist before, just men like Papa. She liked Mrs. Gordon a lot, and wondered how someone so nice could have a daughter as bossy as Suze. It didn't make any sense. She washed the plates and put them in the rack, then laid her time machine out on the table.

She made sure all the pieces were hooked up, set the alarm clock for 3:00, and went into the living room to read. For a few pages she found it hard to concentrate, because all she wanted to do was look at the red plastic clock on the kitchen wall and see what time it was. But then she got caught up in the words, as usual, and forgot all about it.

So she was startled, just for a moment, when "Boogie Woogie Bugle Boy" began playing in mid-song. Then she remembered, dropped her book onto the couch cushion, and ran into the kitchen. The clock said 3:00, straight up. It worked! Dewey did a little skipping dance and laughed out loud. She could hardly wait to tell Papa.

She moved the machine back into her bedroom and reassembled it on the bookcase by the wall, where there was a plug for the radio. She set the alarm part for 8:00 in the morning and smiled, thinking about how nice it would be to go from dreaming to music. Then she returned to her book.

When it got dark outside, about 6:00, she turned the lamp on. She looked up every few minutes, or when she heard a noise, hoping it was Papa coming home and she could tell him her news. She waited and waited, but after a while gave up and made dinner.

Lighting the kerosene stove was not one of Dewey's favorite things—if you didn't do it just right, it could explode, and that was scary. So she was always careful. The macaroni and cheese burned a little on the bottom, but after she scraped off the brown crunchy parts, it was pretty good. She rinsed the pot under hot water, using the scrub brush to get the last bits of sticky burnt cheese off, and found herself humming part of Bach's *Toccata and Fugue in D Minor*. It was one of Papa's favorite songs, one of the few phonograph records they owned, and he had been playing it a lot in the last few weeks.

But when she turned off the water and stopped humming, the music continued. She walked into the living room and looked at the record player. It was closed and silent. Not that she expected it to be playing itself, but where else could the music be coming from? The Sandovals played only mariachi music, or big bands.

She walked back into the kitchen to dry the dishes and saw that the clock said 8:05. Eight! Dewey hit herself in the forehead with the heel of her hand. Oh. The music was her radio! The Hill's station, KRC, always played classical music after dinner. An alarm clock couldn't tell the difference between 8:00 in the morning and 8:00 at night. At least not a civilian clock. Army clocks did. 0800 was morning. 2000 hours was night.

She turned off the radio and reset the gate and the ball bearing and the dowel. Just to make sure, she waited half an hour, then set the alarm for 8:00 again. Eight in the *morning*.

Dewey stayed up as long as she could, waiting for Papa to come home and tell her about his meeting. But at 10:30 she finished her book, the third book that day, and didn't feel like starting another one. She was tired, and if he *had* gone back to his lab, he could be there for hours. She brushed her teeth and went to bed, falling asleep to the slow, steady tick-tock, tick-tock of the mechanical clock that seemed to echo in the empty house.

DRINK SWIRLY-
BIRD COLA

DEWEY'S RADIO CAME on at 8:01 Sunday morning. Church music, which was pretty, but not her favorite. She put on her glasses and loped down the hall to Papa's closed door. Breathing, and some snores. Good. He'd come home. She went back to her room. Papa liked to sleep in on Sunday mornings, because he could.

Dewey got dressed in corduroy pants and a heavy wool sweater that was warm but itched a little and was too long for her arms. In the kitchen, she scrunched up the sleeves and poured another bowl of Kix. She really wanted oatmeal, because it was a chilly morning, but that meant lighting the stove, and she wasn't sure she was awake enough for that.

Papa finally got up around ten. He came into the kitchen barefoot, his blue bathrobe flapping over the striped legs of his flannel pajamas. He needed a shave, and his eyes looked red and watery behind his glasses.

"Morning, Dews," he said. He lit the stove and poured water into the Chemex carafe, then sat down and ran his fingers through his hair, leaving it standing up in little tufts.

"Are you okay?" Dewey asked. He looked tired. He always looked tired these days. But this morning he looked worse than usual, like he was getting a cold.

He smiled, a little smile that barely moved his mouth. "I'll live."

"Are you sick?"

"No, I, uh—" He took off his glasses and rubbed his eyes. "I was working in the lab, a little after ten, I think, and I heard a thud out in the hall. I went to see. Three guys were trying to carry this big lab fixture, a glass bowl about four feet across, over to a party in the men's dorm. For a punch bowl. They asked me to give them a hand, and once I got there, I had a couple of drinks. It wasn't real punch—I mean, the boys were just dumping liquor bottles willy-nilly into the bowl. I think there might have been a can of pineapple juice too. I don't really remember."

"You got *drunk*?" Dewey asked in surprise. Papa often had a beer when he got home from work, or a whiskey after dinner, but she'd rarely seen him have more than one.

"A little," he admitted.

"How come?"

He shrugged. "I just didn't want to think about the war for a while. I didn't want to think about any of this." He gestured with his hand, but Dewey knew he didn't mean their kitchen.

"Then we're not going on a picnic today." Dewey looked down at the table and picked at a flaking bit of paint with her thumbnail.

"No, no, Dews. We'll go. Don't worry." He patted her hand, then got up and poured steaming coffee into a thick china mug. It smelled like burned nuts.

"Would you see if there are any aspirins in the bathroom?" he asked. "Bring me two—no, make that three."

Dewey brought him the chalky white tablets, and he swallowed them with a gulp of coffee and a grimace, then sat back down. "There. When those kick in, I'll be right as rain," he said. "We'll leave in an hour or so."

"Okay," Dewey said. "I got my time machine to work."

"That's great. Sorry I didn't make it back for dinner."

"I know. How was your meeting?"

Jimmy Kerrigan sighed and rubbed his face with his hands. "Long. It was long. I don't like politics." He looked at her for a minute, then reached out and stroked her cheek with the back of his knuckles. For a second,

Dewey thought, he looked like he might cry. Then he dropped his hand and took a drink of coffee. He sighed again. "I'm going to take a shower, see if I can get my head to stop pounding. Then I'll tell you every—" He stopped himself. "Then I'll tell you what I can. We'll have a long talk."

Dewey loved talking to Papa, more than just about anything. But his voice sounded odd—sad, and a little distant.

"Okay, Papa," she said, and wrapped the bulky arms of her sweater tight around her, as if she were shivering.

He came back from the Lodge at 11:00 carrying a white box tied with string.

Dewey looked around, but there was no one with him. "Is it just us?" she asked. Gas was such a scarce commodity, even on the Hill, that Sunday drivers rarely left the gate without stopping at the Lodge to round up a full load of passengers—soldiers, women from the dorms, and other people without families.

"Not very patriotic, I know. But I thought it would be nice if we could be by ourselves today. Just the two of us. Hop in." He held the car door open for her.

They drove slowly through the populated part of the Hill, turned right at the Tech Area, and took the winding road through scattered trees and green buildings to the West Gate. Many sites that had been wooded last fall were now cleared, and there were more buildings every week as the labs spread out farther and farther.

The Hill was a natural fortress, a flat mesa fissured with canyons on three sides. The land didn't slope down, it dropped off abruptly, vertically, with sheer cliffs that ended in tree-lined streams hundreds of feet below. It was pretty, but a little alarming. Dewey moved to the middle of the seat, away from the canyon-side door.

She looked out at the tall Jemez Mountains to the west, peaks covered with white snow against the blue sky. It seemed to her that the sky was bluer than the sky back in St. Louis. The light was different too. Everything seemed crisper, clearer, as if the world up here were a little more than three-dimensional. Maybe it was the altitude.

They drove southwest for almost an hour as the road skirted the edge of canyon after canyon before Dewey saw the sign for Bandelier National Monument. A red sign nailed diagonally across it said LODGE CLOSED.

"It's not open," she said, disappointed.

"Not to the public," said Papa. "It's closed for the duration. We took over the lodge for housing in '43. That is, the government did. I don't think anyone in the project's still living here, but until the war ends, we've pretty much got the run of the place."

Dewey nodded. By now the army probably owned most of New Mexico.

Two adobe-style buildings flanked the entrance road, a dirt track that wound steeply down into the canyon. At the bottom, Papa parked the car in front of another adobe building that was dwarfed by the towering cliffs behind it. He got his knapsack out of the trunk and put a blanket, a flashlight, and a green metal thermos into it, then stacked the lunch box on top and cinched the top shut. "Let's take a walk," he said, and threw the pack over his shoulder.

The path led away from the broad parking area, and the world soon narrowed to a V. The blue sky was a triangle with low brown mountains on one side and steep brown cliffs on the other. Except for a fringe of gray-green oak trees along the creek, and some low scruffy bushes, everything was one of a thousand shades of brown, from pale beige to reddish ochre to chocolate in the shadows. The cool air smelled like pine and juniper, and was so dry that Dewey could feel its sting in the middle of her head when she breathed through her nose.

It was quiet, still. The gritty dirt path scritched under the soles of her shoes, and she could hear the creak of the leather straps on Papa's pack as they walked. A hundred feet to their left, unseen, Frijoles Creek murmured gently as the water flowed over stones on its way down to the

Rio Grande. On their right, knee-high grass and saltbush grew around rough-pitted angular boulders at the base of the cliffs. Dewey had to bend her neck as far as it would go to see the cliff tops, where the road was.

At the base of the cliffs, the rocks looked like they had been sculpted out of wet clay, squeezed into formations by giant hands, like geologic snowmen left to dry in the New Mexico sun.

"What kind of rock is this?" asked Dewey. She picked up a small chunk lying in the path and found that she could crumble bits off between her palms.

"It's called tuff. It's volcanic ash, compressed for thousands of years, and it's pretty soft. Porous, like the pumice stone I use on my feet."

"There's a *volcano* here?"

"There was. Still hot springs around, so some thermal activity's going on, but nothing to worry about. Hey, look," he said, pointing at the cliffs. "Take a look at that!"

Dewey looked, but didn't see anything to get excited about.

"Gotta get closer," Papa said. He boosted her up onto a low ledge a few feet above the path and clambered up after her. "Now can you see it?" He pointed to a flat place on the rock wall, in the shadow of an overhang.

Dewey stared into the dimness. It just looked like

ordinary rock, with faint veins of other minerals. Then she saw it, a cluster of crude drawings. A spiral, a stick-figure man, a bird. Or maybe a dog. It was hard to tell. She moved closer and ran her fingertips gently along the incised outline of one of the figures.

"Who drew these?" she asked.

"The people who used to live here. The Anasazi."

"People *lived* here?"

Papa nodded. "A long time ago. They vanished without a trace. Maybe they got sick. Maybe there was a war. Nobody really knows, but they've been gone for about four hundred years."

"Is this their art?"

"Possibly. Or it could have been a message. For all we know, it's all that's left of an Anasazi billboard. Drink Swirly-Bird Cola."

"*Papa.*" Dewey giggled.

"Well, maybe not." He looked up at the cliff face. "C'mon. Let's have lunch in one of their houses."

"Okay," agreed Dewey. She looked around, but didn't see any buildings. "Is it much farther? I'm getting kind of hungry."

"It's right here." Papa pointed to a narrow path that led up the cliff. "You up for a little bit of climbing? Not too far."

"Sure," said Dewey, although she wasn't really sure.

Not about the climbing part, that was okay. But she still didn't see any house.

They were puffing a little when they got to the top of the path, which opened out onto a small ledge. A crude ladder about eight feet high, thick branches lashed together, leaned against the wall of the cliff. Its top rested inches below a dark opening. A cave?

"After you," said Papa, and reached out one hand to steady the ladder.

Dewey climbed. The ladder was sturdier than it looked. It didn't even creak under her weight when she put her foot on the first rung. But the rungs were pretty far apart for someone her size, and she had to stretch to climb up each step.

At the top, she stepped into a small rounded room, about six feet on a side, and tall enough that she could stand up without ducking. Papa climbed up behind her and tossed his knapsack onto the crumbly stone floor.

"Hey, it's a suite," he said. He ducked through another opening in the right-hand wall. Dewey followed, and was surprised to find a second room, and a third beyond that. The air was cooler and felt a little damp, although the stone walls and floor looked dry. Dewey was glad she had her plaid wool jacket on.

Papa spread a green army blanket on the floor of the

first room and put the lunch box on it. He sat down, cross-legged, and opened the thermos.

"Tea? I made it the way you like, lots of milk and honey. It'll warm you up a little, while I go get some wood to make a fire." He poured some of the steaming liquid into the metal top and handed it to her.

He climbed back down the ladder and was back in a few minutes with an armful of big sticks and branches. He piled them against the opposite wall, where the dirt was blackened, making a loose teepee shape with the larger branches on the outside. He scratched a kitchen match on the rock wall and held it to the base of the teepee. Dewey watched the little yellow flames lick the dry wood and change to orange as the fire grew. She wondered about the smoke, and was surprised to see that it rose straight up into a small soot-rimmed hole in the ceiling of the room.

They sat on the blanket, their backs against the other wall, passing the tea back and forth because there was only one cup. Dewey felt snug and cozy, and could almost imagine people living like this, waking up every morning to the sky and the mountains just outside the door.

"I like this," she said. "It feels like a secret hideout."

"Our special private place," said Papa. He nudged the lunch box over with the toe of his boot, then reached down and opened it. "Looks like they gave us ham-and-cheese sandwiches, a couple of apples, and . . . what's this?" He opened the wax paper around a dark square. "Mmm. Chocolate brownies. A fine feast." He handed Dewey a sandwich.

She ate in contented silence, listening to the crackling of the fire. Then she noticed Papa wasn't eating. He had taken one bite out of his sandwich, but now it lay in his lap, and he was just staring out the doorway into the distance.

"Papa? Is something wrong?"

He didn't respond for a few seconds, then turned to her and sighed. "I need to tell you some things that I'm not supposed to talk about. That's why I wanted us to be alone, and why I wanted to be someplace very private."

"Are you going to tell me about the gadget?"

"No. *That* I can't tell you. But this has to be a secret too."

"I won't tell anyone. Promise." Dewey made an X across her chest. "You can trust me."

"I know I can." Papa leaned back against the wall and closed his eyes. After a moment he took a deep breath and, without opening his eyes, began to talk.

"Before the war, when you were just a tiny baby, I worked on a project with two other men. David was at Princeton, and Josef was in Berlin."

"You worked with a Nazi?" Dewey was shocked.

"No. I worked with a German mathematician. A good man. A good friend. Math is its own language, Dews, its own elegant world. But the rest of the world changed around us. Some professors, like Einstein and Fermi, escaped and came over here. And others, like Heisenberg and my friend Josef went to work for their government, the way I'm working for mine."

He reached into his jacket pocket, pulled out a pack of Camels, and lit one. Dewey was surprised. He rarely smoked, only when he was working on a very stubborn problem, or when he was upset. She didn't say anything, but reached out and held his other hand.

"I didn't want this war. None of us did. But what we're doing here is critical. I believe that," he said, blowing out a stream of blue smoke. "So I came to New Mexico to work on the most challenging problem I've ever been posed. And I love that. I've gotten up every morning excited to go to my desk, hoping it's the day a pattern starts to emerge, and the pieces begin fitting together." He stopped and looked out at the sky.

"If we win this war, I'll always be free to do what I love. To solve problems, to teach, to share my discoveries. A lot of my colleagues can't. Some of them have died for it."

"Because they did math?"

"Because they were Jewish." He shook his head slowly.

"Before the war, we—the scientific community—could talk about our ideas. We were trying to understand how the world works, and borders didn't matter. But they do now. And a lot of the work we're doing here, on the Hill, is based on discoveries German scientists made in the thirties. So it's likely Josef and the others are trying to solve the same problems. But god help us if they get there first."

His cigarette burned down to his fingers and he flipped the butt into the fire. "That's part of what yesterday's meeting was about."

He put his arm around Dewey, pulling her tight to him, and leaned over so his head was touching hers.

"I love you so much," Papa said, his voice barely above a whisper. "But I have to go away again. A couple of weeks. The General's asked me to help them make sense of some German papers they've found."

"It's important?" Dewey asked.

He nodded. "I wouldn't go if it wasn't."

"Okay," Dewey said in a small voice. It wasn't okay at all, but she knew that was what Papa wanted her to say. She curled into his side, her head resting in the hollow of his shoulder. They sat that way for a long time, until the small fire burned to ashes, the rest of their sandwiches untouched.

March 30

PATRIOTIC DUTY

SUZE GOT HOME from school a little before 4:00 on the last Friday in March. She clattered up the back steps and opened the door, thinking about the leftover pie in the icebox and the box of colored pencils Grandpa Weiss had sent her for Hanukkah. She was startled to see her mother sitting at the kitchen table.

"Why are *you* home? Why aren't you in your lab?" she asked, dropping her books on the counter with a thump.

"It's nice to see you too, sweetie," said her mother, putting down her coffee cup. "Sit down and have a Coke with me." She patted the chair next to her.

Suze nodded, but her radar was on alert. Something was up. She wracked her brain to see if there was anything she'd done in the last week that she might have gotten caught at, but came up blank. Things had been pretty boring lately. Just school.

Her mother arched one eyebrow and cocked her head in the direction of the Coke bottle. Suze sat.

"How was school?" Her mother lit a Chesterfield and put the match into the ashtray Daddy had given her for Christmas, a square of glass with a picture of a skunk with Hitler's face. JAM YOUR BUTTS ON THIS SKUNK, it said.

"Okay," Suze said warily. "We're doing all the states around here. The West. Cowboys and buffaloes. It's pretty interesting." She took a drink of Coke. "And long division and spelling in the afternoon."

The subjects in this school were about the same as she had in her old one, except there was hardly any science. Suze thought that was weird, because the Hill had more scientists than any place in the whole world, probably. But they were all too busy working on gadget stuff to teach kids, and most of the mothers who had been to college worked in one of the labs as a computer or a secretary. Suze figured that was because they could understand what they were typing.

"That's good," her mother said. She tapped her cigarette, even though the ash wasn't very long at all, and Suze realized that she was stalling. Her radar jumped to red alert.

"I think there's enough space in your room for a second bed, don't you, Suze? I mean, if we moved your dresser over against the other wall and put the desk out in the living room, I think we could fit another twin bed, or at least a cot, in there."

Her mother was talking fast and giving her lots of useless information, which wasn't normal. Suze suspected that she knew what was coming next.

"Are you going to have a baby?" she asked. Half the wives on the Hill were pregnant, it seemed.

"What?" Mrs. Gordon put her coffee cup down so hard it sloshed onto the oilcloth. "God, no! I mean, not now. Not here." She shook her head and laughed. "Nothing that earthshaking. We're just going to have a visitor for a little while, that's all."

"Like who?" No one on the Hill was allowed to have guests from outside, except Oppie, and that was only VIPs from Washington or Chicago, who stayed in the Big House by the Lodge. The Hill was pretty crowded, but they wouldn't make a big shot sleep in a *kid's* room, would they?

"Well, you remember Jimmy Kerrigan, the tenor in my singing group? We went to his house in Morganville last summer once, right before school started? Anyway, he has to—"

Suze didn't hear the rest of the sentence because she felt like she was going to throw up. That was Screwy Dewey's father. No, Mom couldn't mean *her*. It had to be someone else. It had to be—

"*Suze*? Have you heard a word I've said?"

Suze bit her lip and nodded.

"Okay, then." Mrs. Gordon took a puff on her cigarette, ground it out in the ashtray, and continued. "So Jimmy's going away for a couple of weeks. Washington, I think, although he couldn't say. Top secret, very hush-hush, even for this place. Doesn't matter, really," she said. "The point is he's going to be gone for a while and of course he can't take his daughter with him. Poor guy didn't know what to do. But I told him it would be no trouble at all for Dewey to stay with us. You girls are in the same class."

Suze winced. She'd said it. Her mother had said the name, out loud. "Dewey?" Suze said, in a voice that came out as more of a squeak.

"Yes, Dewey. I told Jimmy we have plenty of room— well, we don't really, I mean no one does, but the poor kid can't stay by herself, and your room is big enough—so I told him we'd love to have her come and stay."

Suze stared at her mother with her mouth open. "You want to let Dewey Kerrigan sleep in my *room*?"

Mrs. Gordon looked at Suze, her lips in a tight line that was almost a frown, definitely not a smile. "That's the idea, yes."

"No," said Suze.

"What?"

"No. Not Screwy Dewey. I don't like her. No one does." Suze looked away and took a drink of Coke.

"I do," said Mrs. Gordon. "I think she's a very interesting little girl." She was silent for a minute, then put her coffee cup down on her napkin, centering it, and turned it so the handle pointed precisely into one corner. Suze knew then that she was in trouble. Her mother only did that when she was really mad and about to give a lecture.

Mrs. Gordon lit another cigarette, took a puff, and put it into the ashtray, aligning it so that the glowing tip was in the exact center of the square of glass.

Big, big trouble.

"I've had just about enough, Susan," Mrs. Gordon said. "First of all, I don't want you using that terrible name ever again. Screwy Dewey. My Lord. The poor girl hasn't had it easy, and she doesn't need you tormenting her. Got it?" She looked hard at Suze, who nodded her head just a fraction.

"Second—and I don't know how this could have escaped your notice—but for your information, there's a war on. And to win that war, everyone has to pitch in. Daddy and I have put our careers on hold to come and work in the labs here. And you, young lady, are going to do your part by sharing your room. For a few weeks. What a huge sacrifice we're asking of you. *Huge*." Mrs. Gordon stopped and took another puff of her cigarette, blowing the smoke out with an annoyed hiss.

"What kind of person," she continued, "what kind of patriotic American, would be selfish enough to force one of our best scientists to choose between keeping his daughter out of an orphanage—or worse—and saving the world from Hitler? Just so you can have your own room? How do you think—?"

Suze slumped down in her chair and let her mother's rant wash over her. She didn't think that even Mom really believed the Nazis would win if Screwy Dewey didn't sleep in her room. But she knew when she was licked.

"Well, do you have anything to say for yourself?" asked Mrs. Gordon when she had finished.

Suze sighed. "When's she coming?"

"Monday. I'll go down to the housing office and see about getting another bed." Mrs. Gordon stubbed out her cigarette and stood up. She went to the back door, then stopped, one hand on the knob, and turned around, attempting a smile. "It'll be fine," she said. "You'll see."

Suze said nothing. Life as she knew it was over. Again.

CHANGING OF
THE GUARD

JIMMY KERRIGAN PUT the brown suitcase down on the floor beside the fireplace in the Gordons' living room.

"That's the last of it, Terry," he said. "If the weather warms up much, she'll need to go back to our place and get some lighter clothes, and she may want some books that didn't make her first cut. But I think she's basically covered for the next couple of weeks." He sat down on the arm of the nubby green sofa. The red metal box of Dewey's Erector set lay on the seat. "I can't tell you how much this means to me."

"I know," said Terry Gordon. "It's hard. But I'm glad she's here. She's a bright, interesting kid. I'm happy to get the chance to know her better. In my copious free time," she laughed. "And I think Suze will enjoy the company— once she gets over the snit she's in."

"Are you sure it's not going to be a problem for her?"

"I'm sure. It's just that she's an only child, and she's pretty used to getting her own way. I think this will be good for her. And even though she hasn't said anything, I suspect she's been getting kind of lonely, especially in the evenings, what with both Phil and me working until all hours."

"Tell me about it. I don't think I made it home for supper two nights in a row all last month. I'm sure Dewey will be glad to have someone to talk to over the macaroni, won't you, Dews?" He turned to the kitchen doorway where Dewey was standing motionless.

"I guess so," she said.

"I should get going," he said to Terry. "The train leaves Lamy at six, and I still have to swing by the lab and get my briefcase." He picked up his hat and brushed a few tufts of white cat hair off the pants of his dark blue suit.

"Don't worry about a thing," Terry said. "We'll all be fine. Really." She patted his arm. "I'll stay up here, let you two say good-bye in private. Or what passes for private in this goldfish bowl."

She turned to Dewey. "You go on down with your dad—with your papa. I'll fire up the Black Beauty and make us some Ovaltine, okay?"

"Okay," said Dewey. She didn't move.

Jimmy put his arm around her. "C'mon, Dews. It's not the end of the world. I'll be back in a couple of weeks. Walk me to the car?" He held out his hand.

Dewey nodded and took his hand. They walked slowly down the stairs to the road. There were no other kids around, no other people, because it was the middle of a Monday afternoon, and everyone was in school or in the labs.

They stood for a minute on the bottom stoop in an awkward silence. Dewey didn't know what to say. She was trying very hard not to cry. Papa had gone away before, lots of times. Her whole life. It was an ache she ought to be used to by now. But she never was.

He crouched down so that they were eye-to-eye. "I love you, Dews," he said quietly. "I love you more than anything else in the world. You're my girl." He pulled her into a hug and kissed the top of her head.

Dewey hugged him back fiercely, holding on to him as if she could imprint the sensations of that moment onto herself—the touch of his arms, the smell of his aftershave, the soft scratchy wool of his suit, the warmth of his breath against her ear—to save them for later. She hugged him for a long time, until he finally pulled away, gently, and whispered, "I have to go. But I promise, I'll be back as soon as possible." His eyes shimmered with tears. He kissed her again, once on each cheek, and stood up.

"I'll write when I can," he said. "If I can." He brushed his hand across her curls, then got into his green Studebaker and drove down the road toward the Tech Area. His tires kicked up a little plume of dust as he went around the corner, then he was gone.

Dewey stood on the concrete stoop, staring at the road until the dust had settled back to dirt. A tear trickled down her cheek, and she pushed her glasses up and wiped it away with the back of one wrist.

"Dewey?" Mrs. Gordon was at the top of the stairs. She came down, one careful step at a time, as if trying not to make any sudden moves that might startle Dewey. She paused on the last riser, put out a hand, and touched Dewey's shoulder. Dewey wondered for a moment if Mrs. Gordon was going to try to hug her, and wasn't sure if she wanted that. But Mrs. Gordon just rested her hand on Dewey's sweater for a few seconds and squeezed her shoulder a little. "I'm glad you're going to stay with us," she said. "Let's have some Ovaltine, then we can get you unpacked."

Dewey sniffled once, then nodded and turned around, following her up the steep wooden stairs.

"I expect Suze will be home about four," Mrs. Gordon said, pouring the Ovaltine from a saucepan on the front burner of the big black iron stove. "But you knew that, didn't you? I keep forgetting that you girls are in the same class. Except for math? Suze says you take math with another class?" She put two teacups full of the malty chocolate on the table and sat down.

"Yes, ma'am. I do algebra with the high-school kids," Dewey said, sitting down in a chair on the other side of the table.

Mrs. Gordon raised an eyebrow. "That's a big jump, from sixth grade to high school."

"I guess so. But Papa started teaching me numbers when I was little. He says I could add before I could read." She took a sip. "This is very good. Thank you, Mrs. Gordon."

"'Mrs. Gordon' sounds so formal," she said. "If you want, you can call me Terry. Everyone else does."

Dewey thought for a minute. She called Dick Feynman and some of the other scientists by their names, because they were her friends, even if they were grownups. But they were all men. Nana Gallucci had told her that it was very rude to call a grown-up woman by her first name. And besides, Dewey was pretty sure that Suze didn't call her that. "I don't think Suze would like that," she said finally.

Mrs. Gordon chuckled. "Probably not." She lit a cigarette and snapped her silver lighter shut with a click. "Tell you what. Officially, I'll be Mrs. Gordon. But if it's just us, and no one else is around, Terry is okay." She winked at Dewey.

Dewey felt oddly pleased, like she'd just been made a member of a secret club. "Deal," she said, and tried to wink back, but ended up just kind of squinting. She wasn't very good at winking.

Twenty minutes later, Dewey felt the floor shake a little and heard stomping feet on the outside stairs. Suze was home. Dewey reached down and gripped the chair seat with both hands, bracing herself for what might come next. Suze had glared at her all morning in class. "It wasn't *my* idea," Dewey had wanted to say, but she had kept quiet.

Suze slammed the back door open and dropped her books on the counter. She stood by the stove for a second, looked at Dewey, then opened the icebox door. "We're out of Cokes," she said.

"I know," said Mrs. Gordon. "But I made Ovaltine. I saved some for you, on the stove." She pointed to the saucepan. "Why don't you pour yourself a cup, and then we'll show Dewey your room and get you girls settled."

Suze scowled and opened the cupboard with a bang, found a mug, and filled it from the saucepan, spilling some in the process. She did not sit down at the table, but drank it standing up. "Okay, let's go," she said when she was finished, and walked out of the room.

"Oh, dear," said Mrs. Gordon. She looked over at Dewey, who just shrugged and stood up. In the living room, Mrs. Gordon picked up the brown suitcase. "Suze's room is the one on the right," she said, pointing down the tiny hallway.

Dewey picked up her Erector set and stood beside the couch, holding the metal box in front of her like a shield. The box was bright red, brand-new, and very heavy. It was a little larger than her arms could comfortably encircle.

"Here, let me take that," offered Mrs. Gordon. "It looks like it weighs a ton." She put down the suitcase.

"No, that's okay," said Dewey. She clutched the box a fraction tighter, as if it were full of the last eggs of an endangered bird. "I've got it." She walked a few awkward steps, trying not to stagger under the weight of the box.

"Don't be silly." Mrs. Gordon reached out a hand and touched the edge of the metal box. Dewey didn't let go. Mrs. Gordon looked at her for a long second, then said gently, "Jimmy gave you this, didn't he?"

Dewey nodded.

"I thought so. Why don't you let me take it in and put it on the bed for you? I'd hate to have you drop it." She left her hand on the box but didn't pull any harder. "I'll be very careful. I promise," she added.

Dewey wasn't really sure if she could make it all the way to the bedroom. And if she did drop the box, it would never be the same. Mrs. Gordon was a scientist. Maybe she understood how important it was. Dewey eased one hand off. When she was sure Mrs. Gordon had the box securely, she let go with her other hand and followed.

Mrs. Gordon carried the box and put it down on the foot of the closer of the two twin beds. Its bright red metal looked out of place against the pink chenille bedspread.

"After you've unpacked, we'll figure out a good safe place where this can live," she said. "Maybe under your bed? I think we've got a piece of linoleum left over from putting in the bathroom floor. It ought to slide in and out pretty easily on that."

Dewey smiled, just a little. Mrs. Gordon *did* understand. Behind them, in the doorway, Suze sighed dramatically and thumped down the brown paper sack she had been carrying.

"What's in here, bricks?" she asked.

"Just books," said Dewey.

Suze unfolded the top of the bag. Dewey started to say something, started to shake her head no, then shrank away from the protest like a turtle pulling its head back toward its shell.

Suze reached in and picked up a book, riffling the pages with a thumb. "*The Boy Mechanic*," she said, snickering. "Why do you have *that*?"

"They didn't make one for girls," Dewey replied. She held out her hand for the book, and after a second, Suze gave it to her.

The bedroom was small and square with thin plasterboard walls painted a waxy yellow. The paint was already beginning to flake a little in the corners, even though the whole building was less than two years old. The pair of twin beds, a nightstand between them, took up most of the space. At the foot of the two beds stood a pine dresser, painted a pale robin's-egg blue.

"Suze cleaned out the top two drawers," Mrs. Gordon said. "So those can be yours." She put Dewey's suitcase down at the foot of her bed, then sat on Suze's bed and lit a cigarette, blowing the smoke out in a blue cloud. Suze leaned against the window, her arms crossed over her chest.

"If it's okay, I'd rather have the bottom drawers," Dewey said. "I'm not as tall as Suze, and it's hard for me to stand on tiptoe, because of my leg."

"Oh. Oh, of course," said Mrs. Gordon. "I'm sorry, I should have thought of that. Suze—let's move your things up top again."

Suze walked across the room and started to pull things out of the bottom drawers, glaring at Dewey. So, Dewey thought. She'd wanted the top drawers to begin with. That made sense. Suze Gordon was the kind of girl who'd always want the top, whatever it was. She was one of the loud runaround kids at school, and bossy at recess, although nobody really listened. She'd probably be even bossier about her room. But Dewey was used to that. She'd lived in other people's houses most of her life, and boarders never got to make the rules.

Suze pulled an armload of clothes out of the bottom drawer and kicked it shut, then plopped them into the top one in a heap. She stared at Dewey. "So what's wrong with your leg, anyway?"

"Susan!" Mrs. Gordon said sharply. "What a rude question. Apologize to Dewey this minute."

Dewey looked up from her suitcase, a pair of rolled-up white socks in each hand. "It's okay. It's kind of better when people just ask instead of staring at me when they don't think I'm looking." She turned toward Suze. "It was an accident when I was a baby. My leg got broken in a couple of places. Papa says I was in the hospital for a month, but I don't remember. When I got out it wasn't broken anymore, but it was a little shorter than my other leg, so I have to wear a special shoe and I can't run very well."

She looked at Suze and waited for the other girl to look away first. When she did, Dewey walked over to the dresser and began to line her socks in an orderly row along the left side of the bottom drawer.

DRAWING THE LINE

SUZE WAS RELIEVED to see that Dewey hadn't brought very many clothes. That made it feel more like she was here for the weekend, not like she was going to stay. Dewey only had two pairs of pants, dungarees and cords, and a couple of sweaters. The rest of her stuff—a pair of pajamas, underwear, and socks—only took up one drawer of the dresser. A single left shoe, a white sneaker, sat next to it on the floor. One shoe. That was so weird.

That was all she'd brought, except for the sack of books. Most of them were the school kind of books, math and science. The sack also held some letters and a wooden cigar box and a Mason jar, both full of junk. Wires and batteries, string and rubber bands and springs, parts of an old clock, a whole bunch of screws and nails, and a pair of pliers. Junk. *None of it better get on* my *side of the room,* Suze thought.

"There's not a lot of extra space in here," said Mrs. Gordon, when Dewey had taken the last of her clothes out of her suitcase. "I'll take your bag out and store it with our things, okay?" A little closet-sized room, off the back stairs, was where Suze's roller skates, some boxes of summer clothes, and their own suitcases lived.

"Okay," Dewey said. She closed the brown leather lid and pushed the brass latches down until they snapped shut.

"Are you going back to work now?" Suze asked her mother. It was the second time in a week that she'd been home after school, which was strange, but kind of nice.

"Later on," Mrs. Gordon said. "I thought we could all have dinner together, this first night. After I've stowed Dewey's bag, I'm going to put a chicken in the oven." She turned to Dewey. "Do you like mashed potatoes? They're one of Suze's favorites."

"Yes, ma'am," said Dewey. "I like pretty much everything, except beets."

Mrs. Gordon laughed. "Well, good. That's at least one thing you girls have in common."

"Is Daddy coming home too?" Suze asked.

"He said he'd try, but I wouldn't count on it. He's been down at Anchor Ranch with X-Division all month, and that's miles away. My bet is if they can't hear the siren, none of them will stop working until it's too dark to see. We'll set him a place, but I suspect it'll just be us girls."

"Is there someplace I can put my books?" Dewey asked.

Suze looked at the bookshelf over her bed, where she kept her Oz books and *Treasure Island* and the fairy tales with Maxfield Parrish drawings. If she moved the bookends, there might be room for a few more books. But she didn't want Dewey's books on her shelf. Besides, Dewey would have to stand on *her* pillow to reach. Suze shuddered and looked around the room. "I guess you can put them on top of the dresser," she said. "On *your* side."

"Don't be silly," said Mrs. Gordon. "I'll get a shelf for over your bed too, Dewey. For now, why don't you just leave them in the sack?"

Dewey nodded, and Mrs. Gordon picked up the suitcase and left the room.

But Suze had an idea. She used her foot to pull out a flat wooden box from underneath her bed. Inside were her art supplies—colored pencils, crayons, a compass, a ruler, a pad of paper. She peeled layers of loose drawings aside until she found what she was looking for: a small red cardboard box of colored chalk. In Berkeley, she had used it to draw hopscotch lines on the sidewalk. Since there were no sidewalks on the Hill, it had drifted to the bottom of the art box, useless.

Until now.

The floor was wood, the dresser was blue. Suze wanted a color that would show up against both. White would, but white was boring. She finally decided on yellow. That way if some got on the walls by accident, it wouldn't show.

Suze stood in the alley between the two beds, in front of the polished pine nightstand. She closed one eye, squinting and measuring, then, starting at the back of the stand, right at the wall, drew a straight yellow line down the middle, continuing the line down across the front of the drawer. It wobbled a bit on the round knob.

Behind her, she heard Dewey turn around and huff in surprise, but Suze didn't stop. She squatted, put the chalk on the floor directly under the knob, then bisected the length of the space between the two beds.

She was aware, peripherally, that Dewey had moved away from the dresser and was sitting on top of her bed, watching silently. Suze ignored her and continued the yellow line up the center of the blue dresser, ending with an audible tap of the stub of chalk on the yellow painted wall.

"You and your stuff stay on *your* side," she said, turning around to face Dewey. "Got it?"

Dewey was leaning against her headboard, her arms around her drawn-up knees. She looked at Suze for several seconds. "Yeah, I got it," she said. "Don't worry. I *never* color outside the lines."

Dinner was quiet. Suze watched Dewey eat. She even *ate* weird. She cut her chicken up into a little pile, ate it, then ate her peas, then her potatoes, keeping all the food on separate parts of the plate, not touching. Suze wanted to reach over with her fork and squash the peas into the potatoes, break the dam of gravy so that it would run all over Dewey's plate. But her mother was sitting next to her, chatting as if nothing was different, so she didn't. She gnawed on a drumstick and then, when she was sure Dewey was watching, mingled her own food into a slurry. Dewey said nothing.

A little before 7:00, Mrs. Gordon stood up. "I don't think Daddy's going to make it," she said. "We'll save him some leftovers." She cut off the other drumstick and a thigh and put them on a plate, adding a dollop of mashed potatoes. Then she covered the plate with wax paper and put it in the icebox. She poured the last of the coffee out of the percolator into her cup, and sat down.

"Will you girls be okay if I go back to the lab for a while? Not too long. An hour or two. What time do you usually go to bed?" She looked at Dewey.

Dewey put down her fork. "It depends," she said. "Most school nights, about nine. If Papa's home, he lets me read in bed for an hour or so. If he's at the lab, I sometimes read until he gets home. Or until I fall asleep."

She folded her napkin in half and stood up, carried her plate over to the sink, and ran water.

Suze rolled her eyes. Little Miss Helpful.

"Nine. Okay, I'll try to be back by then," Mrs. Gordon said. She stacked her own plate on top of Dewey's. "Just leave the dishes," she said. "I'll do them when I get back. It helps me unwind, and gets the chemical stink off my hands."

"Okay," Dewey said. "Where should I do my homework?"

Was she always this good? Suze rolled her eyes again, although she had been thinking the same thing. "Dibs on the desk," she said quickly.

"*Su—*" Mrs. Gordon started to say, but Dewey spoke first.

"Good. Then I'll take the kitchen table. That way I can spread my papers out."

The two girls looked at each other, but neither said a word.

Mrs. Gordon shook her head. "Well, I'm glad we got that worked out. I'm going to the lab now, where the explosives are carefully marked. It's probably safer there." She pulled her jacket off its hook by the door and put it on. "I'll be back in a little while."

For the next two hours, Suze did her spelling words, and tried to read the geography chapter about the Spanish coming to New Mexico, but she couldn't concentrate. The apartment felt crowded. Every time she made a noise—rustled papers, dropped her pencil—she wondered if Dewey was listening.

Once she heard Dewey get up from the table, heard the soft rumble of a chair being pushed back across the linoleum, the click of the cupboard latch, the rush of water running, and she stiffened. Dewey was in the kitchen, *her* kitchen, opening private cupboards without even asking. She probably wasn't doing anything bad like stealing, just getting a drink of water. But it bothered Suze that she might be using a juice glass, or even a teacup, not a water tumbler, disturbing a routine Suze hadn't known she was attached to.

By quarter of nine, Suze was tired and ready to go to bed. But she didn't want to go first, didn't want to leave Dewey unsupervised. She went to the bathroom and brushed her teeth, running the water a little harder than she needed to, so it would make more noise and Dewey would maybe get the hint that it was bedtime. She flushed the toilet, twice, in case the water hadn't registered.

It worked. When she came out of the bathroom, Dewey was standing in the hall, holding a red plastic toothbrush and a shiny new tube of Pepsodent.

"Are you done in there?" she asked.

"Yeah," replied Suze.

Dewey nodded, and shut the door. Suze heard the unfamiliar sound of the lock turning.

When Dewey came into the bedroom, she was wearing yellow flannel pajamas patterned with little red and black Scottie dogs. She carried her shoes, which she put just under the end of her bed, and her clothes, which she put into the dresser drawer. Barefoot, she didn't walk too gimpy, Suze noticed, just a little bit of a lope, like a cowboy after a long day.

Dewey climbed into bed. "Do you mind if I read for a little while?" she asked, picking up a book from the nightstand.

"No. My mom'll be home any minute, and she'll probably turn off the light, but until then it's okay." Suze leaned over and got a *Captain Marvel* comic off the floor, and began to read herself. She sneaked a few sideways glances, but couldn't see the title of Dewey's book.

Half an hour later, Mrs. Gordon hadn't come home. Dewey shut her book and put it back on the stand. "G'night," she said. "You can keep the light on if you want. It won't bother me much." She took off her glasses, folded them, and put them down on top of the book. She looked different without them. Her face was oddly naked and exposed. Suze wondered how much she could see. She'd looked through her mother's glasses, and everything was all blurry. Dewey's were even thicker.

"I guess I'm done," she said. She dropped *Captain Marvel* to the floor and reached over to turn off the light.

It was late when she finally heard her parents come in the back door. She hadn't been able to fall asleep. Dewey wasn't making any *noise*, but Suze wasn't used to someone else being in her room.

Through the thin walls, she could hear her parents talking in the living room. She heard her name and got up, stepping carefully across the yellow line so her feet didn't erase it, and tiptoed to the bathroom for a drink of water. She turned the water on, barely a trickle, and stood in the open doorway to listen.

"—asked right out," her mother said. "I guess you can't really blame her. I'd be curious if I didn't know." Suze heard the click of a lighter, but couldn't tell if it was for her mother's cigarette or her father's pipe. "Poor lamb," her mother continued. Suze figured that was probably Dewey, not her. "She just said it was an accident."

"Wasn't it?" asked her father.

"My aunt Sally! Jimmy said Dewey's mother was drunk as a skunk—apparently as usual—and one night she dropped her baby on the stairs. Dewey was barely two. Can you imagine? Then she left, just up and left, while her little girl was still in the hospital. Jimmy hasn't seen her since. Said she's called a couple of times. Not here, of course. In Chicago. And just to ask him for money. Not a

word for Dewey, not in ten years. Poor brave little lamb."
A pause. "Did you hear something?"

Suze heard someone put a glass down, then footsteps.
She ducked back into the bathroom.

"Suze? What are you doing up?" Her mother appeared
in the doorway. "It's nearly midnight."

"I was thirsty."

"Well, okay. Drink up, then I'll tuck you back in."

Suze nodded. They walked quietly back into the bedroom and when she was in bed, her mother tucked the
wool blanket up under her arms and kissed her on the
cheek. "Sweet dreams, pumpkin," she said, and tiptoed
out, pulling the door almost shut behind her.

The thin sliver of light fell across the girl sleeping in
the other bed. Suze thought about what she'd heard. She
saw stairs in her mind and felt goosebumps all over her
arms. She burrowed deeper under the covers and as she
drifted off, wondered if weird old Dewey's dreams were
ever sweet.

April 12

UNDER THE FENCE

DEWEY NOTICED THAT Suze put a big red X on
the calendar in the kitchen every morning after breakfast.
She thought at first that it was to count down the days to
some occasion—a birthday, or a trip to town. Then she
realized that the first X was on the day that Papa had left.
Suze was tallying the days Dewey had been there, like a
convict in a *Saturday Evening Post* cartoon marking off
his sentence on the stone prison walls.

"You better not walk *with* me," Suze had said on their
first school day together. "And don't even think about
eating lunch with me." Dewey had only nodded. She'd
never hung around Suze before, and staying at the Gordons' hadn't changed that. She left for school ten minutes
early and stayed ten or fifteen minutes after the 3:30 bell,
finishing some of her homework.

The third day of her visit, Dewey packed a thermos

of milk and a deviled-ham sandwich and went for a walk at lunchtime, a picnic in the woods, where it was quiet and she could be by herself. Really by herself, without Suze in the next room sighing and thumping and letting Dewey know in a hundred small ways that she was just an unwanted intruder.

Then it rained for a week, pouring, drenching rains, and it was too wet and muddy to go outside. The boys sat in one corner of the schoolroom, eating and trading baseball cards and reading comics, and some of the girls pushed their desks together and played euchre. Dewey brought her cigar box with the bits and pieces of her latest project and sat at her desk near the window, ignoring Suze's stares and working on it in between bites of her sandwich.

Thursday afternoon, finally, the sky cleared, and the breeze was soft and held the promise of spring. When the school bell rang, the other children ran, yelling, out into the playground. Dewey lingered behind.

When she walked out of the school building about quarter of four, Betty and Joyce and some other girls were playing jacks on the concrete, in a space where there were no puddles. Suze stood a few feet away, watching. Dewey was pretty sure she wasn't playing *with* the other girls, just standing nearby and pretending that she would be, any minute. Sometimes Dewey felt sorry for Suze, because the other girls didn't ask her to play very often. But she knew better than to say anything. It would just make Suze mad.

Suze was between her and the gate. Dewey thought about going back inside, but then Suze looked up and saw her. Suze's posture changed. She stiffened, just a little, the way Rutherford sometimes did when another cat walked by the base of the stairs.

Dewey took a deep breath, gripped her cigar box, and focused on a spot about ten yards beyond the gate. She walked toward it, not slow, not fast, not looking at Suze. She was almost past when Suze casually, elaborately, pretended to sneeze, flinging out her arm at the moment of *katchoo*. Her wrist hit the edge of the cigar box, sending it flying.

It landed on the concrete about six feet away with a loud crack and a clatter like hailstones as its lid popped open and its contents scattered. Bolts and screws rolled into puddles and half a dozen corks bounced off in every direction.

"Oh," said Suze. "*I'm* sorry. It was an accident."

Dewey almost believed her for a second. But then she saw Suze look over at the other girls, to see if they were watching. When Suze saw that they were, she smiled. A smile of bravado, overdone and insincere. And Dewey knew it had been no accident.

She thought of a dozen things to say, and said none of them. The other girls were watching, waiting to see if anything would happen. And Dewey knew if there were sides to be taken, the girls with the jacks would, for once, be happy to pick Suze.

Papa had told her that no good ever came from fighting, that it was better to walk away with dignity than to stoop to that level. Dewey suspected it had been a long time since Papa had been picked on. She didn't like being a patsy, but she cared more about the project in the cigar box than what the other girls thought. She bent down and began to gather up the pieces, her body angled so she could still see Suze out of the corner of her eye. Suze just watched the other girls.

Dewey tumbled screws and a gearbox and some round typewriter keys into the box with a rattle that grew more muted as the box filled again. She hadn't found all the pieces, but she'd found the important ones, and if she'd lost a few nuts and bolts, that wasn't too bad. There were more in the jars under her bed. It might be a good idea to take some of them back over to Morganville, although she didn't think that Suze would do anything at home that she might get *caught* at. Suze didn't know whether Dewey would fink to Mrs. Gordon, and that gave Dewey a little bit of protection.

She went back into the school to get a rubber band

to hold the box together. The wood on one edge had cracked, and the paper hinge holding the top was loose. When she came out, Suze had left, and the other girls were busy with their jacks again.

Dewey sighed with relief. The woods were probably a little muddy, but they would be peaceful, and there might be mushrooms. It had rained enough. She pushed her left hand under the rubber band and carried the box down at her side, walking west from the school. She had just crossed the road that separated the populated parts of the Hill from the wooded canyon beyond when she heard footsteps behind her. Had Suze followed her? She ducked behind a tall ponderosa pine and tried to make herself small. But it was just Charlie and Jack. Charlie had a brown Boy Scout knapsack over one shoulder. It sagged as if it was full of something heavy.

"Hey," she said, stepping away from the tree.

"Hey, Dewey," Charlie said. They stopped and Jack nodded his head in greeting. "Where're you going?"

"Just into the woods," Dewey said. "With all the rain, I figure there might be mushrooms to look at."

"Maybe," Charlie agreed. "But we've got something even *more* interesting to look at." He patted the bulging knapsack. "Somebody in the enlisted men's barracks threw out a whole stack of magazines."

"We're going to the tree house, to read 'em where

nobody else can see," said Jack. He sounded excited.

"What kind of magazines?"

"Really good ones. *Lots* of pictures," said Charlie. "You wanna come along? We've got Cokes."

Dewey shook her head slowly. "It sounds like fun, but I'm not supposed to go outside the fence."

"How's your dad gonna know—unless you tell him?" Jack said.

She thought for a minute. That was true. And she hadn't *promised* Papa she wouldn't. "What about the MPs?"

Charlie smiled. "They don't care anymore. They used to patch the holes, and we just dug more. But now they leave us alone. I guess they figured it's easier to keep track of holes you know about than to keep looking for new ones." He looked at his watch. "Besides, it's just after 1600 hours. If we see anyone, it'll be Tommy—Sergeant Nelson. He's okay. He lets us feed his horse apples."

Dewey thought about it again. She wanted to, but— She was about to shake her head no when she looked down at the cracked cigar box. She was tired of being pushed around. "Okay," she said. "Where do we go?"

"Just follow me," said Charlie.

They set off on a narrow, well-worn path. The ground was spongy, but not too muddy, because of all the pine needles. It smelled good, cool and damp and earthy, and Dewey took a deep breath and felt her shoulders relax.

About five minutes in, they came to the chain-link fence, topped with strands of barbed wire.

"This way," Charlie said. He jerked his head to the left, and they walked single file along the fence. The path wasn't as clear, but there was a corridor of trampled grasses and wet underbrush. Dewey's pants cuffs were getting damp, and a few springy branches had snapped her in the arm, but she felt pretty good.

"This is it," Charlie said, holding up his hand.

The grass and pine needles and leaves had been cleared away and the dirt scooped out to form a hollow more than a foot deep and about three feet wide, directly under the fence. Someone had taken pliers and bent up the sharp points at the bottom of the chain link.

Charlie took off his knapsack and, with a small grunt, tossed it underhand onto the ground on the other side of the fence. It bounced a few feet in the leafy undergrowth, and Dewey heard the muffled clink of the Coke bottles inside. He lay on the ground, feet first, and wriggled under the fence, then stood up and brushed leaves and mud off the backs of his jeans.

"Well, c'mon," he said. "What're you waiting for?"

Jack went next, and then Dewey, who handed her cigar box through first so she could use both hands to scoot.

"It's only a few minutes," Jack said, pointing ahead and

to the right. He started walking eagerly in that direction.

Dewey saw it before they said anything. A huge red oak had fallen across the thick branches of two others, about fifteen feet above the forest floor, and the boys had built up, over, and around the natural crossbar. The tree house was a patchwork of lumber in shades of natural wood, white lead, and army green. An eight-paned window, set on its side, formed most of one wall, and a wooden housepainter's ladder was nailed securely to the trunk of the largest oak.

Jack nimbly scrambled up.

Charlie glanced at Dewey's foot, just once. "Do you need help getting up?" he asked.

"No," said Dewey. "I can climb pretty okay. But I'll need both hands, I think." She looked at the cigar box.

"No problem. There's room on top of the magazines." He slid the box under the top flap of the knapsack.

Dewey climbed up the ladder, not as fast as Jack, but without any hesitation. Charlie appeared a few seconds later, the knapsack on his back. He took it off and dropped it with a thump, raising a spray of dust motes that sparkled for a few seconds in the afternoon sun. He sat down with his back to the wall and opened the knapsack, pulling out three Coke bottles by their necks.

In the warmth of the little wooden house, the sides of the green glass bottles speckled with tiny round dots of moisture, like a toad's skin. Charlie pulled a pocketknife out of his jeans, unfolded it to a stubby opener blade, and deftly popped off the three bottle caps. He handed the drinks around. "So, whad'ya think?"

Dewey took a long swallow of Coke, pleasantly cool, and looked around as the bubbles stung the underside of her tongue.

The tree house was a rough cube, about six feet on a side, the plywood floor almost covered with a square of confetti-flecked dark linoleum. The walls were plastered with posters and cut-out magazine pages: *LIFE*, all army and planes and soldiers, no movie stars; WHEN YOU RIDE ALONE, YOU RIDE WITH HITLER!; WIPE THE JAP OFF THE MAP; and color pictures of half a dozen Boston Red Sox baseball players.

The only furniture was a bookcase made from two orange crates, with a pile of comic books, two *Smilin' Jack* Big Little Books, a flashlight, and a tall Premium Saltines tin. On the floor was a big Zenith radio, its pebbly beige case closed. A wooden shelf over the orange crates held two folded army blankets and a flat, metal-capped glass refrigerator bottle filled with water.

"Do you ever sleep here?" Dewey pointed at the blankets.

"Nah," said Jack in a disgusted tone. "Ma won't let us. But sometimes it gets kind of cold, on rainy days and stuff. You know."

"Yeah," said Dewey. She looked around again. The afternoon light, dappled by the forest canopy, slanted in through the window, all gold and shadows, making the little room warm and cozy. "It's great," she said after a moment. "Really great. You guys did a lot of work. How'd you get the big stuff here on your bikes?"

"Our brother Joey—Joe—helped. He did most of the heavy stuff for us," Jack said. "He's a senior. Gonna graduate next month."

"Oh." Dewey hadn't known there was another Reilly brother. "Is he going to go to college, or into the army? After, I mean."

"College," said Charlie. "He won't be eighteen until October, and Pops won't sign the papers to let him enlist early. Ma hopes the war will be over by then. But Joe's having a hard time getting any schools to accept him."

"Not because he's stupid or anything," said Jack quickly. He took another swallow of Coke and belched dramatically.

"Then what's the—?" Dewey asked.

Charlie shrugged. "He's graduating from a high school that doesn't officially exist. No name, no address. Just 'P.O. Box 1663,' like everything else. I guess it makes colleges suspicious."

"Yeah, I guess so," Dewey said. "The army probably should've thought of that."

"The army should've thought about a lot of stuff, if you ask me," said Charlie. "Want a cookie?" He pulled the saltines tin off the shelf and pried off the blue metal lid. "Ma baked 'em last week, but with the rain, we haven't been up here, so it's still pretty full." He took two cookies and tilted the container toward Dewey.

She took a fat cookie bursting with raisins and nuts and bit into it. "Your mom's *good*," she said.

"The best," Jack said. "Let's look at those magazines."

"Sure." Charlie handed Dewey her cigar box, then upended the knapsack onto the middle of the floor. A dozen magazines with loud, garish covers slid out in a fan across the linoleum.

"See," Jack said. "What'd we tell you? Great pictures, huh?"

Dewey picked up one that had slid near her feet. A streamlined yellow-and-red boat that looked like a rocket ship was firing a silver torpedo into impossibly blue water. "Wow," she said. "*Popular Mechanics* from—" she looked at the spine "—1941. You found these in the *trash*?" She put her Coke bottle on the floor, within easy reach, and began to read.

For a long time the only sounds in the tree house were cookies crunching, pages turning, and the occasional creak of a tree branch outside. Dewey felt happy for the first time in weeks.

Every few minutes one of them would interrupt with a "Hey, would you look at this!" Charlie liked building projects, and Jack was drawn to exciting predictions for the future, like personal zeppelins, which Dewey had to admit would be pretty nifty, although not as practical as her "Microtubes, the Future of Radio."

Dewey was on her third magazine and fourth cookie when Charlie looked at his watch and whistled in surprise. "Oh, jeez. It's almost six. I guess we didn't hear the siren." He put down his magazine—"Averting Death from the Skies." "We gotta go." He stuffed the empty Coke bottles into the knapsack. "We eat in half an hour, and if we're late, Jack and me get stuck with K.P.," he explained. He stacked the magazines into an uneven pile and scooted it over next to the bookcase.

"You can take that one with you, if you want," he said. "You just started it."

Dewey looked down at the magazine in her lap. She was reading about a new kind of record player called a HiFi, and she did want to finish. "Okay," she said. "Thanks." The magazine was not much bigger than the top of her cigar box, so she slipped it under the rubber band and tucked the whole package into the waistband at the back of her pants, leaving both hands free for the ladder.

They retraced their steps through the woods to the hole in the fence and beyond. When they reached a fork in the path heading back toward the buildings, the boys stopped. "See ya, Dewey," Charlie said, gesturing to the right. "We gotta go this way."

"Me too," said Dewey.

Jack wrinkled his forehead in confusion. "I thought you lived in Morganville."

"I do. But Papa's in Washington for a couple of weeks, so I'm staying with a family in the Sundts."

"The Schultes?"

"No." Dewey hesitated for a moment. She looked down at the yellow robot on the cover of her magazine, then back at Charlie. "The Gordons."

"You're staying with *Truck*?" Jack said, his mouth open in surprise.

"Who?"

Charlie gave his brother a shove on the arm. "Be nice," he said. He turned to Dewey. "That's what some of the guys call Suze Gordon. 'Cause she's kind of big and likes to push people around."

"Truck." Jack nodded.

Dewey tried not to smile, but it was hard. Truck. She kind of liked the idea that, in some circles, Suze was the one they called names.

"Yep," she said. "That family. Her mom's great, though. She's a stinker. A real one, not just a secretary. She—" Dewey stopped and bit her lip, hoping she hadn't said the wrong thing. She didn't know what Mrs. Reilly did on the Hill.

"Nice," said Jack. "More help with homework than *our* Ma." Both the boys chuckled.

They walked through the darkening forest, Dewey happily humming to herself. She spotted a fallen log with a line of pale conical mushrooms that looked like Keystone Kops hats, and a few yards later, a patch of flat ones that were bright cartoon orange, as vivid in the setting sunlight as if they were flames.

Ten minutes later they were at the edge of the dirt road that ran behind the Sundts. No one was out on the stoops, but then the road was still pretty muddy, and it *was* dinnertime. The boys stopped at a building with two bikes leaning against the wooden railing.

"This is us," Jack said, putting one foot on the stairs. "Up there."

"Okay," Dewey said. "Well, thanks for letting me come up and—" She paused, feeling awkward. She'd had more fun than she'd had in weeks, but wasn't sure how to be polite to other kids. The grown-up line *I had a very nice time* seemed really lame.

"It was good," Charlie said, nodding. "You can come back. But next time," he pointed a stern finger at her, "next time *you* bring the Cokes." He grinned and Dewey grinned back.

"Deal," she said. "See ya."

"Later, alligator," said Charlie, and ran up the stairs, two at a time.

A few minutes later, Dewey climbed the green wooden steps to the Gordons' apartment, her cigar box under one arm, and opened the screen door to the kitchen. She stopped, stock-still, her good mood vanishing in a instant.

Mrs. Gordon was sitting with her arms around Suze. Both of them were crying.

Dewey had never seen Mrs. Gordon cry. She wouldn't have thought Suze could.

Mrs. Gordon looked up at her over Suze's shaking blonde head. "There you are," she said, sniffling. "Come over here and sit down." She moved her arm and patted the chair next to her.

Dewey stared at her for a moment, then sat down woodenly, as if her legs had never bent that way before. She gripped the edge of the table and waited.

"President Roosevelt died a few hours ago," said Mrs. Gordon. "I came as soon as I heard." She patted Dewey's hand. "None of us wants to be alone right now."

For the rest of her life, Dewey would recall that moment as a series of disconnected memories—the taste of oatmeal-raisin cookies in the back of her throat, a square of yellow-checked oilcloth, the slow, deep voice of Edward R. Murrow, and the almost-painful sensation of Mrs. Gordon's wedding ring pressing into the skin on the back of her hand. Dewey was aware of nothing else.

Her eyes stung, but she was too stunned to cry. She couldn't make the news seem real. Roosevelt had always been president. He was president before she was born, had been president her whole life. Everything else in the world had changed, over and over, but not that. FDR and his Fireside Chats and his dog, Fala. And his legs. Dewey had always felt close to him because of his legs. How could he be dead?

"Was it the Nazis?" she asked finally. "Did they shoot him?"

"No, nothing like that." Mrs. Gordon shook her head. "He . . . he wasn't well, you know. And the stress of the war . . . He had a stroke."

"Like my Nana."

"Like your Nana. But much worse." Mrs. Gordon sat very still for a minute, then kissed the top of Suze's head and eased her arm away. She rolled her neck to get the kinks out, wiped her eyes, and reached for her pack of Chesterfields.

Suze sniffled and laid her head down on her arms as if she might take a nap. A few minutes later she got up and walked slowly out of the kitchen.

Dewey listened to the uncharacteristically soft padding of Suze's feet on their way back to the bedroom.

"I think she needs to sleep," said Mrs. Gordon.

Dewey nodded. "Who's president now?" she asked after a minute.

Mrs. Gordon lit another cigarette and blew out a stream of smoke. "The vice president." She thought for a moment. "Christ, I should know the man's name. I work for him now. But Roosevelt's had so many." She tapped a tiny circle of ash off the end of her cigarette in frustration. "Oh, what *is* his name? Henry Wallace? No, that was the last one. Henry something." She shook her head again. "I guess it'll be in the papers."

They sat at the table for almost an hour, watching the stars appear outside the window, and listened to the radio, reporting the same news, over and over. When she'd stubbed out her last Chesterfield, Mrs. Gordon stood up. "Nothing's going to change," she said, turning off the radio. "We might as well have supper."

She pulled the frying pan out of the cupboard and scrambled some eggs, but neither of them was hungry.

April 13

MAXWELL
AND ELEANOR

WHEN DEWEY GOT up the next morning, all the
flags on the Hill were flying at half-mast. Nothing else
looked any different, but everything had changed.

Women sat on the stoops of the apartment buildings,
talking softly, hugging each other, weeping. Most of the
people Dewey saw had been crying, even the soldiers. The
sight of an army MP with a rifle in his hands and tears
in his eyes was both unsettling and reassuring. They were
all in this together.

It was Friday, but there was no school. It felt wrong
to run around, laughing and playing tag or Red Rover,
so kids sat in small groups with board games or jigsaw
puzzles. Even Suze was quiet. She cut out a photograph
of Roosevelt from *LIFE* magazine and pasted it to a piece
of black construction paper. She propped it up against the
teapot in the kitchen and spent most of the day looking at

it while the radio droned on from the counter. From every open window on the Hill, the sonorous voices of newsmen describing the progress of the northbound funeral train filled the spring air.

The new president's name was Truman. Harry Truman. Dewey had stared at the picture of him in the paper for a long time that morning, a bland-looking man with a round face and round glasses. He didn't look like he'd be much of a match for Hitler, and that worried her. She lay in her bed Friday night, thinking about him. She didn't think Harry was a good name for a president. Not very dignified. Franklin was a much better name. It was—

"Are you asleep?"

Dewey wasn't sure for a minute if she'd really heard the whispered question, but when she looked over at the other bed, she could see the vague outline of Suze, propped up on one elbow.

"Not really," Dewey said.

There was a silence then, as if the conversation, such as it was, had ended, but neither girl moved to turn over. The ticking of the clock on the nightstand seemed unusually loud.

Another whisper. "I'm, um, sorry about your box."

Dewey wasn't sure what to say. "That's okay" was a lie. "Yeah," she said after a few seconds.

"I shouldn't have done that. The president was dying," Suze said, and Dewey could hear the tremble in her whisper. "Maybe if I hadn't . . ." She let the sentence drift off.

Dewey flinched in surprise. Not just because Suze had apologized, but because she had been feeling that same uncomfortable sense of "what if?" She'd disobeyed the rules, and something terrible had happened. She didn't really think that sneaking under the fence had killed the president, but the two events were linked so tightly together in her mind that they *seemed* connected.

"I don't think it was your fault," she said quietly, as much to herself as to Suze. "The president, I mean."

"I know. But I can't stop thinking about Eleanor Roosevelt. I don't think she'd like me. *She* wouldn't have knocked your box down."

Dewey giggled. She couldn't help herself. Suze sounded very serious, but the idea of tall, dignified Mrs. Roosevelt standing on the playground with a cigar box was just too funny. "No, I can't quite see that," she said. "'I shall bat away your cigar container,'" she continued, in a high-pitched voice that was a pretty good imitation.

It was Suze's turn to giggle. "Is it busted up really bad?"

"Not too much. And I've got another one, if it cracks more." Dewey hesitated, then said, "But don't do it again, okay?"

"No," Suze said. "I don't think I will." A pause. "What are you making with all the junk inside it?"

Dewey bit her lip in the darkness. Suze sounded a lot

different tonight than she had on the playground, but was it safe to tell her about the project? It was private.

"I won't tell or anything," Suze said. "Really." Her voice sounded a little sad.

"I'm trying to make a wind-up guy," Dewey said after a minute. "Kind of like a robot, except it doesn't walk right yet."

"Oh." Silence. "You like inventing stuff, huh?"

"Yeah," Dewey said. "Especially trying to get the pieces to fit together. It's like doing a puzzle, except I'm making it up as I go along."

"That does sound kinda like fun," Suze said. She pushed her pillow behind her and sat up against the headboard. As she did, a dark shape fell off her bed and hit the floor with a muffled thump. It slid on the wood, ending up just under Dewey's bed.

Dewey reached down to pick it up and peered at it in the dim light from the window. It was some kind of stuffed animal. A teddy bear? Dewey had never seen it before. She smiled. Most of the time, Einstein the duck sat on the shelf over her bed, because she was really too old to sleep with him anymore. But tonight she had taken him down and tucked him under the edge of the covers, for comfort. Suze must have had the same idea.

"What's your bear's name?" Dewey asked. She handed it back across the gap between the beds.

There was a small pause, and then Suze said, "Maxwell."

Dewey immediately thought of James Maxwell, who formulated the first equations about electromagnetic fields. But she doubted Suze knew about him. Maybe after Maxwell House coffee. Or maybe she just had an uncle Maxwell who'd given her the bear. She—

"Because of the scientist guy, Maxwell," Suze said.

Dewey just about fell out of bed.

"See, my mom's a chem—a stinker—you know," Suze continued. "His name used to be Fuzzy, when I was little. But Mom used to laugh and say, 'Maxwell was right, opposites do attract'—I guess 'cause he's a dark brown bear, and I've got blonde hair—and she and Daddy started calling him Maxwell. It's really a more interesting name than Fuzzy, if you think about it. Mom's big on giving things science names. Our cat is Rutherford, and even my—"

Suze stopped abruptly in mid-sentence, and Dewey heard her make a funny noise with her mouth, like she was trying hard to think and stop herself from talking at the same time.

Dewey waited.

"If I tell you something, will you promise *never* to tell anyone else?" Suze asked slowly.

Suze's face was just a sort of pale blur under paler blonde hair, but even without her glasses on, Dewey could tell that Suze was very serious. "Yeah, I promise," she said after a moment's hesitation, during which curiosity won out over anything else.

"Scout's honor?"

"I'm not a Girl Scout," Dewey said. "So I don't know if it would count. But pinky swear. That's what my Nana did if something was *real* secret." She held up her right hand, pinky extended, and kissed its fingertip. "Pinky swear I won't tell."

"Okay." Suze took a deep breath. "I was sort of named after my mom's favorite scientist, Marie Curie."

"I thought Suze was short for Susan," Dewey said, puzzled.

"It is. My first name's fine. But my *middle* name . . ." Suze sighed.

"What?"

"Okay. You know Marie was Polish before she married Mr. Curie?"

"Sure."

"Well, Mom gave me *that* name. My middle name is Sklodowska."

"Wow," said Dewey.

"Yeah. I don't think I'd mind—much—if she'd given me Marie. It's not the greatest middle name but—" She stopped because Dewey was laughing.

"I'm not laughing at you," Dewey said quickly. "It's

just that—" She giggled again. "See, my middle name *is*
Marie. After my Nana, though, not Madame Curie."

"Dewey Marie Kerrigan?"

Silence.

"Well, kind of." It was Dewey's turn to think hard.
Ever since yesterday afternoon when she'd heard the news
about the president, nothing had felt quite real, as if she'd
stepped out of ordinary time. Lying here talking in the
dark, Suze was very different from the bossy girl on the
playground. But who would she be in the morning? Would
she try to show off with this?

"I won't tell either," Suze said after a minute. "Scout's
honor. Brownie's, anyway." She held up her fingers in
what Dewey supposed was the Brownie salute.

It was Dewey's turn to sigh. "See, Dewey's not really
my name. It's a nickname, like Suze."

"I wondered about that. But I thought you could have
been named after a librarian or something. Like the
Dewey Decimal system. So what's it short for?"

"You said your mom's nuts about chemistry?" Dewey
ran a nervous hand through her hair. "My papa's the same
way about math. And puzzles and codes. All his letters to
me have parts I have to unscramble or decipher. It's kind
of fun, but sometimes he gets a little carried away."

"What does that have to do with your name?" Suze
asked.

"*Every*thing. See, my birthday is December twelfth. The twelfth day of the twelfth month. Twelve-twelve. That was too good a number for Papa to pass up. So instead of giving me a normal name, *he* picked the Latin word for 'twelve.'" Dewey paused, then said, slowly and deliberately, "Duodecima. My real name is Duodecima Marie Kerrigan."

"Jeez," said Suze. "Dewey's *lots* better. Do teachers ever call you the whole thing?"

Dewey made a face. "Not here. But the nuns did. I had to go to Catholic school when I lived with Nana. Nuns don't like nicknames. And they *love* Latin. I hated Catholic school."

"I can see why," Suze said. They sat in silence for a minute or two digesting this new information about each other.

"So look," Suze said finally. "I won't tell anyone about Duo—about your name, if you won't tell about mine. Deal?"

"Deal," said Dewey.

"Spit on it?"

"Sure," Dewey said, although she'd never spit on anything before.

They sat up onto the edges of their beds, legs dangling, and each girl spit into the palm of her right hand, then extended it. They shook hands across the narrow gap between the beds, then disengaged with a faint moist sound.

"G'night . . . Twelve," said Suze with a chuckle.

"G'night, Curie," Dewey replied. She tucked Einstein under her arm and settled down to sleep.

April 21

FINDING
THE PIECES

WHY DID IT always rain on Saturday afternoons? Suze sat at her desk in the corner of the living room, listening to the water hit the glass of the window and spill over the sill. The building didn't have much insulation, and a few times the downpour was so intense that she felt as if it might come right through the walls.

She got up and got a glass of milk from the icebox. The kitchen windows were fogged up so that she couldn't see anything outside. She took a handful of saltines from the tin on the counter and went back to her desk.

She'd already finished her homework—a page of long division that was pretty easy, and a list of spelling words that weren't. They were tricky, because they were words that came from Spanish, and didn't spell anything like they sounded.

Some of them meant something. Like Los Alamos, which was the name of the ranch that had become the Hill, and meant "the cottonwood trees." She picked up her pencil and began to doodle. She drew a few stick trees, and underneath wrote ΛΟΣ ΑΛΑΜΟΣ. That was *Los Alamos*, in Greek. Greek letters, anyway. It was almost recognizable, even in another alphabet, when she used capital letters.

She drew another clump of trees and wrote λοσ αλαμοσ underneath it. That was better. More mysterious in lowercase letters. If you didn't know, it could be almost anything. She wrote her name, Συζε Γορδον. She liked her name, because the Z, *zeta*, was fun to draw. It had taken her a long time to get it right. It was the second-hardest letter. Lowercase *xi* was the hardest: ξ. She drew a skeleton hand and wrote ξ-ραψ, "x-ray," beside it.

Her favorite letter to say out loud was *omicron*. It sounded like the name of a villain, someone Wonder Woman might have to battle for the safety of Earth. Omicron the Magnificent. "Omicron the Terrible," she said out loud. She drew a crown on the paper, and then sighed. It was fun to say out loud, but it was the most boring of all boring letters to draw. O. It just looked like a stupid O, and what was the point of having secret writing if it didn't *look* different?

She continued to doodle idly, singing under her breath, "Omi-cron. Pi. Pi. Omi-cron. Pi. Pi," sort of to the tune of the flying monkeys song from *The Wizard of Oz*. She wanted the letters to be bolder, stand out more from the white of the paper. She drew a larger *zeta*, an outline, and began to fill it in, pressing as hard as she could with the pencil. But she pressed too hard, and the lead snapped off, ripping a small furrow in the paper.

Stupid pencil.

She opened the drawer of the desk to see if there might be an ink pen. She pushed aside the papers and rubber bands and other odds and ends that had accumulated there, and uncovered the score pad from the gin rummy games. It had been so long since her mother had any free time in the evenings that Suze had almost forgotten about it. She wondered if they would ever play again. Some of the penciled scores had faded so much they were nearly illegible.

Suze sighed. She rummaged to the bottom of the disarray, but came up empty and shut the drawer. The she remembered that there *was* a nib pen and a bottle of black ink in the art box under her bed. It would make a nice dark line, and she could even make the thick parts of the letter look different from the thin parts, the way it showed in the chart in the encyclopedia at school. That was almost impossible with a pencil. Suze thought longingly about the dark ink, and about the pad of thick, bright white paper that was also in the box.

But Dewey was in the bedroom. Mostly, for the three weeks she'd been living there, they had kept to themselves, in separate rooms, between school and bedtime.

They didn't talk to each other much, unless Suze's mother was around, which wasn't very often. Then they both pretended until she went back to the lab.

She sighed again. She really wanted the pen. And it was *her* room, after all. She got up off the hard desk chair and marched into the bedroom, her red socks making muffled thumps on the wood floor.

Dewey was sitting on her bed, her back against the headboard, working on one of her gadgets. Suze wasn't quite sure what any of them *did*, but Dewey always seemed to be working on one of them. She kept the half-finished ones in her empty dresser drawer. It didn't look like any of them were completely done yet.

This one was flat and thin, with wheels and a wind-up box on top. One of the wheels was bolted on, and the others dangled loose. Dewey had dumped out her whole Mason jar of screws and nails and junk onto the bedspread and was pushing them around with her fingers, looking for something. The littlest pieces had rolled and lined themselves up in the ridges of the chenille like beans in a furrow.

Dewey's face was all screwed up and wrinkly, the way it was in school sometimes when she was thinking of the answer to a hard question. Her tongue was sticking out of the corner of her mouth, and she looked even weirder than usual. Suze thought about saying something, but she wasn't really in the mood.

But Dewey never seemed bored, Suze thought, even when all she was doing was staring at rusty junk. "What are you hunting for?" she asked.

Dewey glanced up, surprised.

"I need six of these little bolts," she said after a minute. "And the nuts to go with them. I'm pretty sure I've got more in here somewhere." She looked down at her fingers, which had continued moving pieces aside.

"Oh." Suze looked at the pile of junk on the bedspread. It was kind of interesting junk. "Can I see?" she asked, without really thinking about it.

Dewey shrugged. "I guess so."

Suze hesitated for a second, then sat down on the end of Dewey's bed, carefully, so that none of the little piles would spill onto the floor. Even so, the bed sagged where she sat, and a few tiny round balls, BBs or something, slid down the chenille, making tiny rattling noises and stopping at a fold in the fabric.

"Show me the thing you want," Suze said.

Dewey handed her one of the pieces she had been holding in her fist. The metal felt warm against Suze's skin. The bolt had a flat head smaller than a pea and was about half an inch long.

Suze leaned over the pile in the middle of the bed. After a few seconds, she reached in and pulled out a bolt. "Is this one?"

Dewey held out her hand, curved, palm up. Suze dropped the bolt into it.

"Yep, that's it." Dewey peered at Suze. "How'd you find it so quick?"

It was Suze's turn to shrug. "I just looked at it and tried to find another. It's easy. Like those puzzles where only one of the shapes matches exactly, but in real life." She looked at the pile, then pulled out another bolt from a haystack of intercrossed nails. "Here's another one."

"You're *good* at this," Dewey said.

Suze felt an odd sense of pride at the compliment, even if it was coming from Dewey. "I'm good at puzzles," she said. "Especially the kind where you have to find something. Jigsaw puzzles. I'm good at finding pieces for those too." She pulled two more bolts out from the pile. "See. What else do you need?"

Dewey handed her a nut, and within a few minutes, Suze had found five more of them and poured them into Dewey's hand as if she had uncovered uncut diamonds.

"Is that all you need?" Suze asked.

"For now, anyway. Now I can put all the pieces together and see if the wind-up part will work the way I want it to." Dewey swept her empty hand across the pile and scooped up a handful of metal bits, dumping them with a clatter into the Mason jar.

"Wait," Suze said. She bit her lip. "Uh, before you put

them all away, can I look through them? Some of them are kind of interesting."

"Okay. I'm not going to need them right away." Dewey dumped the contents of the jar back onto the bedspread.

For a long time the bedroom was quiet except for the sounds of small metal parts clinking and tunking together. Dewey sat on the floor near the door, the parts of her gadget arranged around her in a semicircle. She had a pair of pliers and a screwdriver, and would pick one tool up, fiddle with a metal piece, then put it down again and pick up the other tool, making minute adjustments to something Suze couldn't see.

Suze sat on the bed, Indian-style, and sifted through the assortment of tiny metal objects, making piles of her own. She liked the shapes. She separated out the straight and pointy pieces, like nails and tacks, and put them on her left. Next to them she made a line of straight, blunt things. Bolts and small metal rods. On her right she put the round things, divided into silver washers, bronze gears, and tiny bearings and marbles of graduating size. In front of her she made a much smaller array of odd bits that didn't fit with anything—a gob of molten lead that reminded her of the lumps Daddy used to bring home, a small black knob, an electric plug with no cord.

When she had sorted the contents of the jar into families of shapes, she looked at them for a while, moving some from one pile to another, selecting others that she especially liked, displaying those up on the platform of Dewey's pillow.

She began to fit pieces together, nesting one against another in a way she found very satisfying. It wouldn't *do* anything, not like Dewey's gadgets, some of which actually wound up with a key and moved. But she liked when her eye found an angle or a particular curved edge and she pulled that piece out of the pile, fitting it into the metallic composition that was forming.

She heard Dewey stand up and come over to the side of the bed, but didn't pay much attention.

"That's kind of pretty, what you made," Dewey said. "You're good in art. Mrs. Nereson almost always puts your pictures up on the corkboard."

It was true, but Suze didn't know how to reply. Finally she just nodded her head.

"I'll be back in a sec," Dewey said.

Suze nodded again, and looked back down at the pile of nails she'd been assessing. The composition needed more pointy things. A few minutes later, when she heard footsteps coming back, she was absorbed in making a stylized cactus out of a J-hook and some carpet tacks.

Dewey came over and stood next to the bed again, this time with the lid of a shoebox proffered in both hands.

"What's that for?" asked Suze.

"So that when I go to bed tonight you have someplace to put your picture. That way you can keep making it better tomorrow. If you want."

Suze hadn't thought about it as a picture. She hadn't planned any of this. But when she looked at the arrangement forming on the pillow, she realized how much she didn't want to break it up into pieces of metal junk again and scoop them back into the jar.

"You mean I can *keep* these?" she asked.

"Sure. They don't really do anything. At least not anything I'm working on now. And there's always more around, if you know where to look. This place is lousy with perfectly good stuff people just throw away." Dewey shook her head. "This way you don't have to wreck it unless you want to. You don't, do you?"

"No," Suze said slowly. "I guess I don't." She looked at Dewey, who didn't seem quite as weird, right then. "Thanks," she said.

Dewey smiled, just a small grin, and went back to work on her gadget while Susan Gordon carefully moved her first collage, piece by piece, onto the cardboard frame of the shoebox lid.

April 24

SPECIAL DELIVERY

DEWEY CLIMBED THE stairs to the apartment automatically, not even looking where she was walking. She'd had an idea for a new project while she was eating lunch in the woods, and the pieces hadn't quite come together in her mind. It would need a mainspring, and a worm gear, and she thought there was one in the cigar box, but it might not be the right size, unless—

She stopped in the kitchen doorway. Propped up against the napkin holder was a note that said DEWEY in capital letters. Below it, lying flat, was a large brown envelope. Army, very official, with lots of rubber stamps and dates and signatures.

A typed paper label said: "Miss D. Kerrigan, c/o Marjorie Gordon, P.O. Box 1663, Santa Fe, New Mexico." The note, scribbled on the back of a PX receipt, said:

Dewey—

A courier brought this to the lab. I didn't think you'd want to wait.

—T.G.

Mrs. Gordon must have left it at lunchtime. Dewey sat down and carefully unwound the figure-eight of red string and paper circles that held the envelope closed, then smiled in delight. Inside was a flimsy V-mail envelope, unsealed, with no postmark. But Dewey recognized the angular handwriting instantly.

Papa.

It wasn't a long letter, not even a whole page. Dewey read it through twice quickly, and then a third time, taking in every word, every comma.

Hello Dews—

Hope you're having an okay time at the Gordons'. They're nice people. Don't stay up too late. If you go over to the house, be a good Munchkin and look for my pocketknife, the one with the three blades and the can opener and the screwdriver. No one seems to be able to find another one.

I went to see "Casablanca" and visited with Uncle T. the other day. That was a treat. But since he's just moved, things are a bit hectic and disorganized,

*and he needs some help finding where things go. I
may be here for longer than I'd planned.*
    I miss you so much.
    OOXOXOXX,
    Papa

Dewey ran a finger gently over the blue ink signature
from Papa's fountain pen. She sighed and carefully refolded the letter, sliding it back into its envelope. He wouldn't
be back this week. But at least he'd written.

Humming under her breath, Dewey took the letter
back to the bedroom. She hid it under the paper lining
of her dresser drawer, with her Hill pass—her important
papers—then opened her cigar box to look for a good,
strong spring.

May 8

TANGLED LIKE SPAGHETTI

IT WAS FINALLY spring, and Hitler was dead. Suze felt like the world was a giant jigsaw puzzle, and in the last month all the important pieces had been removed, one after another, leaving blanks and unfamiliar names. Roosevelt, Mussolini, Hitler. All dead. It just didn't seem real.

Because nothing in her life had changed much at all. She went to school, she came home. Daddy hardly ever left his lab until the middle of the night—if then—and Mom skipped supper more often than not. She missed having Mom cook. Sometimes there were leftovers in the icebox, but lately Suze had been stopping by the PX for a hamburger on the way home from school. It was either that or cold cheese sandwiches for supper.

Well, *that* had changed, a little. Last week, Dewey had made them macaroni and cheese, on the stove and everything, and it was pretty good. Better than cold sandwiches, for sure. Then Mom came home later and made a big fuss over Dewey, and how great it was that she was grown-up enough to make supper. Big deal. The directions were right on the box.

So on Tuesday, after school, instead of going home, Suze went to the Commissary to get something *she* could make for supper. The store was a lot smaller and dingier than the Piggly-Wiggly back home, and there wasn't a lot of choice. But she found Chef Boy-Ar-Dee spaghetti. The sauce and everything was in the box, so how hard could it be? On the way home, she thought about how surprised her mom would be, what she'd say. Suze smiled and juggled the box up in the air, catching it and throwing it up again. It made an interesting shooshing noise, with the long dry noodles inside.

Dewey was sitting at the kitchen table, taking something apart, as usual. Some kind of wind-up toy, a chicken or a duck, that she was prying apart with a butter knife.

"Hey," Suze said.

"Hey."

Suze put the box of spaghetti down on the table and watched Dewey for a minute. She was making that weird face she did when she was thinking really hard. "What're you doing?"

"Trying to get the spring out. I wound my other one too tight, and it got sprung."

"Oh. Do you have to bust the toy up to do that?"

"Yeah," said Dewey. "But it's pretty snafued anyway." She held it up, and Suze could see that its bill was almost rusted off, and it only had one foot.

"It doesn't waddle anymore, it just falls over," Dewey explained.

"Junk," agreed Suze. "I'm going to make spaghetti tonight. You can have some too."

"Okay." Dewey resumed her prying.

Suze waited for more of a reaction—gratitude, excitement, something—but Dewey didn't say anything else. Suze turned on the radio. It was almost 5:00, and she'd overheard Barbara tell Joyce that KRS—the only station on the Hill—was going to play some Top 40 music this afternoon, instead of the classical stuff they usually played. Suze didn't really mind classical, but it was hard to sing along to.

". . . gonna take, a sentimental journey—" crooned Doris Day. Suze made a face. She didn't like that song much. Too slow and sappy. She went into the living room to get the collage she was working on.

She was trying to make a picture of her old life in Berkeley. Not like a drawing of her house or anything. That was kind of baby. Besides, she couldn't draw that well. The people one Sundt over had thrown out some old magazines—*Saturday Evening Post*s and *Ladies' Home*

*Journal*s. They had big colorful ads, and she was cutting some of them out, like paper dolls from real life. Men in hats and women with baby carriages and the sign from a Texaco station. A Buick and a Plymouth. Sort of a street scene, but some parts were bigger than they ought to be. Her favorite so far was a tiny woman with a shopping basket filled with a giant bottle of Dr. Pepper. Suze hadn't glued anything down yet, just stuck the cutouts onto a big piece of cardboard with thumbtacks to see how they fit together.

She plopped the stack of magazines onto the seat of the empty chair and propped some of the finished figures up against the napkin holder. She leafed through the pages of a *Ladies' Home Journal*. It was really boring to read, but it had good pictures. She cut out a full-page shiny chrome Sunbeam toaster and held it up next to her people. It was the size of a building. That made her laugh, and she started to make up a comic book story to explain it while she leafed.

Unbeknownst to the innocent people of Flat-ville, the evil scientist Linoleo had created an army of giant toasters that were now ringing the city. Linoleo laughed his evil laugh. Soon the people of Flatville would slide into the flaming slots of death, where they would burn—

Suze stopped herself with a shudder. That wasn't funny. She didn't want to think about that. It was too close to what had happened to real people in Germany. Jews, like Gramma and Grandpa Weiss. There were stories in the newspaper that week, about GIs finding bodies stacked in piles, and big brick buildings that were really ovens. She'd had nightmares from just reading about it.

She crumpled the picture of the toaster into a tight ball and tossed it, hard, into the trash can by the back door. She picked up the Chef Boy-Ar-Dee box and busied herself reading the directions, so that her brain would fill up with something else, something easy.

The chugging opening bars of "Chattanooga Choo Choo" came out of the radio, and without thinking about it, Suze started shaking the box to the rhythm. Shoosh-pah, shoosh-pah, shoosh-pah. Spaghetti made a pretty good train sound. She stood up, keeping the box in motion, and began to march around the kitchen in time to the toe-tapping music. Shoosh-pah, shoosh-pah.

And then, in mid-song, the music stopped abruptly, replaced by the voice of Bob Parton, the disk jockey, sounding excited.

"The Germans have surrendered!" he said. "The war in Europe is over! President Truman announced this morning that General Eisenhower . . ."

Suze stared at the radio in shock for a minute, then

began shaking the box of spaghetti furiously, like a New Year's Eve noisemaker. She jumped up and down so hard that a paper Toto dog, only partially cut out, fluttered off the table and glided across the linoleum. Suze paid no attention.

"It's over! It's over!" Suze half sung, half shouted. "It's over, it's over, it's *o-ver*!" She jumped to Dewey's side of the table, and without thinking about it, grabbed her arm and pulled her into the celebration.

They danced around the tiny kitchen, arms linked together, both shouting, "It's over!" to the cacophony of the box of spaghetti, until the radio began to blare out "The Star-Spangled Banner."

Suze dropped Dewey's arm and put her hand over her heart, automatically, the way they always did in school, and closed her eyes. When the anthem was over, she was standing in the kitchen again, looking at Dewey.

Suddenly everything felt awkward.

"The war's over," Suze said in a normal tone of voice.

"Yeah," Dewey said. "I'm glad." She looked around for a second, then sat down.

Suze felt a little out of breath, but she didn't feel excited anymore. Not the same way. The radio droned on and on about generals and treaties and terms, and Suze turned the volume down, picked the Toto dog up off the floor, and sat back at the table. She fiddled with her scissors.

"I bet there will be a lot of parties tonight," she said after a minute. "Maybe my dad will even come home early. He can stop working for one night. It's the end of the war, after all."

"Maybe," Dewey said. "I guess they'll have to keep making the gadget, though, because of the Japs. *That* war isn't over."

"Oh. I forgot about them."

"Yeah, but I bet the army hasn't. On the other hand," Dewey said, smiling, "now maybe Papa can come home from Washington, and stop looking for a Nazi gadget."

Suze stared across the table. "The Nazis have a gadget?"

"Probably not, or the war wouldn't be over," Dewey said, shaking her head. "But Papa said that before the war, scientists all over the world talked to each other, all the time, so the ones that turned into Nazis *could* have known the same stuff."

"How do *you* know about that?" Suze glared suspiciously at Dewey. "It would be top, top, *top* secret."

"I don't know much. Just what Papa said in his letter."

"Oh, right. Like the censors would let something like *that* get through," Suze said scornfully. Dewey was just trying to sound big.

"It was in code."

"Code? Like a spy?" Suze snorted. Now she was sure Dewey was full of baloney.

"It's not like he's passing on war secrets or anything," Dewey said quickly. "He just lets me know what he's doing." Dewey got up and went back to the bedroom. She returned a minute later with a flimsy piece of paper and spread it out on the table. It had been folded and refolded so many times it was almost in pieces.

"See, Papa's letters have always been in code. Ever since I was little. He says it exercises my brain. When I was in first grade, it was mostly rebuses—you know, the puzzles where the pictures sound like words?"

Suze nodded impatiently.

"Then later, it was mostly numbers. Like . . ." Dewey wrinkled up her forehead. "Like 4-5-23-5-25 would be D-E-W-E-Y. Alphabet code. That's an easy one. Most of them were trickier."

Suze looked down at the letter. "This is just words."

"Well, yeah. Like Papa's going to send a number code by the censors? That would just make them pay attention."

"I guess so." Suze read the letter and smirked. Code? What a bunch of bushwa. This was just a boring old letter. "There's nothing secret in here."

"Sure there is. Look." Dewey pointed to a line. "He says he saw *Casablanca* with Uncle T. But Papa doesn't go to movies, and I don't *have* any uncles. So it must be a clue."

"About what?"

"Well, that one's not really code. It's just Spanish."

Suze muttered under her breath. Casablanca. *Casa blanca.* House. White. House— "White House? You think your dad went to the White House?"

Dewey nodded. "With Uncle T., who has to be Truman."

Hmm. That was pretty good, even for baloney. "But what about the Nazis? There's nothing at all about Nazis, in any language," Suze said. Let her try to explain *that.*

"Yeah there is. See here, where he calls me a little Munchkin? Papa never calls me cute names, so that's gotta be code too."

Suze thought for a minute. What would Munchkins have to do with Nazis? Well, *Oz. Nazi.* They both had Zs. Was that it? "Because Oz sounds kind of like Nazi?" she said. "The Zs?"

Dewey raised her eyebrows in surprise, so high that Suze could see them above her glasses. "Wow. That's good. I hadn't thought of that at all." She looked down at the paper. "Wow," she said again.

Suze felt oddly pleased. "So what did you think it meant?"

"Munich," Dewey replied. "Munchkin, Munich."

That made sense too. Suze wished *her* father would write secret notes. This was kind of fun. "What about the rest?"

Dewey shrugged. "I figure a pocketknife with that many blades is a useful gadget, right? But since Papa doesn't have a knife like that—"

"—and no one can find another, it means—"

"—Nazi scientists aren't building a gadget," Dewey finished. "I told you."

Suze whistled through her teeth. "That's really clever."

"Papa's good at puzzles," Dewey nodded. She looked down at the letter, then up at Suze. "You won't tell anyone, will you? I don't want Papa to get into trouble," she said seriously.

"Nope. My lips are sealed," Suze said.

"Thanks." Dewey gave the butter knife a hard twist and the two halves of the duck split open with a pop and rattled onto the tablecloth. She pulled the spring out and looked at it in triumph. "Finally."

Suze stared at the letter and the demolished duck. "It's a good thing you Kerrigans are on *our* side," she said after a minute, and went over to light the stove and boil water for spaghetti.

May 26

HEROIC FIGURES

THE AFTERNOON EVERYTHING changed
started out pretty ordinary. Suze sat on the couch in the
living room, a stack of comic books on one side of her,
and the big yellow bowl full of buttered popcorn on the
other. A green bottle of Coke balanced on the wooden
arm of the couch.

"What are those about, anyway?" Dewey asked from
the chair across the room. She'd been reading a book
about geometry—Suze wasn't sure why, since school was
almost over for the summer—but she'd come to the end
of it. A cereal bowl of popcorn was wedged between her
leg and the side of the chair.

"What are what about?"

"Your comic books. What kind of stories do they
have?"

"Just the usual," Suze said, without taking her eyes

off Wonder Woman, who was about to lasso a very evil-looking Jap.

"I don't know what that means."

"You've never read a comic book?"

Dewey shook her head.

"C'mon. You've *never* read a comic book?" Suze asked again. That was unbelievable. How could anybody, even Dewey, grow up in America and never read a comic book? It was just the sort of thing that spies got trapped by. *Who is Clark Kent?* And a Nazi wouldn't know, would he?

"Classics Illustrated. *Treasure Island*. Once," Dewey said sadly. "Then my Nana took it away. She said they'd rot my brain and give me nightmares." She looked wistfully at the pile at Suze's side.

"Says her. *Treasure Island*?" Suze shook her head. "That's pretty tame. Even these," she patted the top of the stack, "even these won't keep you up nights. They're just adventures. Superheroes with special powers."

"Like what?" Dewey moved the bowl of popcorn to her lap and slid forward to the edge of the chair.

"Well, like when Captain Marvel says 'Shazam' he turns from an ordinary guy into"—she looked at the comic on the top of the stack—"the World's Mightiest Mortal. Captain America got shot up with some sort of secret army serum, and Superman's super because he came from another planet. I'm not sure about Captain Midnight. But he can do nifty stuff too."

"There are a lot of captains," Dewey said. "Are all the heroes men?"

Suze nodded. "All the captains, yeah. Most of the others too. But there's Wonder Woman. And Sheena, Queen of the Jungle. And Brenda Starr, but she's boring because she's just a reporter. Mostly she just gets rescued. Or kissed." Suze made a face. "I like Captain Marvel and Superman best. Superman can melt steel just by staring at it the right way."

"That would be kind of useful," Dewey said.

"Yeah." Suze crammed a handful of popcorn into her mouth and wiped her hand on her pants leg. "You want to read a couple?" she said as she chewed.

"Really?"

"Sure." Suze swallowed and took a drink of Coke. "I've read all these a bunch already. Just don't wreck 'em, okay?" Dewey gave her a funny look, and Suze realized that had been silly. Dewey was about the neatest person she'd ever met. She even used a bookmark when she was done reading, instead of turning down the corner of the page, like everyone in *her* family.

She thumbed through the top of the stack, and pulled out the third one down, which had a man in a red cloak and tights standing with his foot on a Nazi's head. "Here.

Start with Captain Marvel. This one's pretty good." She tossed the comic across the coffee table, spine first, so that it sailed into Dewey's lap.

"It looks swell," said Dewey. She ate a single piece of popcorn and settled back into the armchair with a contented smile.

Suze put the stack of comics on the coffee table, and went into the kitchen, where she'd been working before she decided to take a break and read. The table was covered with cutout pieces from shiny magazines—people mostly, and some cars and a tank. A Pyrex baking pan corralled an array of seemingly random objects: five bottle caps, a chip of green-painted wood, a marble, the cardboard top off a milk bottle, a red rubber ball, and a wax-paper square with a small mound of reddish dirt.

Her first collage, life in Berkeley, had turned out pretty okay. She'd glued everything to a big piece of cardboard, the side of a carton of cereal from the PX. This one was going to be the Hill, so she had cut out a lot of soldiers. Magazines were good for soldiers, and army-green trucks and buildings, because just about every ad was about being patriotic and the war. So that was useful. It was harder to find pictures dressed like people on the Hill—almost everyone in magazines looked like they were on their way to a party. Most of the women had dresses and lots of makeup, and didn't look like *anybody* she knew in real life.

She had spent a week walking around the Hill trying to figure out what she'd want to show, and another couple of weeks begging old magazines from people and cutting out enough pictures. She'd gotten pretty excited the night she found a water tower in an ad, and had spent most of another morning cutting carefully around the strands of a black-and-white barbed-wire fence.

Suze started laying out pictures on the kitchen table, layering them so it looked like trees behind buildings behind people. On the very top, she put some of the objects from the Pyrex pan—a Coke bottle cap near the building that looked like the PX, the red rubber ball on top of some playground swings.

She moved the pictures and the objects around for almost an hour, but no matter where she put them, they didn't quite make what she could see in her head. Everything was too flat. She wanted the people to be at the front—not just a paper's thickness away from the background, but sticking out from it. She tried taping a marble to the back of a soldier, but it only made his middle bulge. His head and feet drooped down, as if he'd been draped across a tiny, invisible barrel. She cut a strip from a piece of shirt cardboard, taped it down the soldier's back, then taped the marble to *that*. He was stiffer, but teetered head-foot-head-foot like an army seesaw. Suze sighed, put the soldier down onto the oilcloth, and went to the bathroom.

When she came back, Dewey was standing next to the sink, a juice glass of water in her hand. "Are Billy Batson and Captain Marvel the same person?" she asked.

"Yeah. Billy Batson's just his secret identity."

"But . . ." Dewey frowned. "But Billy's just a kid. And Captain Marvel's a grown man. How can—?"

"Shazam," Suze said confidently. "Solomon, Hercules, Atlas, Zeus, Achilles, Mercury. The ancient wizard gives him all those guys' powers when he says the word." She smiled. She didn't get to explain much to Dewey, and it felt kind of good. When it came to comic books, Suze knew her onions.

"Oh," Dewey said. "Well, I guess it works." She turned to go back into the living room, but stopped as she passed the table and looked at the teetering soldier.

"Why did you do that?"

Suze followed her gaze. "The marble?"

"Yeah."

"I want that guy to stick out, but it didn't really work."

"Stick out how?"

"Like this." Suze picked up the soldier and held it about an inch away from one of the buildings. "I want it to look like he's standing in front of the PX, not just pasted to it. Like in the shoebox dioramas we made for school, except these people are too big for a shoebox."

Dewey nodded, then scrunched up her face, thinking. "What about a bigger box? From a department store?"

"Hmm." Suze looked at the tabletop. "That would work. Except," she said, sighing, "there isn't a department store for like two hundred miles."

Dewey nodded and looked around the kitchen. "A drawer, then," she said.

"What?"

"A drawer." Dewey put *Captain Marvel* down and pulled out the shallow silverware drawer to the left of the sink. "See. It's about two inches deep, so you could paste some stuff to the bottom, and some on the sides. When you were done, you could probably even hang it on the wall, like a frame."

"Yeah," Suze said slowly. "Yeah. That might work." She stepped over to the counter and looked into the drawer for a long minute before she sighed again and pushed it back in with a thunk.

"What?"

"Even *my* mom would probably notice that the silverware drawer was missing," Suze said. "Or the desk drawer. Or any other drawer." She slumped against the counter. "It was a good idea, though."

"You just need one that nobody's using."

Suze looked around the small, cluttered apartment. "Around here? Fat chance."

"Not *here*," Dewey said, sounding like it was the most obvious thing in the world. "The dump."

"There are drawers at the dump?"

"There's just about *every*thing at the dump."

"Drawers?"

"Probably. There's usually a busted-up desk or two. You should check it out." Dewey picked up *Captain Marvel* and turned to go.

Suze bit her lip. She knew there was a dump, of course. But she didn't know exactly where it was, or how it worked, and she didn't want to admit that. Maybe if she went for a walk, she could find it? Not likely, since she hadn't stumbled across it in two years of wandering.

"Uh, where exactly *is* the dump?" she asked, as casually as she could.

"You've never been to the *dump*?" Dewey made it sound as if she'd never eaten cheese.

"*You'd* never read comics," Suze countered.

Dewey shrugged. "True." She held up *Captain Marvel*. "So we'll trade. Let me finish this one, then I'll take you, if you want. I'm always up for a trip to the dump. It's about my favorite place on the Hill, and I haven't been this week."

"Sure, I guess so." Suze's voice came out sounding as if she was doing Dewey a big favor by going, which wasn't what she'd meant, exactly. But Dewey didn't seem to notice.

By the time Suze had found her shoes—one under her bed and one under the dresser—Dewey had replaced *Captain Marvel* on the top of the stack and was waiting by the back door.

They walked to the bottom of the stairs. Suze turned right and was five feet down the dirt road when Dewey said, "Hold up a sec." She ducked under the angle of the stairs and came out a few seconds later pulling the handle of her red wagon.

Suze looked at it and frowned. Walking with Dewey was one thing. Everyone knew she was staying with the Gordons and nobody had made too big a deal. It was kind of old news. But a little red wagon? Suze was almost twelve. "Do we have to take that?"

"No," Dewey said. "But it takes about twenty minutes to walk to the dump, and it's kind of hot today. *I* wouldn't want to carry a wooden drawer all the way back." She looked at Suze, looked back at the wagon, and waited.

Suze was pretty strong, but she was already starting to sweat a little, just standing there in the sun. Maybe Dewey had a point. "Okay. Let's take it," she said after a minute. "Do you want me to pull?"

"You can have the way back, when it's full," Dewey said.

"Deal. As long as you don't want to bring back an anvil or something."

"Promise," said Dewey.

DUMP DRAWERS

SUMMER HAD FINALLY come to the Hill. The trees had thick green leaves, although there wasn't much shade anywhere near the road. At least there was a little bit of a breeze coming through the pines and scrub oaks to the west. The sky was a bright, storybook blue, with high, puffy white clouds. They could hear a baseball game in progress near the school—the crack of a bat and cheers—the sounds only slightly muffled by distance in the clear mountain air. It was the kind of summer day Suze loved, the kind that just might turn into an adventure.

The wagon bumped and squeaked on the dirt road, rattling over ruts left from last week's rains. Most of them were as dry and brown as crusts of old bread now, but a few muddy puddles remained where the potholes were deeper.

It was quiet. A lot of the men were gone, off to some-place in the southern desert called Base Camp. Suze didn't know where, or why. It was even more secret than the usual secret stuff. Her father had gone down the day before and was going to be away for the next week.

"Wait up," Dewey said. She dropped the wagon's handle and bent down to tie her shoe. Her left shoe, not the odd brown one that laced up the sides. Suze had almost forgotten about Dewey's shoes. Maybe she'd just gotten used to them while they'd been sharing a room.

"Will you have to wear one of those shoes forever?" she asked after they'd started up again. "I was just wondering."

"I hope not," Dewey said. "The doctor in St. Louis said there's an operation I can have that'll make my legs the same size again, but they can't do it until I'm eighteen, until I stop growing for sure. Then I can wear normal old shoes, like everybody else."

"That'll be good."

"Yeah, real good." Dewey looked down at her feet. "I mean, I'm kind of used to it, but no one else ever is. I get tired of having to explain all the time, or pretending that I don't notice when people are staring."

Suze felt her cheeks redden, and was suddenly glad that no one paid much attention to *her* feet. "Yeah," she said after a minute, which seemed lame, but she couldn't think of anything else to say. They walked along past the post office, the PX, the Pond.

"After this picture's done, do you know what you're going to do next?" Dewey asked as they turned onto the main road and headed east.

"I'm not sure." Suze had a whole pile of loose pages to cut out, and some ideas had been floating around her head as she lay in bed at night, falling asleep, but nothing had quite jelled. Maybe a grocery store—there were more food ads than anything else—or a circus. Not with the same pictures, but those were the two ideas that kept coming back. "Maybe something with a circus," she said finally. "How 'bout you? Are you gonna make another gadget thingy?"

It was Dewey's turn to think. "I don't know. I just finished a wind-up guy that rolls around, sort of in a circle. I might make a better one of those, now that I've figured out most of the hard parts, but I'm not sure either." She smiled. "Maybe I'll get a good idea at the dump. It depends on what I find."

"Are there magazines there?" Suze asked.

"Not usually. Mostly army and science and building stuff. But you never know. It's kind of like treasure hunting, except *some*body thought it was just junk."

Suze nodded. "Like drawers," she said. "Not quite pirate treasure, but I hope I find one. A wooden drawer, about two feet wide. Oak would be nice." Suze could almost see it, a polished square full of bright colors and shapes, hanging on the bedroom wall, the wood glowing in a beam of sunlight. "What about you?"

Dewey bit her lip and Suze saw her fingers drum for a moment on the handle of the wagon as she thought. "What I really want to find is a record player. Not the needle part, that could be busted. Just the turntable, the go-round."

"How come?"

"It would be fun to mess with. Like if I put magnets on it, so they went around, and then put a piece of glass over it, or thin enough wood, and put some BBs or ball bearings on the glass, I could see how they'd move."

"Would it do anything?"

"Maybe," Dewey said. "But I'd have to play with it for a while and see what happened before I decided."

"Yeah. I know what you mean." Suze hadn't put it into words, but that felt like what she'd been doing for the last couple of days. Playing with the images until they almost seemed to go where they belonged, fitting together into a puzzle she hadn't ever seen before.

She looked at Dewey out of the corner of her eye. She'd never had a conversation like this with another kid. She didn't feel like she had to be funny, or try to show Dewey how smart she was. She could just—

"This is it," Dewey said.

The dump looked like a vacant lot, fenced on three sides. On the right were organized bins of different kinds of lumber, but the rest was seemingly random piles of recognizable objects in unfamiliar configurations—a stack of wall-less windows, pieces of motors and other machines, shovels with splintered handles, a steering wheel, a stack of stenciled ammo crates, the front grill to a Buick.

"The furniture stuff—if there is any—is usually in the back corner," Dewey said. "I'm going to check out the little junk boxes over here." She pointed to her right. "You can take the wagon. Yell if you need help yanking something out."

Suze nodded and picked up the handle of the red wagon. She'd had one like it when she was in kindergarten. But she was much taller now, more than five feet, and had to bend her knees a little as she pulled it around the corner of a wall of construction metal, some rusty, some shiny in the afternoon sun.

Her eyes widened and her heart raced, just a little, when she saw four desks lined up against the chain-link fence. Three of them were metal, army green and battleship gray, but one was wood, like the teachers' desks in her old school in Berkeley, except painted a pale institutional green.

To get to the desk, Suze had to abandon the wagon

and climb over a stack of fluorescent light fixtures and around a varnished wooden door propped up against them. She barked her shin on the edge of the door, but it just scraped off a little skin and didn't bleed. She tried to remember if she'd had a tetanus shot. But that was for rusty nails, and the door was only wood. It wouldn't matter, she hoped.

The desk had a huge piece missing from the back corner—which was probably why it was at the dump—and seven drawers. Three deep ones were stacked along each side, and a wide, shallow one ran across the middle, above where her knees would go. That one was perfect, not quite two feet across and two inches deep. She tugged at it, but there was some sort of catch at the back, to stop a person from accidentally pulling it all the way out, spilling paper clips and rubber bands all over the floor. By the time she'd crawled underneath and released the catch, her hands and knees were covered with dirt.

Suze pulled the drawer out, admired it for a minute—it might be oak, under the paint—then lifted it over the stack of fixtures, propping it carefully on the other side so it wouldn't get scratched up. She looked at the other desks, and decided, after some deliberation, that they were too metal and ugly, and there wasn't anything to do about *that*. She clambered back over the fixtures and put the good drawer into the wagon.

Dewey knelt in front of a line of gray metal boxes with lots of dials. She was using a screwdriver to pry off a black Bakelite knob. The stubs of metal on the fronts of the boxes were all that was left of their other knobs, which lay in a small pile next to her knees. The wagon's wheels crunched in the dirt, and Dewey looked over her shoulder.

"Find one?" she asked.

Suze grinned and pushed a strand of hair off her sweaty, dusty face. "Yeah. The rest were metal, or way too deep."

The knob came off in Dewey's hand with a small popping sound. She dropped it onto the pile with the others, and stood up. "That's a good one," she said, wiping her hands on a bandana from her pocket.

"It's great," Suze said. She ran a finger lightly over the smooth painted front of the drawer. "I can't wait to get home and see how everything fits. Are you gonna look for any more jun—?" She'd been about to say "junk," but that sounded like an insult she didn't mean. She groped for a word. "Any more, uh, paraphernalia?" She grinned. It was one of her favorite big words.

Dewey laughed, an explosive little laugh that came out part snort, part Bronx cheer. "Yeah, right," she said. She looked around. "Nope, I think I'm done for today. It's *hot*." She bent down, scooped up the little pile of black knobs, and put them inside the drawer. She patted her pockets. "I'd say let's go get Cokes, but I didn't bring any money."

Suze reached into her own pocket and held up a nickel. "This is enough for a pack of Kool-Aid. We can make it when we get back."

"Not the lemon-lime." Dewey made a face.

"No. Ick." Suze pulled the collar of her shirt over her face and wiped some of the sweat off, tasting gritty salt and hot cotton, then picked up the handle of the wagon.

They walked back along the road in a satisfied silence punctuated by the slightly arrhythmic sound of the wagon's mismatched wheels and the staccato clatter of the knobs in the wooden drawer.

Suze felt good. She'd found treasure, and she'd been to a brand-new part of the Hill. New to her, anyway. An adventure. She began to whistle, sort of in time with their steps, "The Colonel Bogey March." As she launched into it a second time, she was astonished to hear Dewey begin to sing the words the boys sang on the playground—if no teacher was within earshot:

Hitler *has only got one ball.*
Goering *has two but they are small.*
Himmler *has something sim'lar,*
But poor old Goebbels *has* no balls *at all!*

Suze joined in on the second line and they sang it together, then both burst out laughing. Suze reached down and slung her free arm around Dewey's shoulder, then they sang it a third time, at the top of their lungs, like pirates returning home with a trunk full of particularly glorious booty.

As they rounded a corner, Suze took a deep breath and started another chorus. "*Hitler* has only got—"

She stopped singing and stood stock-still. Joyce and Barbara, in full Girl Scout regalia, stood on the porch of the post office.

"Well, my stars and garters," said Joyce, in a fakey grown-up voice. "What *do* we have here?" She stepped off onto the hard-packed dirt and smiled a little half smile that made Suze nervous.

"Look, Barb," said Joyce. "It's the Sad Sack Club. Screwy Dewey, founder and president. Or have *you* taken over now?" she said, looking at Suze.

Suze didn't answer, but she felt her cheeks going red, and felt Dewey stiffen under her arm. Neither of them moved.

"Why, they've been rag-picking. It must be the initiation into the club," Joyce said. She took another step toward them, and her gold trefoil Girl Scout pin winked in the bright sun.

"Mind your own beeswax," Suze said. She gripped

the wagon handle tighter, and felt Dewey start to move out from under her arm. Suze almost let her go. Because maybe there was still time to—and then she stopped. To what? To pretend that she hadn't been to the dump with Dewey? But she had, and it had been fun. Suze looked down at the drawer in the wagon. Just a minute ago, she'd been excited to get back home, to start fitting the pieces of her collage into it. That had been a good feeling, and she wanted it back. Wanted it more fiercely than she'd known, wanted it a lot more than she cared if Joyce liked her or not. She took a deep breath and squeezed Dewey's shoulder, just once, and Dewey stood still.

"We should get going," Barbara said, to Joyce's back. "The other girls are coming at five, and we still have to make the tea."

"Oh, we've got time. Don't you want to see what the trash of the day is?" Joyce took a quick step over to the wagon and reached down toward the pile of knobs. "Knobs," she said. "Now *there's* something every girl needs."

"Leave 'em alone," said Suze. She dropped the wagon handle.

Joyce ignored her. "And a drawer. I guess they don't have real furniture over in *Morgan*ville." She looked at Dewey.

"That's mine," Suze said through her teeth. "Leave it alone."

"Oh, it's a *special* drawer," Joyce said in a talking-to-babies voice, and reached for it.

Without thinking, Suze let go of Dewey, took a step forward, grabbed Joyce by the knot of her big yellow Girl Scout neckerchief, and pushed her away. Hard.

Joyce stumbled back. Her feet hit the edge of a puddle, and she went sprawling into the mud, landing with a great *splosh* and sat there, stunned. Nobody moved.

After a few seconds Barbara walked over and offered her a hand. Joyce stood up, glaring at Suze. The back of her green Girl Scout dress was soaked with mud, and her beret had fallen off when she landed. It lay in the puddle, sodden as a wet toad.

"Now you've done it, Truck," Joyce said in a tight, angry voice. "*I'm* telling my mother. I bet she'll make you pay for a whole new uniform."

Suze stared at her. "What did you call me?"

"Truck," Barbara said. She stood next to Joyce. "That's what everyone calls you."

"Big fat pushy steamroller truck," Joyce said, enunciating each word.

Suze stood by the wagon, her arms hanging at her sides. *Truck?* She felt her eyes sting, and wiped her face brusquely with the back of her hand. She took a deep breath. "Sticks and sto—"

Then Dewey stepped forward and spit, right onto Joyce's brown oxfords.

"You're all *wet*," she said, and crossed her arms over her chest.

"Barbara's father's gonna put you scrags in the brig. Just wait," Joyce said in a low voice.

"Color me so yellow," Dewey replied. She turned to Suze. "Kool-Aid?" she asked, and without a glance back, began to walk toward the PX.

Suze nodded, but said nothing. She picked up the handle of the wagon and followed Dewey, looking over her shoulder every few seconds, just in case. But the other girls didn't move.

They were almost to the PX before either of them spoke.

"You knew?" Suze asked. "Truck?"

"Yeah. I'd heard." Dewey shrugged. "But not as much as I'd heard 'Screwy Dewey.' I've been wanting to spit for a long time."

"Yeah."

"But now we're fubar, aren't we?"

"Completely fubar," Suze agreed. "Barbara's dad's brass." She thought for a minute. "I don't think there's really a brig, though. At least not for civilians."

"Probably not. But I bet your mom will think of something."

Suze groaned. "Yeah, that's the truth. You still want Kool-Aid?"

Dewey shook her head. "I'm thirsty, but we oughta get back and clean up before the Tech whistle blows."

Suze looked down at her dirty knees. "It couldn't hurt."

They pulled the wagon under the stairs of the apartment building. Dewey shoved most of the knobs into her pockets, and Suze cradled the drawer in her arms.

"For once I'm glad there aren't any phones," Suze said. "We're probably safe until after dinner. If Mom even comes home." But just the same, they tiptoed up the stairs and let themselves into the kitchen without banging the screen door.

Suze put the drawer down on the tabletop. She turned toward the living room doorway and then stopped, her mouth open in shock.

Her mother was already home, sitting on the living room couch. She looked like she'd been crying. And that wasn't all. Oppie was sitting next to her, looking skinny and tired. Dr. Robert Oppenheimer, the head of the whole Hill, his expression official and serious.

It wasn't possible. Joyce *couldn't* have told already.

"We're *really* fubar," she whispered to Dewey. "Look."

Dewey dropped her knobs into the drawer and came up behind Suze. "Oh jeez," she said, shaking her head. "This isn't good."

Suze looked at the back door. Maybe they could—

then she sighed. "We might as well get it over with." She squared her shoulders, took a deep breath, and walked into the living room, Dewey right behind her.

Her mother looked up at the sound of her footsteps, bit her lip, then looked at Dewey.

"Girls, sit down," Mrs. Gordon said, and her voice quavered. Suze had never heard her sound like that before. They sat, one on each chair, and Suze braced herself for the biggest lecture of her whole life. Then Oppie spoke.

"I'm sorry," he said quietly. He held up a piece of flimsy yellow paper, a telegram. "There's been an accident."

FOR THE DURATION

SUZE STARED AT her mother, her stomach full of sharp ice. In her mind, she could see fire, explosions somewhere in a desert, her life blowing apart. "Something's happened to Daddy?" she asked. Her hands gripped the sides of her chair so hard that she could feel a blister of varnish crackle under her fingernail.

Her mother looked startled, for a moment. She started to smile and shake her head, another moment, and then the smile disappeared and there was only the head-shake. "No, sweetie," she said in a soft voice. "Daddy's fine." She turned to Oppie, who nodded.

"I saw him late last night. He's tired, we're all tired. But, no—" He stopped and looked down at the telegram in his hand. "No," he said. "Phil's fine."

"But?" Suze said, and as she said it, her mother got off the couch and walked toward her chair. Suze leaned forward, lifting her arms fractionally for the anticipated hug, but her mother only touched her cheek with the back of a hand, and went over to the chair where Dewey sat with her hands clenched in her lap.

"Dewey," Mrs. Gordon said, smoothing a hand across Dewey's dark curls. "Honey—" And then her voice broke.

Suze felt a wave of relief wash over her, as if a huge weight had been lifted off her chest.

Dewey bit her lip, so hard it was white all the way around. She looked over at Oppie and said, "Papa."

Oppie nodded.

"Bad?"

Suze heard her mother give a little cry, a squeak from somewhere in her throat.

"He was hit by a car," Oppie said. "Crossing the street in front of the Capitol. Soldiers, just back from France. Drunk and celebrating." He looked down at his hands. "An accident," he muttered. "A stupid goddamn accident."

"He's—?"

"Yes." Oppie shook his head slowly, sadly. "I'm sorry. He—the police say he was killed instantly, that he never knew what hit him."

Suze began to cry without a sound, tears rolling down her cheeks. Her mother was crying too, shaking, touching

Dewey's hair with one hand, the other resting on Dewey's shoulder.

Dewey didn't move. She stared at a place next to the front door and seemed to get smaller, as if she were sinking, shrinking into the chair.

"I'll have to leave now, won't I?" Dewey said. Her voice was flat. Not angry or sad, or even cold. Just flat. "I guess I should go pack."

"Oh, no. No!" Mrs. Gordon looked over at Oppie, who seemed startled by what Dewey had said. "Robert, she won't—?"

He sighed. "I really hadn't thought," he said. He looked at Dewey. "Is there someone we should call?"

Dewey barely moved, but shook her head a minuscule no.

"Grandparents? Aunts? Uncles? Anyone?"

Another tiny shake. No.

Oppie blew out a stream of air. "Well, nothing needs to be done tonight." He tried to smile, but he just looked weary. "Don't worry," he said. "Don't worry. We'll work it out." He looked at his watch. "But I've got the general waiting." He stood up and picked his porkpie hat up off the end table. "Walk me out, Terry?"

"Sure, let's grab a smoke." Mrs. Gordon stroked Dewey's hair once more, then got her Chesterfields from the coffee table, and the two adults went out the front door, leaving it open a few inches. Suze could hear the murmur of talking, too low for individual words. She sniffed and wiped her eyes with the back of her hand.

"I'm really sorry," she said to Dewey. She wanted to say something else, something more, but what was there to say?

Dewey nodded. "Thanks," she whispered. She didn't look at Suze. She didn't look at anything. She just sat there for a minute, two. Then, as if she'd just decided something, put both hands on the arms of the chair and pushed herself up.

"I'm going for a walk," she said in that soft, flat voice.

"Okay." Suze thought about asking if she wanted company, but was pretty sure she knew the answer, and didn't. She looked at the clock on the mantel.

As if reading Suze's mind, Dewey said, "I don't think I'll be hungry."

"Yeah. Okay."

Dewey walked slowly, almost formally into the kitchen. Suze heard the screen door open, and then a faint padding as Dewey went down the outside stairs.

Suze sat in the living room, staring at the pattern of the rug she'd never really noticed before, listening to the murmur of the grown-ups' voices. She heard a pause, the click of a Zippo, and then the murmuring continued.

Eventually, she got up and went into the kitchen, for no other reason than that she didn't want to sit in that chair anymore.

She was surprised by the small wooden drawer that lay on the oilcloth of the kitchen table. She had forgotten it, as if it had been a hundred years since she put it there. It had only been twenty minutes. Suze remembered being excited about it, but now it didn't seem important.

She poured herself a glass of orange juice. Her throat was sore from being thirsty. And from crying. The juice stung a little going down, but the cold and sweet felt good. She closed her eyes and held the cool glass against her face, hot from the sun, flushed from tears.

"Sweetie? How're you doing?" Her mother's voice came from the living-room doorway and sounded, right then, as sweet and soothing as the juice.

"Okay, I guess." Suze snuffled once and opened her eyes.

"I know. It's so hard to believe." Her mother pulled a chair out and sat down, close enough that Suze could smell the comforting, familiar smokiness of her hair. "You read about the war. Somewhere else. Hundreds of people probably died yesterday. We knew this one."

Suze nodded. She felt so strange, as if a big piece of the world had vanished, even though she'd only met Mr. Kerrigan once. She sat down. "I'm glad it wasn't Daddy," she said finally, and then put her hand over her mouth, because that seemed like the exact wrong thing to say. It was true, but it felt rude to be glad about anything.

"Me too," her mother said. She put an arm around Suze's shoulder and kissed her cheek. "Seems like a crummy thing to think right now, but I guess that's human nature. There but for the grace of god—" She looked around the kitchen. "Where's Dewey?"

"She went for a walk," Suze said. A pause. "How come she didn't cry?"

"It hits everyone differently. Maybe she wanted to cry by herself. Dewey's a pretty private person, you know."

"Yeah." Suze wouldn't have said it that way, but it was true. "Mom?"

"Yes, sweetie."

"What's going to happen to Dewey now? *Will* she have to leave?"

Her mother lit a Chesterfield and blew out a long stream of smoke before she answered. "That's what Oppie and I were talking about, outside. Poor kid. I don't think there's anywhere for her to go. Her grandmother's in a home, and no one's seen her mother for almost ten years."

"Nobody knows where her *mother* is?" That seemed impossible to Suze. How could a mother get lost?

"Not since Dewey was a baby." She looked for the

ashtray. "What's this drawer?" she asked, moving it aside. The glass ashtray was underneath, and she tapped her cigarette into it.

"It's for my art project. Like a frame." Suze put it onto an empty chair. "So what's going to happen?"

"It's a muddle. That's what Oppie said. Dewey could easily fall through the cracks."

"How come?"

"Well, Jimmy—her dad—her papa—was a civilian. If he'd been Army there would be official government channels. And under normal circumstances, there are state agencies to take care of an orphan. But since this place is so goddamn secret, the state of New Mexico can't even know that Dewey Kerrigan of Los Alamos exists."

Orphan. Suze was startled by the word. Even though it was eighty degrees outside, she imagined Dewey in the snow, in rags, begging, or being locked away in some huge stone building, cold and forbidding.

"She's not really an orphan though, is she? Not if she's got a mother."

"Not technically. But for all practical purposes, she is."

"So what's going to happen to her?" Suze asked for the third time, sounding a little impatient.

Her mother let out another stream of smoke. "Well, legally, no one knows right now. But she can't go back to Morganville, not by herself, and the duplex can't stay empty long. There's still a housing shortage. Oppie says he'll take care of the paperwork so nothing has to be done immediately, but that only buys her a couple of weeks."

"And then what?"

"I guess I'll have to box up Jimmy's things, put them in storage." She looked like she was going to cry again, and busied herself stubbing out her cigarette as if it were the most important thing she'd ever done.

"But where will *Dewey* go?" Suze asked.

"Sweetie, I really don't know."

"Can't she stay here?"

"For now, yes. Would that be all right with you?"

Suze glanced at the drawer she and Dewey brought home from the dump, and her thoughts seemed to carom around its corners. If anyone had told her two months ago that she'd be *asking* to let Dewey stay with her, she'd have told them they were nuts. But it felt right.

"Yeah. There's plenty of room."

"Good. I like her too. That's settled, at least for the duration."

"How long is that?"

"Till the war's over. No one's going anywhere until then."

Suze started to ask another question, but her mother answered it before she'd gotten the first word out.

"If the tests that Daddy and the other fellows are

working on are a success, we might see an end to it by fall. Maybe even sooner."

"What if the gadget doesn't work?" Suze asked, because it was obvious that was what they were testing, whatever it was.

"Oh Christ, sweetie, don't even *think* that. If it's a dud, we're all back to square one, and they'll be invading Japan within a month." She drummed her fingers on the oilcloth as if trying to make up her mind, then lit another cigarette. "Thousands more American boys dead, and the war could go on for years. It'll work. It has to."

"So what happens when the war ends?"

"Well, now there's the $64 Question. I haven't a clue. I suppose we'll fold up our tents here and go back to Berkeley."

"Good," said Suze. She wondered if their neighborhood had changed, if the war had made everything different, or if she could just slip back into her old life. "Would we take Dewey home with us?"

"Well, Daddy and I will have to talk about that." Her mother shook her head. "And I don't even know if we can. There are laws. She's got a mother out there—somewhere." She rubbed her eyes with both hands. "But let's cross that bridge when we come to it." She stubbed out her second cigarette, this time without even looking. "In the meantime, she's more than welcome here."

"For the duration?"

"For the duration."

"Thanks," Suze said.

"I'm glad you feel that way, sweetie." Her mother smiled, the kind of smile that made Suze feel warm all over, like she'd won a prize for being a good kid. A good—And then, for the first time since she'd seen her mother and Oppie on the couch, she remembered Joyce and the mud, and gave a little involuntary groan.

"What is it, Suze?" Her mother patted her hand gently. "I'm sorry. This is all happening so fast. It's tough for all of us."

"It's not that. . . ." Suze said, and let the *that* drift off because she wasn't sure what she was going to say next.

"What? Whatever it is, it's okay, sweetie."

Suze was pretty sure that wasn't going to be true, but she took a deep breath and said, "I kind of pushed Joyce into the mud this afternoon."

In the next two seconds, her mother's face went from startled to almost amused, just her eyes, to a more typical Mom look.

"I see." She raised one eyebrow, a signal Suze knew meant "Tell me the rest."

"Okay, well, Dewey and I went to the dump to get this drawer," Suze said quickly, patting it on the chair next to her, "and then Joyce and Barbara saw us and Joyce called

Dewey 'Screwy Dew—' you know, that name—and tried to take the drawer away so I pushed her and she kind of fell into a puddle. I didn't *mean* for her to fall down or get her Girl Scout dress all dirty but she called me a big fat truck and—"

Suze burst into ragged sobs that she hadn't known were coming. Not at all.

She felt her mother's arm around her, felt a soft kiss on her forehead. "What a miserable afternoon," Terry whispered. She held Suze while she cried, and when the sobs faded to sniffles and tears, pulled a hankie from her pocket.

"Blow," she said.

Suze blew.

"I'll talk to Joyce's mother tomorrow," she said. "Under the circumstances, I think we're going to let this one slide. But, Suze—"

"I know, I know." Suze nodded. "You don't even have to say it."

"Okay. I won't." She patted Suze on the shoulder and stood up. "You want a hamburger? I need to eat something."

"Yeah, sure." Suze wasn't really hungry, but it was nice to have Mom home for supper.

WALKING

DEWEY WALKS AROUND the Hill without thinking, without seeing anything but the ground in front of her feet, each step. She walks because as long as she is moving, she doesn't have to do anything, say anything, feel anything. She doesn't want to talk to anyone, answer questions. She doesn't trust her voice to speak without breaking.

She walks by the post office, by the mud puddle that looks alien now, a puddle from another life. She touches the barbed wire of the fence that surrounds the Tech offices, but that is too real, too close. She walks away, one foot in front of the other, trying to stay blank. *Tabula rasa.* Who said that? She can almost hear Papa's voice and she won't. She can't. She starts saying the multiplication table, fast, under her breath, as if it were a chant that will keep all other thoughts at bay.

Dewey puts her hands in her pockets. Her fingers curl unexpectedly around a small black Bakelite knob and caress it as if it were a talisman, the ball of her thumb tracing the smooth curve over and over and over.

She walks around the edge of the Hill, without intention, looping east, then north, until she finds herself in Morganville. She walks by the small empty house, touches the glass of the front window gently, her palm flat against the cool pane. She remembers the feel of Papa's rough-bearded cheek, the smell of wool and aftershave, and pulls her hand away as if she were burned.

Dewey begins the multiplication table again, out loud, starting with the twelves, because the bigger the number, the more power it has. Numbers don't change. Numbers don't leave. Numbers don't die. They go on for eternity, infinity, and there is comfort in that.

She walks and chants until the sky in the west is streaked with orange and the margins of the forest have grown dusky blue and indistinct in the twilight. She walks until the lights of the apartments wink on, until the stars begin to appear at the edge of the world.

When she can no longer see the ground in front of her, can barely make out the shapes of her own shoes, Dewey returns to the road that leads past the Sundts. She would walk all night, but someone would come looking for her, and that would make it harder. She counts her steps—one, two, three, four—and at three hundred seventeen, she is at the foot of the Gordons' stairs. The kitchen light is on, but she does not hear voices.

She climbs three steps, then sits down in the darkness, in the shadow of the building where she is nearly invisible. She rests her head against the wood siding, slightly warmer than the night air. Dewey closes her eyes and leans against the solidity of the wall, her fingers curled protectively around a small, smooth knob, softly murmuring numbers until her lips are barely moving, chanting herself into a stillness that soon becomes sleep.

When Dewey wakes the moon is high in the night sky, and her glasses are askew on her face. Why is she on the stairs—? and then she remembers, all in a rush, and she feels as if she is dissolving from the inside out. She holds her arms across her chest and shudders. Her neck is stiff from sleeping against the wall.

"Hey, kiddo," a voice from above her says softly.

Dewey twists to look up the stairs. Mrs. Gordon is sitting on the top step, in a wedge of light from the open kitchen door. She is wearing her reading glasses, a sheaf of papers in one hand, a cigarette in the other, its tip glowing as bright as neon in the darkness. An amber beer bottle rests by her thigh.

"I fell asleep," Dewey says.

"I know. I've been keeping an eye on you." Mrs. Gordon pushes her glasses up onto her hair. She shakes the beer bottle, then drops her cigarette into the neck. There is a quick hiss, then silence. "I made some lemonade. I thought you might be thirsty when you woke up."

"What time is it?" asks Dewey.

"A little after midnight."

"Oh." Dewey is not usually up this late. But nothing is usual. She swallows, testing her throat, and nods. She stands up awkwardly, bracing herself against the wall, her leg all pins and needles, and slowly climbs the stairs.

She pauses two steps from the top, eye level with Mrs. Gordon, uncertain whether to continue and sit down next to her. Mrs. Gordon smiles. "It's okay," she says, and puts her hand on Dewey's shoulder, pulling her into a hug.

Dewey is surprised, but lets her. It feels nice, Mrs. Gordon's arms around her, her face against the soft cotton of the plaid shirt.

"There, there, kiddo," Mrs. Gordon whispers. "I miss him too. He was one of the good guys."

Dewey trembles and closes her eyes. She feels Mrs. Gordon's arm under her knees, feels herself being lifted, then cradled, and allows herself to sink into Mrs. Gordon's lap. She feels the faint brush of a kiss on her forehead, and then she is gently rocked. No one has held her like this since Nana, when she was little, in those first lonely weeks in St. Louis. Something inside Dewey lets go. She finally begins to cry, a slow, steady trickle, as if she is leaking.

MORGANVILLE PURGE

FOR THE NEXT few weeks, Dewey rarely left the apartment. Her gadgets lay untouched in shoeboxes under the bed, her Erector set gathered dust. She spoke when she was spoken to, ate when she was hungry—which was not often—and sat by herself in the bedroom, reading and rereading Suze's comic books.

Billy Batson was an orphan. So was Superman. So was Batman. They became superheroes because of it. Orphans with capes. And now they can never die, no matter what danger they get into. Trains, bombs, spaceships from other planets, Nazi spies, machine-gun gangsters. Nothing can kill them. That was better than real life, where there was war, and drunken soldiers.

In real life, almost everyone was gone. Dr. Gordon had gone off with the other men, south to the desert where Charlie said they were going to test the gadget. Charlie and Jack were going away too, to their grandmother's in Oregon for all of July, because, Jack said, their mother was afraid that what was in the desert might set fire to the world, or at least New Mexico. They said they'd leave their comic books with her for safekeeping, more than two hundred of them. She'd read most of Suze's.

Finally one evening in the middle of June, Mrs. Gordon sat down on the end of Dewey's bed and cleared her throat. Dewey put down *Captain America* and looked up.

"Dewey? Honey? I think it's time to bring the rest of your things over here. From Morgan—from your house."

Dewey nodded. She had known this was coming. "I'll take my wagon over after breakfast tomorrow. It may take a couple of trips," she said in a small voice.

Mrs. Gordon smiled and patted Dewey's knee. "Well, if you'd like some help, some company, I've got a car. I thought we could stop by the Commissary and get some empty boxes. Norma says she'll cover for me at the lab tomorrow." Dewey thought about it. Mrs. Gordon was the nicest grown-up lady she had ever known. She understood about experiments, because she was a scientist, and about not wanting to put down your book when the clock said it was bedtime. And she wore glasses to read or do the crossword puzzle, and that was kinship.

"I'd like that," she said finally.

They went over after breakfast Saturday morning.

Mrs. Gordon wore a bandana over her hair, and a flannel shirt with the sleeves cut off, in case they had to clean up dust. They packed the easy things in the kitchen first. The canned beans and tuna could go into the Gordons' cupboards, along with the bowls and plates. Mrs. Gordon admired the glass Chemex coffeemaker, and Dewey said that she could have it. Dewey didn't drink coffee.

There was not much in the living room. The furniture all belonged to the army and was kind of ugly. Dewey didn't mind leaving it behind. One of the pictures on the wall was a print of water lilies. Mrs. Gordon said it was Monet. Maybe they could hang it in the living room of the Sundt? Dewey had to think about whether seeing that painting every day would make her too sad, and decided that it would be okay. The other painting was darker, a still life with a dead pheasant and lots of fruit, and when Dewey shook her head, Mrs. Gordon wrapped it in newspaper and put it in a carton. Dewey said to leave the record player for last.

In Dewey's room, Mrs. Gordon asked about the pieces of equipment, and told her a story about getting her first chemistry set, when she was Dewey's age. That was in 1920, when it was even harder to be a girl. "*Our* kind of girl," she said with a wink, as if she and Dewey were part of a club.

Dewey liked that. She leaned against her dresser. "Can

I ask you something?" she said. "A science question? It's been kind of bothering me."

"Sure. I'm about ready for a break." Mrs. Gordon sat on the end of the bed and lit a cigarette. "Shoot."

"It's probably stupid."

"There are no stupid questions, just stupid answers. Try me."

"Okay, well." Dewey rubbed some dirt off the end of her finger. "Jack—he's a boy in my class? He said that Dr. Fermi made a bet with his dad that when they test the gadget, all the air in the world is going to catch fire. And his mom found out, and that's why he and Charlie have to go to their gramma's farm in Oregon next month. Just in case."

Mrs. Gordon looked at Dewey, her eyes wide, her cigarette stopped halfway to her lips. "Jack told you that?"

"Yeah. And I figured it was just hooey, but—" She shrugged. "Is it?"

"Oh, jeez," Mrs. Gordon said. She took a long puff on her cigarette. "I shouldn't tell you anything at all. But if the other kids are talking—" She looked around for an ashtray, sighed, and tapped the ashes into her cupped hand. "I don't think it's something you need to worry about," she said.

"But is it true?"

Mrs. Gordon sighed again. "Partly. Enrico *did* make

a bet with Bob and some of the other fellas. More as a joke, because the calculations the theoretical guys have done really don't bear it out."

Now Dewey's eyes got wide. "You mean it *could* happen?"

"It's a remote possibility. Very remote. A thousand to one."

"Then why is Jack's mom taking them to Oregon?" Dewey asked.

Mrs. Gordon looked off into an empty corner of the room. "To keep her cubs safe," she said softly.

"What?"

"Nothing." Mrs. Gordon shook her head. "Look, I'm going to flush this butt down the toilet and start on the other room. Can you finish up in here?"

"I think so," said Dewey. Mrs. Gordon hadn't answered the way she'd hoped. She took a breath and thought about the air with a worried frown, then shook her head and finished packing. All her equipment fit in one carton, her clothes and a few books in another. A lot of her things had migrated over to the Gordons' in the last two months, and all that was left was heavy winter clothes and a dress she'd only worn once since she'd arrived.

When she went into the second bedroom, Mrs. Gordon had laid everything from the closet out on the bed. The shirts and ties and pants seemed so empty without someone in them.

Dewey bent over to help fold them and put them in a box. She picked up a blue wool sweater and was ambushed by the smell of Papa—tobacco and aftershave and the baked-fruit scent of the Brylcreem he used to slick back his hair. Dewey heard herself whimper. She dropped the sweater and left without a word, sitting in the kitchen until she could walk without shaking and she trusted herself not to cry.

When she went back into the bedroom, Mrs. Gordon held out a small cedar box. "You okay?"

Dewey nodded.

"You sure? We can come back tomorrow."

"I need to get this done," Dewey said, shaking her head.

"Okay. Up to you," said Mrs. Gordon. She hesitated for a moment, then handed Dewey the box. "I think you'll want this."

Dewey sat on the edge of the bed and opened the box. The bottom was lined with dark green felt. Inside were two small photographs, Dewey as a baby and her third-grade picture. She picked up the two heavy silver dollars and saw that one was from 1907, the year Papa was born, and one from 1932, when she was. A pair of silver cuff links with his initials—JPK, James Patrick Kerrigan—lay curled inside the circle of the leather-banded wristwatch that he had rarely worn. Dewey felt her eyes begin to sting, way back in her head, and closed the box quickly.

"I'll put this with my clothes," she said.

She kept a few of his handkerchiefs, white linen with a blue script K embroidered in the corner, and two undershirts. His hats were too big, coming down over her eyes, but when she tried on his cap, a tan-checked wool with a pale silk lining, and glanced in the mirror, she looked like a newsboy. Like Billy Batson. So she kept that too. Dewey would have liked to have his other watch, the silver pocket watch he carried every day. But it had been in his pocket and—and she didn't want to think about that at all.

"I thought we'd just put these boxes down in the furnace room at our place, for now anyway," Mrs. Gordon said. She folded all the flaps on the top of a carton so they interlocked like a Chinese puzzle.

"Okay," Dewey said. She wasn't sure what she'd do with two boxes of men's clothes. If she was a boy, she could grow up and wear them. But she wasn't, and there were poor people in Santa Fe who could use them. They could wait a few months, though. Until the sweaters became ordinary wool and didn't smell like memories.

Mrs. Gordon carried the boxes outside and put them in the trunk of her black Chevy. "I think that's it," she said. She stood in the doorway and pulled her bandana off, running her fingers through her short honey-brown hair. "If you've got the key, we can lock up and get it back to the Housing Office before they close at five. It's twenty of now."

Dewey sat on the arm of the couch. "Do I have to give it back today?"

"I suppose not. I just figured since we're done here and they're still open—"

"I'm not done," said Dewey quietly.

"Oh." Mrs. Gordon looked around the room. "You mean the phonograph? We can put that on the front seat. There's plenty of room."

Dewey shook her head, trying to figure out how to tell Mrs. Gordon to leave. She didn't want to be rude—she liked Mrs. Gordon. A lot. But it was time to say goodbye to her house, Papa's house, and she needed to do that alone.

"I'll put it in my wagon when I leave. It's not that heavy."

"Don't be silly. The car's—" Mrs. Gordon looked at Dewey and didn't finish her sentence. She thumped the heel of her hand softly against her forehead. "Oh. Sorry. I'm a little dense at the end of the day. You need some time to yourself, don't you?"

"Yes, please," Dewey said. "If that's okay."

"Okay?" Mrs. Gordon said, her voice going funny, as if her throat were being squeezed. "Yes, hon. It's okay." She took a step toward Dewey, hesitated, then stopped where she was and jingled her car keys lightly in one hand. "Tell you what. I'm going to go home, open a beer, and make a meat loaf. It'll be done around seven, if you're hungry. But take your time. It'll keep."

"Thanks," said Dewey. Mrs. Gordon started to say something more, then just smiled, a small, sad smile, and went out the front door, pulling it shut behind her with a click.

Dewey waited until she heard the Chevy's engine and the crunch of tires on gravel and dirt fade away with distance. Then she got up off the arm of the couch.

Dewey walks from room to room in the dimming sun of late afternoon, standing still in doorways, memorizing what had been. These rooms are the only places she has lived with Papa since she was a tiny child. A year and a half. She rests her hand on the light switch of the bathroom and wishes she could flip time off and on as easily. One more week. One more day. But it is gone, over.

She says a silent good-bye to the bathroom where her small red toothbrush hung next to Papa's brown one. To the bedroom where she woke to the sound of Papa's tenor as he shaved. To Papa's room, where some nights a slit of yellow light under the door angled out into the hall until almost dawn. To the kitchen where they shared tuna casserole and news of their days. And to the living room, where Papa drank a glass of whiskey and explained music and books and calculus and the moon after the supper dishes were washed and dried.

When she has etched a memory for every room, Dewey lifts the wooden lid and turns on the record player. Through the cloth grill in the front she hears the low humming as the tubes warm up. She pulls the black disk with Nipper the dog out of its paper envelope. Leopold Stokowski. The Philadelphia Orchestra. She holds the record by its edges and carefully lowers *Toccata and Fugue in D Minor* onto the turntable.

Dewey sets the needle gently onto the first groove, then sinks into the armchair. She takes off her glasses, laying them in her lap, and closes her eyes.

Bach's dramatic opening bars fill the small room, and the music strikes her with an almost physical force, raising the hair on her arms with its intensity. It grows and crashes in mournful waves, and when the stairstep oboes sound, Dewey begins to cry. She has not cried since the night Oppie brought the news. There has been no place safe enough to let go.

All her life, Papa has been gone so much, so often, that it has not been hard to pretend he was only on a trip, or working in Chicago, and would be back soon. Not this week, not this month. But soon. It is a hope that has held her together for so many years, an easy lie to believe to get through these last few weeks.

Now Dewey cries with her whole body, letting the music sweep her away. There are no neighbors, no Hill, nothing but sound and sensation. She cries for Papa, for Nana. For loss and for love.

Halfway through the Bach, there is a pause, the end of the first side of the record. The needle moves to the center, scritch, scritch, scritching rhythmically, endlessly on the lacquered disk. Dewey does not move or open her eyes. She lets the record scratch and hiss for a long time, until she feels as empty as this house. She opens her eyes, sits very still for a minute, then pulls a handkerchief out of her pocket, wipes her eyes, blows her nose, and puts her glasses back on.

Dewey lifts the needle off the disk. She does not need to hear the second side. Bach has done what she wanted. But as she touches the record, an unexpected surge of feeling rises through her small body.

"You said you'd come back," she whispers. And then, louder, "You promised. You *promised*, Papa!" Her voice becomes an outraged howl, the loudest noise Dewey has ever made. She is rigid, her breath ragged in her throat.

Then, in one abrupt move, she lifts the record off the turntable with both hands and smashes it with all her strength across her upraised knee.

The brittle black lacquer shatters. Dewey stands motionless in the living room of her former home, her hands tight fists, until her breath is back to normal, then drops the shards onto the wooden floor and turns away.

She closes the lid and carries the record player out to her wagon.

"I miss you, Papa," she whispers, and locks the door behind her.

June 23

SHAZAM

THE END OF June was hot and dry, so dry the air
seemed sharp. What little grass there was turned brown
and withered, and pine needles stood out pale and dead
on the trees. Late in the afternoons clouds gathered over
the mountains, and some nights the sky was alive with
lightning, crackling and booming, but no rain reached the
Hill. Tensions and tempers ran high. Everyone seemed to
be on hold, as if waiting for a phone that refused to ring.

On a Thursday noon, Suze sat at the kitchen table,
the remains of a peanut butter sandwich at her elbow,
fiddling with some bottle caps. She had a dozen or so, all
different colors. They were going into her next picture,
but she hadn't figured out *where* yet. She spun a Lemon
NEHI cap with her thumb and finger, and it skittered
across the oilcloth and plinked into the side of her mother's
coffee cup.

"Oh, for crissakes. Will you *stop*?" Mrs. Gordon snapped. She put down the pencil she'd been using to do the puzzle in last Sunday's paper. "Can't you think of *anything* else to do?"

"Sorry," Suze said, stung. Her mother had been in a bad mood all week. She scooped up the errant bottle cap and put it into the shoebox on the chair next to her. "I'll leave."

"No, no. Look, *I'm* sorry. I'm just cranky. Everything's a deadline these days, and a tight one."

"Why do you even have to go back to work?" Suze asked.

"Because Norma took the night shift running the vacuum separation, and we got good precipitate. I have almost eighty curies to proc—" She stopped and shook her head. "Oops. Shop talk. Anyway, because there's a lot to do today."

"But isn't everything done?" Suze asked. "If Daddy's down there testing to see if it works, it must be finished, right?"

"It ain't over till the Fat Man sings," her mother said.

Suze wasn't sure what that meant.

Terry Gordon looked at her Timex. "The siren's going to blow any second. Why don't you see what Dewey's up to?"

"Dewey's never up to *anything* anymore," Suze sighed.

"All she ever does is sit on her bed and read comics. She talks to me if I go in there, but she doesn't want to do anything, not even invent stuff."

"Suze, she lost her daddy. Can you imagine anything harder? She'll come out from under eventually, but it's going to take some time."

"But it's been more than a month. She doesn't even want to go to the *dump*."

"Imagine that," her mother said, trying not to smile. "Look, sweetie. I'm sorry. I know it's been kind of lonely for you too." She picked up her white T badge and pinned it to the pocket of her shirt. "How about some night this week we play some gin? You and me? We haven't done that in ages."

Suze nodded. "Okay." She'd go dig the score pad out of the desk drawer.

"And in the meantime, you can work on your art project. I like what you're doing with the colors." She ruffled Suze's hair on her way out the door and was gone.

Suze was startled and pleased. She hadn't thought her mother was paying much attention. Maybe she would work on it for a while.

She cut and glued and sorted for an hour. It was hot in the kitchen, even with the windows open. Her sweaty fingers left smudges on the shiny paper, and she was thirsty. Suze started to turn on the tap for a glass of water, then remembered that there was a shortage—too many people on the Hill, in too hot weather—and they weren't supposed to use water except for emergencies. And she'd drunk the last Coke in the icebox the night before.

She found her shoes under the couch and two dimes in the desk drawer. If only there was a Woolworth's on the Hill. It would be nice to just wander and browse. She missed going into a store where she didn't already know exactly what she'd find.

"I'm going to the PX," she yelled from the doorway, in the direction of the bedroom.

"Okay," Dewey answered, but nothing else.

An hour later Suze returned with a Clark bar, the newest *Wonder Woman,* and a bad mood. She slammed the screen door and went back to the bedroom.

Dewey was sitting on her bed, barefoot, wearing a sleeveless man's undershirt and a pair of khaki shorts. A comic was propped up on her knees.

Suze flopped hard onto her own bed and opened the Clark bar. By the time she'd crunched her way through to the end, peeling the wrapper down around the softening chocolate as she ate, her lips were smeared with brown and she felt a little better. "What're you reading?" she asked Dewey.

"*Airboy.*" Dewey held up the comic. Airplanes zoomed

in the background behind a Jap pilot with bug-eyes and lots of blood gushing out of his mouth.

"Ick," Suze said, making a face. "Where did you get *that*?"

"It's one of Charlie's. Or Jack's. I'm not sure which is which." Dewey lifted up the edge of her bedspread and pointed. "There's a ton of them under here. You can read some, if you want."

Suze whistled. There were three or four huge stacks of comics under Dewey's bed. She leaned over and took one off the top. The Sub-Mariner, a pointy-faced man wearing nothing but swim trunks, was beating up Nazis on a busted-up U-boat. "Cool," she said. "How come the boys gave you all their comics?"

"They didn't give 'em to me. I'm just keeping 'em 'cause they had to go to their gramma's last week."

"Couldn't they just leave them in their house?" Suze asked. The boys lived in another of the Sundts, two buildings away.

"Their mom *hates* comics. Especially the war ones. They've been stashing 'em in their tree house, but they were afraid someone might swipe 'em, or they'd blow away if it got real windy." She dropped the bedspread. "Besides, I've read all of yours."

"Are they all war?"

"Mostly. There's some *Flash* and *Blue Beetle* and *Bat-*

man, and lots and lots of war. Boy comics." She looked down at the comic in her hand. "This one's got a girl in it. The Black Angel. But she doesn't really get to do much."

"Girls never do," Suze agreed. She flopped onto her back and sighed. "I hate girls."

Dewey looked startled.

"Not you or me," Suze said. *"Girls."*

"Oh," said Dewey. "Like Betty and Joyce."

"Yeah. All of them." Suze thought about what had happened on the way back from the PX. Dewey would understand. "I had just finished my Coke, maybe twenty feet from Barbara's house on Bathtub Row, when her and Betty and a couple others came out wearing their Girl Scout hats and those yellow neck things. I guess it's too hot for a whole uniform."

"Did they see you?"

"Yeah, they saw me all right. Betty said, 'Look out, here comes a truck,' and they all crossed over to the other side of the road, laughing. Like it was funny." Suze said the F so hard she almost spit.

"Did they hold their noses?" Dewey pinched her own nose with a thumb and forefinger. "Like this?"

"Yeah, like I was a skunk or something." Suze leaned on one elbow and looked at Dewey. "How did you know?"

Dewey just rolled her eyes. "How do you think I know? Was Joyce there?"

"Of course not—oh, you haven't been around. She's in Michigan for the summer. Visiting an aunt or someone." Suze sighed again. "I don't know what I'm going to do when school starts. What if none of them will sit near me?"

Silence, for a moment. "I'll sit by you," Dewey said. "If you want."

"The Sad Sack Club?"

Dewey shook her head. "The Shazam Club. No *girls* allowed."

"Yeah. Shazam." Suze thought about that for a minute, then smiled. "I've got an idea," she said. "I'll be back in a little while." She jumped off the bed and went into the kitchen to get her shoebox.

Ever since she discovered the dump, Suze had been collecting little scraps of her own. Not metal parts, like Dewey's Mason jar full of screws and springs, but random objects whose colors and details caught her eye: a lead soldier with a broken hand, some acorns, a doll's shoe, some stamps with intricately patterned borders, green wooden houses from a Monopoly game, a March of Dimes pinback button, bottle caps, some small smooth stones she'd found in the creek at the bottom of the nearest canyon.

She sifted through these treasures until she found a pale caramel river rock, a little smaller than an Oreo, but thicker. It fit snugly in the curves of her cupped hand, a good shape, a nice weight. A second stone was dark gray, a little bigger and flatter.

Suze reached for her box of colored pencils. She selected a red one and rasped the sharpener around its blunted tip, letting the curls of wood drift into the wastebasket by the side of the table. The scarlet edges stood out sharply against the dark pile of coffee grounds.

The caramel stone wobbled on the hard tabletop, so she put a woven potholder underneath it to steady it, and carefully printed SHAZAM on it. Not quite right. She used her art gum to erase the letters, brushing the rubber crumbs off the table with the edge of her hand.

Solomon for wisdom, Hercules for strength, Atlas for Courage . . . Suze grinned and printed ΣHAZAM, then erased that too, because in capitals it just looked like it was spelled wrong. Lowercase was better. She sharpened the pencil again and printed σηαζαμ.

That was it. That looked magic. But she erased it a third time and printed the last version again, as neatly and carefully as she could, because now it was a sorcerer's stone, and you can't be too careful. The second stone was easier. She blew on both of them to get rid of any art gum crumbs or dust, and went into the living room, returning with two bottles of ink and her tiniest paintbrush. Black India ink for the caramel stone. Silver ink, a Passover present from Grandpa Weiss, for the dark one. It took her ten painstaking minutes to letter each stone:

σηαζαμ

Suze picked up one corner of the potholder and slid it to the other side of the table, where the stones could lie flat and undisturbed until the ink was completely dry and wouldn't smear.

She read her new *Wonder Woman* for twenty minutes, just to be sure, then checked. The stones looked dry. She tilted her head at different angles, to see if there was any wet-ink reflection. Nope. She wiped her hand on the leg of her shorts and gingerly touched one with the tip of a finger. No smear. Suze carried the stones back to the bedroom on the potholder as if they were crown jewels on a velvet pillow.

Dewey had moved on to an issue of *Thrilling Comics*, featuring a bunch of boys called "The Commando Cubs."

"I've got something for you," Suze said. She placed each stone onto the pink chenille bedspread.

"Nice rocks," said Dewey. She tented the comic upside down, using her knee as a bookmark, and leaned forward. "What kind of writing is that?"

"Greek."

"I thought it might be." Dewey peered at the two stones. "What do they say?"

"Shazam," Suze grinned. "Solomon, Hercules—"

Dewey joined in. "Atlas, Zeus, Achilles, Mercury," they said in unison.

"They were almost all Greeks, so I figured this is probably how the wizard spelled his secret name," Suze explained.

"You know what I was wondering?" Dewey asked. "How come Mercury? That's the Roman name for the guy on the dime. The fast guy. The Greeks called him Hermes."

"Yeah, I know, but the H wouldn't work. Shouting 'Shazah!' would be pretty stupid," Suze said.

"That's probably why. I guess the wizard knew what he was doing."

"Wizards usually do." Suze pointed to the stones. "You can have first dibs."

Dewey examined them closely. "I'll take the silver one," she said finally. She picked it up and cradled it in her hand. "What are they for?"

"They're the magic stones of the Shazam Club," Suze said. She picked up the other stone. "We carry them in our pockets, and no one else knows we've got secret powers. Wisdom and strength and—I forget the rest."

"Courage," Dewey said quietly.

"Yeah," said Suze. She looked down at the stone in her hand, then reached over and chinked it against Dewey's. "Shazam," she said.

"Shazam." Dewey tucked the stone into the left-hand pocket of her shorts and picked up *Thrilling Comics* by the spine, pinching it shut. She tossed it onto her pillow. "Wanna see if there's anything good at the dump?" she asked.

Suze pocketed her own stone and grinned. "I'll go find my shoes."

BY THE DAWN'S
EARLY LIGHT

THURSDAY MORNING, the twelfth of July, Dewey stood outside the fence of the Motor Pool and watched two dozen MPs load equipment and horses into a line of waiting trucks. The armed men stood guard while some scientists from the Tech Area, carrying small duffel bags, boarded an army-green bus. Then the MPs got on and the small convoy rumbled through the gate.

"Something going on," she told Suze when she got back to the apartment. They sat on the back steps, a bag of peanuts between them, watching black clouds move steadily in from the west, blotting out the blue summer sky.

"Another thunderstorm," Suze said. She opened the screen door and leaned in to look at the kitchen clock. "It's eleven thirty. Same time as yesterday. I wonder why that is?"

"I don't know, but I hope there's hail again. That was amazing."

"Only because *you* were inside. I got caught by the post office, and it hurt. I'm surprised I'm not black and blue." Suze held out her arm, which showed no sign of hailstone damage.

"Besides the thunderstorm," Dewey continued. "Do you think the MPs are going to the desert? Is it more important to guard than the Hill?"

"That Trinity place is," Suze said. She opened a peanut with her thumbnail. "My dad's down there all the time now. He takes a bag of sandwiches and a thermos of coffee and doesn't come back for two or three days."

Dewey nodded. They were going to test the gadget. It was an open secret. No one was supposed to know anything, officially, but in private, it was all anyone had talked about for weeks.

———

Dewey thinks about the gadget a lot. The gadget that will end the war. That is the truth of the Hill, why they are all here. If the gadget works, the war will end and they will all be heroes.

Dewey hates the war as much as anyone. If not for the war, she and Papa would still be living in their cozy apartment across from Harvard Square. He would never have gone to Chicago or New Mexico. Or Washington. The war has taken everything away, but now it is her only hope. Mrs. Gordon has said that she can stay with them for the duration, and that is only as long as the war.

When the war ends, everything will change again. The Gordons will leave, and Dewey will have to go somewhere else. To a home, to an orphanage. Every day she walks around the Hill, relishing her freedom while she has it. Every day she crosses her fingers that they will not test the gadget. Not yet. She cannot wish for it to fail—that would mean Papa had failed—and she does not want any more soldiers to die. But she does not want the war to end.

This is a secret she can tell no one. Not even Suze, late at night, when they talk in the darkness. It is unpatriotic, it is treason. Dewey hides her thoughts behind the pages of the boys' war comics, full of flags and blood and bravery.

⸻

It rained for the next two days, violent thunderstorms one after another, roaring thunder, splitting the sky with lightning, clattering hail on the wooden shingles of the cheaply built Sundts.

Mrs. Gordon came home late Saturday afternoon, her hair in damp tendrils, her cheeks red with excitement.

Dewey looked up from *Air Aces*. "It's happening, isn't it?" she asked quietly.

"Hmmph. And they call this a top secret project." Mrs. Gordon put her bag of groceries down on the counter. "Not inside the fence, that's for sure. The rumor mill down at the Commissary is buzzing at a fever pitch." She looked out the window at the storm clouds massing once again in the west. "But yes, if the weather cooperates, it looks like tomorrow's the day."

Dewey felt her stomach tense. "Are you going down there?"

"Nope." Mrs. Gordon shook her head. "They offered me a seat on the bus, and it's tempting, but I'm going to stay here with you girls. Phil's going down. He can bring back the skinny." She pulled a large white paper-wrapped bundle out of the bag.

"Pot roast tonight," she said. "He'll need a hearty meal—Lord knows when he'll get a chance to sit and eat again—and it'll make good sandwiches for tomorrow." She pulled a bunch of carrots out of the bag and handed Dewey the vegetable peeler. "If you'll scrape these, I can do the potatoes with a paring knife."

"Okay." Dewey tore the lacy green leaves off the tops of the carrots, then shaved long thin orange curls into the wastebasket. She worked methodically, carefully. She felt like she was preparing her last meal.

When Dewey woke up Sunday morning, the sky outside the window was a perfect deep summer blue, with only a few high white clouds. But by mid-afternoon it was as dark as twilight. Rain lashed at the buildings, pockmarking the dirt roads, then creating swift gullies of muddy water that surged down every slope. The lightning was blue-white and fierce and thunder rattled every window in the apartment.

Dewey sat on her bed reading *Air Aces'* "Raiders of the Purple Dawn," her fingers crossed behind the pages, hoping the storm would continue and the test would be canceled.

But the rain stopped. Mrs. Gordon made a stack of thick beef sandwiches wrapped in waxed paper and rousted Dewey and Suze. By 4:00 they were walking with their neighbors down to the Tech Area.

It seemed as if everyone on the Hill was there, holding a thermos of coffee or a sack lunch or a bottle of suntan lotion. Three buses had been painted so they weren't army green anymore. Dewey wasn't sure why they'd bothered, since the buses were going to be escorted south by three official sedans and a canvas-topped army truck full of equipment—jerry cans of water and gas, radios, big coils of wire, and a box with dozens of welders' goggles.

When everything was loaded, Dr. Gordon kissed Mrs. Gordon and hugged Suze and then, as an afterthought, gave Dewey a little salute from the door of the bus, and disappeared inside. At half past five the convoy headed out the east gate, and it began to drizzle again.

"I want you girls in bed early," Mrs. Gordon said as they walked home, ducking under overhangs and into doorways every few minutes to avoid the brief downpours. "As soon as it's dark."

"How come?" Suze asked. "Have I been bad or something?"

"Not that I know of—" Mrs. Gordon cocked an eyebrow and looked at Suze, who shook her head.

"Then why?" asked Dewey.

"Because unless it's raining cats and dogs, we're going to get up early and have a little picnic."

"A breakfast picnic?" Suze sounded skeptical.

"Earlier than that," Mrs. Gordon said. "A middle-of-the-night picnic."

Suze frowned. "That's kind of strange, isn't it?"

"We live in very strange times, my dear." Mrs. Gordon was smiling.

Dewey put on her pajamas and went to bed a little after 8:00. The light through the bedroom window still cast pale, indistinct shadows. She turned over and faced the wall, and when she closed her eyes, it seemed dark enough. But she couldn't sleep.

She thought about the gadget and the buses full of men driving across the desert. She turned over, scrunched up her pillow, and wondered if the air really could catch on fire. Suze was snoring lightly, because her nose was stuffed up, and the noise seemed to fill the small room. Dewey scooted the blanket around with her feet, tried sleeping on her side, then on her stomach, and worried about how many more nights she would sleep in this bed at all.

Finally she put on her glasses and got up to get a glass of milk. Sometimes that helped.

The apartment was dark except for the light over the kitchen table. Mrs. Gordon wore the same clothes she'd had on earlier. She sat with her feet up on a chair, a cup of coffee by her elbow, a cigarette in the ashtray. Her reading glasses lay on top of an open copy of *The Saturday Evening Post.*

"Can't sleep, Dewey?"

Dewey shook her head.

"I'm not surprised. It's pretty exciting. I knew I wouldn't sleep a wink, so I just stayed up." She looked at the clock. "It's almost two. I was going to wake you in an hour anyway. Why don't you have a cup of Ovaltine and keep me company?"

"Okay." Dewey sat down.

"I filled up the thermos—you girls are still a bit young

for coffee—but there's a little left in the pan." She tilted the saucepan over a thick china mug and put the Ovaltine down on the table. "It ought to be cool enough to drink. I took it off the burner a while ago."

Dewey took a small experimental sip. It was barely warm. She took a deeper drink. "Where are we going?" she asked.

"Out to the south mesa, where it overlooks the Hill road. Some of the guys have been out there all night, but I figure we might as well be comfortable until it's time. The show—if there's going to be a show in this weather—is supposed to be at four."

"The gadget?"

"We hope so."

Dewey sipped her Ovaltine and thought for a minute. "But isn't the Trinity place like three hundred miles from here?"

"Not quite. More like two-twenty."

"But still, we won't be able to *see* anything. I mean, the earth curves too much, doesn't it?"

"Ah, my practical little scientist." Mrs. Gordon smiled. "A good question. Yes, it does. For most normal phenomena. But if everyone's calculations are correct, we'll have visual confirmation, even way up here."

She saw Dewey frowning, biting her lip, and patted her hand. "Still worried about the atmosphere igniting?" she asked gently.

Dewey nodded. It was *one* of the things she was worried about.

"Well, as I said before, I don't think it will. I really don't. But you're in good company. There's half a dozen Nobel laureates out there right now wondering the same thing. A lot of questions are going to get answered in the next couple of hours."

Not all of them, Dewey thought.

They sat in the kitchen for a few minutes staring out into the darkness. Mrs. Gordon smoked a cigarette, Dewey finished her Ovaltine. At quarter of three, Mrs. Gordon stood up and stretched. "Why don't you go get your clothes. Grab a sweater. It may be windy. You can change in the bathroom while I try to wake Sleeping Beauty. That could take a while."

By the time Dewey was dressed, Suze was up, more or less. She stood in her pajamas staring blearily into her dresser drawer as if she had never seen underwear before. Dewey took a *Captain Marvel* into the kitchen to wait.

They trooped down the wooden stairs in complete darkness, carrying blankets, thermoses, and a paper sack of sandwiches and cookies out to the car. The eastern sky was cloudy, but directly above, the night sky seemed to have a million stars, with the haze of the Milky Way arcing across the inky dome.

No streetlights on the Hill. Rectangular patches of light spilled onto the dirt road from a few apartment windows, and when they were past the Lodge, Mrs. Gordon drove with her low beams on. All Dewey could see were the trunks of trees, streaks of bright water in the road, and the occasional green-gold glow from a foraging raccoon's eyes. Everything else was darkness. They drove in silence for ten or fifteen minutes, Dewey figured, Suze half asleep against the passenger-side window, Mrs. Gordon drumming her fingers softly on the steering wheel. Then she pulled off the road and turned off the engine. "We can walk from here," she said.

Dewey opened the car door and was glad she'd brought a sweater. The air was cool and smelled clean, as if the rain had washed the mesa, leaving only the scents of piñon and damp earth.

Mrs. Gordon had a big silver flashlight and walked ahead, shining it on the path, a faint trace slightly more compressed with footprints than the surrounding gravelly sand. Up ahead Dewey could see little pools of light from other flashlights and the smaller metallic glints of eyeglasses and wristwatches. As her eyes adjusted to the dark, she made out a cluster of people, fifteen or twenty rounded shapes against the flat angles of the mesa rocks.

Friends called out greetings, and Mrs. Gordon laid the plaid blanket down in a clear space next to them. People were talking in small groups, some subdued, some excited, and every few minutes a circle of light winked on and off as someone checked his wristwatch for the time.

"Any word, Nance?" Mrs. Gordon asked a woman on her left. Suze lay down and put her head in her mother's lap.

"Still storming, but the meteorology guys say it'll clear within the hour. Zero's been moved back to five thirty."

Dewey heard a crackle of static. "Is there a radio here?"

A man two blankets over—too far for Dewey to see his face—said, "Two of the SEDs brought a shortwave. We were getting transmissions from the observation planes over the site, but the weather's grounded all but one."

"Can I go see?" Dewey asked Mrs. Gordon.

"Sure. Take the flashlight. But point it down and keep your hand over it so no one loses their night vision, okay?"

Dewey nodded and followed the sound of the radio, stepping carefully between the blankets. It was like being on a beach that had no ocean. She didn't need the flashlight. Her eyes had adjusted enough to make out the lighter shapes of shirts and hands and sandwiches.

It was a great radio, a Zenith Trans-Oceanic. The two men operating it seemed surprised when she asked a question about its reception—probably because she was a girl. But they answered it, and Dewey had a very interesting conversation with them about the wave magnet antenna until another transmission came through and the engineers had to go back to work.

Dewey sat on the hard-packed dirt a few feet away, listening to the crackling report from the faraway pilot and looking out over the edge of the world. It was too dark to see much difference between sky and land, except the sharp edges below which the star-speckled black was solid. A thousand feet down, on an invisible road, a single pair of headlights as tiny as pinpoints moved slowly across the featureless darkness.

When she began to feel stiff from sitting on the damp ground, Dewey made her way back to their blanket, Mrs. Gordon's face recognizable in the red glow of her cigarette's tip. She drank a cup of Ovaltine, warm in the cool night air, and ate half a pot-roast sandwich. To her left, a few pale streaks were beginning to appear in the eastern sky when one of the radio men shouted, "This is it!"

Dewey stared out into the darkness, not looking *at* anything, her fists clenched in excitement and fear.

And suddenly there was a bright light, as bright as the sun. It lit up the faces of the people and the leaves of the trees. Dewey could see the colors and patterns of blankets and shirts that had been indistinct grays a second before, as if it were instantly morning, as if the sun had risen in the south, just this once.

Time stood still for a moment, and then the light faded. A minute later she heard—and felt—a long, low rumble, like distant, alien thunder. It faded as well, and after a moment's pause, everyone on the mesa stood and began hugging each other. Conversations grew louder, happier, as their silent vigil became a party. Several men pulled out bottles and silver flasks, which quickly made a circuit of the group. One of the radio men did a spirited Irish jig.

Mrs. Gordon hugged Suze, then Dewey, then took a long swig from the nearest flask. Someone began to sing, and in the commotion, Dewey slipped away. Ten feet from the celebration she sat down against the rough trunk of a pine tree, hugged her knees to her chest, and began to tremble.

The gadget worked.

July 16

CELEBRATING

MRS. GORDON SHOOED the girls off for naps as soon as they returned to the apartment. A nap at 7:00 in the morning? Dewey fretted and tossed and turned for more than an hour, but fatigue won. She awoke again to the sound of horns blaring, a little after 1:00 that afternoon.

Dewey padded out to the kitchen in her pajamas. A makeshift parade had gathered in the road below. Kids pounded wooden spoons on tin pans and blew across Coke bottles for low-pitched whistles. Women waved handkerchiefs and flags, and every few minutes an impromptu song or a cheer swept through the crowd as it gathered more and more members.

The buses had returned.

Dr. Gordon came bounding up the back steps ten minutes later, grinning from ear to ear, his fingers raised in a

V-for-Victory sign. He grabbed Mrs. Gordon and kissed her, then twirled her around the kitchen. He had dark circles under his eyes and needed a shave, but Dewey had never seen him happier.

"We did it!" he said. "My god, Terry, you should have seen it." He saw Suze standing sleepily in the doorway and lifted her off the ground in a huge hug.

"We saw the light, Daddy," she said when he put her down. "Was it brighter down there?"

"It was the most incredible goddamn thing I've ever seen. The light—oh, Jesus, the light—a fireball, gold and purple and blue and red, climbing up into the sky, climbing and climbing. It kept changing colors, like a kaleidoscope, a huge monstrous kaleidoscope of fire and gases. It lit up every crevice of every mountain for a hundred miles, as clear as daylight. Clearer." Dr. Gordon leaned against the icebox and rubbed his fists against his eyes as if he could still see it.

"We were flabbergasted. I mean, we've worked on this thing for two years. We thought we had a good idea of what it would do. But none of us were ready for this. It just kept getting bigger. It was beautiful. It was terrifying. It was—" He shook his head. "No words for it. Nothing like it ever before. Not on *this* earth." He reached up and opened the cupboard, putting two glasses and the bottle of whiskey on the counter. He poured an inch in each, and handed one to Mrs. Gordon.

"To success," he said. They clinked glasses and drank.

"Now what happens?" Mrs. Gordon asked.

He shrugged. "It's out of our hands now. The science worked. It's all Washington from here."

Mrs. Gordon looked at him for a long minute, then put her glass down with a soft but solid clunk. "I think I prefer physics." She wasn't smiling anymore.

"The genie's out of the bottle, Terry. No way to put it back now." He yawned, an enormous yawn, and picked up the whiskey bottle. "I know what's next for me, though. I'm going to have another knock of this, then sleep until the middle of next week." He poured another inch of whiskey in his glass and downed it.

"Why don't you kids get dressed and go join the parade?" he said, looking at Dewey and Suze. "Here." He dug into the pocket of his jeans and pulled out three crumpled one-dollar bills. "Get yourself a couple of hamburgs at the PX. Cokes too. We're all celebrating today."

Dewey didn't feel like celebrating, but she knew a grown-up order when she heard one. She and Suze put on their clothes and went out into the carnival atmosphere of the Hill.

It was as if a dam had burst after so many months of tension and pressure. Everyone was hugging. Some people were laughing, some were crying, some were doing both

THE GREEN GLASS SEA

at once. And finally, everyone was talking about the gadget.

"Magnificent. Horrible too. But magnificent."

"So much for Japan. It'll only take one."

"Cloud looked like a glowing mushroom, eight miles high. Eight *miles*."

The men who had been on the buses were easy to spot. Many of them held whiskey bottles, and they had the same strange expressions on their faces, like space pilots in science fiction comics. Awestruck and solemn, as if they had looked into another world.

On the porch of the Lodge, a small knot of people huddled around a portable radio, listening to the news from Albuquerque that KRS patched in around lunchtime.

". . . at the army air base in Alamogordo reported that an ammunition dump had blown up early this morning. There were no injuries, but the explosion was heard as far away as El Paso . . ."

"Ammo dump my foot," said one man in uniform. "But I guess folks on the outside will believe what the army tells them."

"Will people buy that?" Dewey asked. "I mean, if we could see it from here—"

"Probably," Suze said. "If that's what's on the radio,

I bet it'll be in the papers too. I'd probably believe it, if I didn't know what the gadget really was."

"Okay, what is it?" Dewey asked.

"It's a bomb, goofus."

"Well, yeah. But they've been bombing Japan for a year. And Hitler was bombing London forever. There were bombs all over the war. What makes this one so special?"

"It was *really* big," Suze said confidently. "So now we'll have the Japs on toast." She was skipping along and grinning as if she'd personally won a prize.

"How long do you think that'll take?" Dewey asked. She wasn't skipping and she wasn't thinking about the war. She was wondering if she should start packing.

"I don't know. Soon, I guess. Why would they wait?" Suze pulled the crumpled bills out of her pocket. "Two hamburgers and Cokes is only forty cents," she said. "And Daddy said we should celebrate. We can buy every comic in the PX with the rest of this!"

Dewey hesitated. Three dollars was a lot of money. But what if the army sent her off to someplace where comics weren't allowed? An orphanage run by ladies like Nana, or worse, Mrs. Kovack? This might be her last chance. She fingered the small stone in her pocket. "Sure," she said. "Shazam."

"Yeah." Suze smiled and linked her arm through Dewey's. "Shazam."

August 4
ACHIEVING FLIGHT

EVER SINCE HE got back from the desert, Dr. Gordon had been home as often as he was in his lab, walking around the apartment whistling and singing, although his voice wasn't very good. Mrs. Gordon was home a lot too. Dewey figured there wasn't much to do anymore.

All her boxes had been packed for weeks. Nothing at the Gordons' had changed, but Dewey knew it could be any day. A few other families had already left. It was just a matter of time.

They had even given a party a week ago, a farewell for one of Dr. Gordon's colleagues who was going back to Columbia. A dozen people crammed into the small living room, drinking cocktails and laughing until 2:00 in the morning. Well, mostly laughing. They were making so much noise that Dewey couldn't sleep, and she'd gotten up about midnight to get a drink of water from the bathroom. She heard Dick Feynman talking, and stopped in the doorway to listen. "Well, yes. We *started* for a good reason, and we've been working so hard. It was pleasure. It was excitement," he said. "But you stop thinking about—you know? You just stop. And now . . ."

"And now that we've seen what it can do. My god," Terry Gordon said, her voice raised, sounding angry. "They can't *use* it. Not on civilians. Not on anyone, for that matter. I mean, maybe as a demonstration, but—"

"That's not realistic, Terry," said Dr. Teller in his Hungarian accent. "It's no longer an experiment to be demonstrated. It's a weapon, to end this terrible war once and for all."

"At what cost, Edward? At *what* cost? Look, Chicago's drafted a petition. If enough of us sign it, they'll have to listen, and—"

"Oh for crissakes, Terry—" Dewey heard Dr. Gordon say, and then there were footsteps and she ducked back into the bedroom.

———

The Gordons had been arguing a lot lately. But they'd both gone down to Santa Fe this afternoon, to get presents for Suze's birthday tomorrow, and the apartment was quiet. That was good, because she and Suze were working on a new project. They'd found a pile of cigar boxes behind the PX—men smoked a lot of cigars when they were celebrating—and they planned to glue them together to make what Suze called Shazam Theater.

They'd taken all the lids off, and Suze was in the kitchen covering the boxes, inside and out, with pages from snafued comics that they'd both read—ones that were ripped or had no covers. So far, it looked pretty nifty. Bright red and blue and yellow with lots of black-lined squares that made for a kind of random geometry. Suze had a good eye for that kind of thing.

Dewey's part was to make the insides move. She'd drilled holes through each box so she could attach gearboxes and cams that would make Batman kick and Wonder Woman's lasso spin round and round. One box was almost done. Suze had cut out Captain Marvel and Billy Batson and glued them to shirt cardboard, and Dewey had sandwiched a metal rod in between the two pieces. When she turned a crank on the top of the box, they spun around, Billy changing to Captain Marvel and back to Billy as fast as her eyes could follow.

She was having more trouble with Superman. She wanted him to fly from the painted street up to the top of a cardboard building, and had cut a hole in the back of the box for a lever. It was simple, and it worked—up, down, up, down—but she wasn't satisfied. With a gearbox and a cam, she could wind him up and he would fly on his own. That would be so much better.

Dewey looked through her supply cache—a former ammo box with a sturdy latch—but didn't find what she was hoping for. She went into the kitchen. It smelled like rubber cement.

"I'm almost done with this one," Suze said, pulling bits of sticky rubber off her fingertips. "One more and we can start to put stuff in them."

"They look good," Dewey said. "I'm working on Superman, but I need some more parts. I'm going down to the machine shop." She looked at the clock. "I'll be back by dinner."

Suze nodded and reached for the scissors.

———

Dewey was on her way back when the Tech siren sounded at 5:30, her pockets full of odd gears and shafts and mainsprings. She spun a tiny lazy-susan device in her hand, admiring the soft precise clickings of the ball bearings. It was perfect for Wonder Woman's lasso. Sergeant Morton, like many of the GIs on the Hill, wasn't very busy these days, and he'd spent almost two hours with her, listening to her ideas and making suggestions. He'd even drawn some sketches for her, construction diagrams, then helped her rummage through the shop's inventory to find the necessary parts.

As she climbed the steps to the Gordons' apartment, Dewey was thinking about how to rig up a battery so that Wonder Woman's lasso could spin at the flick of a switch. She climbed slowly, picturing the wiring. A few steps from the top, she heard Mrs. Gordon say, "Well, I guess you'll have to finish your project some other time. You can pack after supper. I want to get an early start, and there's some paperwork to sign before we can leave."

Dewey felt as if she'd been hit. She stopped, stock-still, and felt a prickle of icy sweat under her arms. After a moment she turned and walked slowly back down the stairs, to the shadows under the steps, and dropped bonelessly onto the edge of her wagon.

The Gordons were leaving? She'd been braced for that, ever since the gadget had worked. The duration was over, and the grown-ups had been talking about "after the war" for three weeks, at night, when they thought she was asleep. But Dewey hadn't been sleeping very well. Worrying about when it would happen and how long the army would let her stay on the Hill after the Gordons had gone. Not long, she guessed.

Dewey knew that no one, no place is forever. But it hurt that they hadn't told her, hadn't given her any warning at all. Tomorrow morning? Dewey thought about watching Suze pack up Captain Marvel and the cigar boxes and felt her eyes sting. That was too hard. She couldn't just sit on the porch in the morning and watch her drive away. She wasn't that brave.

Dr. Gordon yelled from the kitchen door. "Suze, will you get a move on? I want to get over there while they've still got steaks left."

Dewey stepped out from under the stairs and walked to the edge of the building, then turned and walked back, as if she were just returning from the machine shop.

"Oh, there you are," Mrs. Gordon said, coming down the stairs. "I wondered when you'd be back." She looked at the bag of parts Dewey carried. "We're going to the Lodge for supper. Go ahead and take your things upstairs. We'll wait."

Dewey's stomach knotted at the idea of eating. She looked down at the ground and scuffed her sneaker in the dirt, thinking fast. "Um, well, the machine shop was closing, and Carlos—Mr. Sandoval—said he'd show me how to make a reciprocating cam if I came over to his house. His wife's making enchiladas, and he invited me to eat with them. I just came back to get the Superman box," she lied.

"They were your neighbors, over in Morganville, right?" Mrs. Gordon asked.

Dewey nodded.

"Well, all right," she said. "Phil and I are going to a party tonight, but I left a paper sack on your bed so you can pack."

There it was, bald and cold. And Mrs. Gordon was smiling? She'd always been so nice. Dewey stared at her in disbelief.

"Oh, that's right, you don't know," she said. "Well, we've decided to—"

"Terry, we have to get going," Dr. Gordon interrupted, tapping his watch. "I don't want to be last in line and get shoe leather." He started walking in the direction of the Lodge.

Mrs. Gordon raised her hands in a what-can-you-do? gesture and started to follow him. "Suze will explain when you get back, won't you sweetie?" she said over her shoulder.

Suze nodded vigorously. "Yeah, we're finally—"

"Susan!" Dr. Gordon yelled. Suze looked at Dewey, shrugged, and ran to catch up.

Dewey wanted to run after them, ask them *why*. But that would only make it harder. She climbed the stairs as if her feet were made of lead and went back to the bedroom. Sure enough, a paper sack lay on the end of her bed. Even old Mrs. Kovack wouldn't have been that rude.

Her eyes blurred with tears, Dewey opened the sack and added a pair of pants, a clean shirt, two tightly rolled balls of socks. She carefully tucked the wooden box with Papa's things into a fold of the pants, then took Einstein the duck and *The Boy Mechanic* off the shelf over her bed, and put them on top. She kneeled down and reached under her bed. The Erector set was too heavy to carry. She'd have to come back for it later. After. She took the cigar box that held the special parts, her best finds, and wrapped it closed with a rubber band.

Dewey rolled the sack closed and picked it up, staring at the other, rumpled bed. Suze Gordon hadn't wanted her to come here. Dewey knew that. But she'd thought, in the last few months, that they'd gotten to be—Dewey shook her head. People don't change. Not really. Suze was going back to her old life, and that was all that mattered to her now. Dewey pulled the dark stone with the silver lettering out of her pocket and looked at it for a long moment. Then she tossed it onto the center of Suze's pillow.

"Shazam yourself, *Truck*," she said, and left the Gordons' apartment.

INTO THE WOODS

AFTER DINNER, SUZE left her parents at the
Lodge, talking with a bunch of people who were all going to the same party. Her mother had told her to pack as
soon as she got home, but since she'd be twelve tomorrow,
she could decide things like that for herself. Besides, she
wanted to get the last cigar box covered before they left
in the morning.

She worked for an hour and put the box aside to dry
before stacking it with the others. She tossed one of the
cut-up comics into the trash, its tattered pages flapping,
then fished it out again. That was a pretty good picture
of Clark Kent. She cut him out, got an idea, and leafed
through the rest of the pages in search of an image of
Superman the same size. She had to look through six
more comics before she found what she was looking for,
but it was perfect. She could hardly wait to tell Dewey.

Why wait? It was 8:30, not quite dark. Maybe she'd go over to Morganville and walk Dewey back. It was too good an idea to keep to herself for long, and Dewey could talk about machine parts for hours.

The road was mostly shadows, just enough light to see where she was walking, a few stars winking overhead in the deepening blue. She passed a group of boys, bats and mitts slung over their shoulders, heading home from the baseball field. She nodded to Jack and Tom. Tom nodded back.

Suze had only been to Morganville a couple of times, including the visit to the Kerrigans' house a year ago. She didn't really remember which one it had been, and all the barracks-like duplexes looked exactly alike. But Dewey's neighbors' door had been surrounded with cactus plants in clay pots. That ought to be easy enough to spot. She walked up and down two rows of houses before she found it. In her memory, there had been a lot more pots, but she shrugged and knocked on the glass window of the back door.

A tall blond man in khakis and an open cotton shirt answered. "Can I help you, kid?"

"Mr. Sandoval?"

"Nope," he said. "Ken Johnson."

"Oh. Sorry," Suze said. "I guess I got the wrong house." She looked around at the identical buildings.

"Nope," the man said again. "Right house. But it's

mine now." He gestured at a row of open cartons just inside the doorway. "The Sandovals moved back to Albuquerque last week. If you need a forwarding address, the housing office may have one."

"No, that's okay," Suze said. "Thanks." She turned away and shook her head. Dewey had said Mr. Sandoval had invited her to dinner. Enchiladas. Had Dewey lied? Dewey never lied. Suze wasn't sure she even knew *how* to lie. But she sure hadn't had dinner with the Sandovals.

Suze kicked a pebble across the rutted dirt in frustration. Everyone was acting strange these days. She hadn't seen much of her parents in months, and now that they were home, they just argued with each other. Mostly at night, after she'd gone to bed. But the walls were thin. They talked about the gadget and the war, and her mother's voice was often loud and angry.

But Daddy sounded excited again, the way he used to be in Berkeley when he could still talk about his lab and his lumps of metal melting and snapping. A lot of what he was saying was nuts, though—building rockets and sending men to the moon. Science fiction stuff. Maybe he had worked *too* hard?

Suze hoped they'd both be in a good mood in the car tomorrow. It was going to be a long trip. But Mom had said there would be a surprise too, for her birthday and—a *surprise*. Suze snapped her fingers. That had to be it. Dewey was off somewhere making a surprise present for her birthday.

Suze walked quickly back home, smiling to herself, making up a lie of her own, in case Dewey was already there, so Dewey wouldn't know that *she* knew about the Sandovals. She ran up the back stairs, muttering, ". . . to the PX after dinner, then I went by the dump to see if—" She opened the screen door and called out. "Dewey? I'm back." But there was no answer. Good. She could pretend she'd been here all along.

Suze hummed to herself, thinking about her birthday, wondering what Dewey was making, and went to the bedroom to pack. She unfolded the paper bag at the foot of her bed with a flick of her wrist and a sharp *snap* and plopped a pair of green socks into it, and a sleeveless cotton shirt. She'd pack her toothbrush in the morning. Maxwell? He was a kind of baby thing, but he'd make a good pillow in the car. She reached over to the shelf above her bed and stopped, her fingers deep in the bear's chocolate-colored plush.

A dark gray stone with silver lettering lay in the center of her pillow. Dewey's Shazam stone. The hair on the back of Suze's neck prickled. Then she smiled. It had to be a clue. A scavenger hunt?

She let go of Maxwell and looked around the room. Nothing seemed different at first, then she noticed that the little cedar box was missing from Dewey's shelf, and her duck was gone. Suze pulled up Dewey's bedspread and looked under the bed. No stacks of comics, because the boys had come back from Oregon when the air didn't catch fire, and reclaimed them. The big red Erector set box sat on its square of linoleum, but the cigar box of metal junk wasn't on top of it. Dewey always put her things away, always in the same place.

So Dewey hadn't hidden clues. Dewey had already packed. But how? Dewey didn't *know* yet.

Suze looked at the dark stone in her hand. It felt like a message, but now she had the uneasy feeling it might not be good news.

Where was Dewey? Suze walked from room to room and back, looking for—looking for what? She wasn't sure. But Dewey's red toothbrush wasn't in the holder in the bathroom, and when Suze opened the bottom dresser drawer, there were two gaps in the precise line of rolled-up socks.

Dewey had packed up and left. Where would she go? Suze lifted up a corner of the paper that lined the bottom of the drawer. Dewey's pass was still underneath, and no one got through the gate without their pass. So Dewey had to be somewhere inside the fence, and that meant—

The fence.

Lots of people went outside the fence without a pass.

Lots of kids, anyway. Jack and Charlie had a tree house somewhere outside and—

Suze looked at the rucked-up spread on Dewey's bed, which had concealed four huge piles of comics all last month. War comics. Boys' comics. If the boys knew Dewey well enough to trust her with their entire comic collection, had they also shown her their secret tree house?

She was halfway down the back stairs, the screen door banging shut behind her, before she thought of the flashlight. The light from windows was enough to walk on the roads, but it would be *dark* in the woods. She dashed back upstairs, grabbed the big silver Eveready from the counter, and took the steps down two at a time.

Jack and Charlie lived in an apartment two Sundts over. Suze crossed her fingers that their parents had gone to the same party as hers. She didn't want to have to explain anything to a grown-up this time of night. The apartments weren't marked or numbered, and she wasn't sure which one the boys lived in, but when she got to the bottom of the stairs, a voice said, "Whadda *you* want?"

Jack sat on the top step, whittling a stick with his pocketknife. In the light from their kitchen door, Suze could see a small pile of bright shavings at his feet.

"I need to ask you something," she said, a little out of breath. "Can I come up?"

Jack snorted, but motioned with his stick. Suze climbed

the stairs and leaned against the wall, three steps down from their porch.

"I need a favor," she said.

"What?"

"I need to go look in your tree house."

Jack looked startled, then shook his head, sneering. "No. No way. It's secret, or haven't you heard. No girls allowed."

"I've heard. But Dewey's been there, right?"

"Yeah," Jack said. "But Dewey's different. There's no way we're letting *you*—"

Charlie appeared in the doorway in a T-shirt and a pair of chinos. "Who're you talking to?" He held the unfinished wing of a model airplane in one hand.

Jack jerked a thumb in Suze's direction. "Her. She wants to see the tree house, but I told her—"

Charlie stepped onto the porch and looked down at Suze. "Tonight?"

She nodded. "It's important."

He laid the airplane wing down on the stair post and folded his arms across his chest. "Sell me."

"I can't find Dewey, and a bunch of her stuff is gone too. I think she might have run away."

"Why'd she leave? You push *her* in the mud too, Truck?" Jack said.

"No." Suze clenched her fists but kept her voice steady.

"I don't know why. Last time I saw her she was all excited about a project we were working on. But when I got home from dinner at the Lodge, she was gone."

Charlie frowned. "Why do you think she went to the tree house?"

"I don't know. 'Cause I can't think of any other secret hiding place." Suze looked at Charlie. "But I'm getting kinda worried. Will you tell me where it is?"

She watched him think about it, and when he shook his head, her heart sank.

"You'd never find it in the dark, even if I told you." He paused and looked at her. "But Dewey's a good kid, so I'll take you. Got a flashlight?"

Suze held it up.

"Okay then." He patted Jack on the shoulder. "You stay here, little brother. In case the folks come home early. Tell them I went down to the PX for Cokes with Nella and Alice."

"But—" Jack protested.

"Somebody's gotta stand watch. If Ma gets wind of this, she'll call out the army, make a federal case of it. I don't know what's going on, but I don't think Dewey wants that kind of fuss."

Jack glared at his brother, but nodded. "Okay. But if you're not back by midnight—"

"Then something really *is* wrong," Charlie said. "Sit tight till then." He gave Suze a two-finger salute. "Let's go."

They walked along the path at the front of the Sundts, the quiet part, away from the road. Suze was a big kid, but she felt small next to Charlie, who had grown over the summer and was close to six feet tall. Twenty yards from the last lighted windows she could barely see anything, and the moon was just a slivered crescent over the mountains to the west.

She clicked the switch on the flashlight, but Charlie put his hand over the lens. "Don't turn it on unless we have to. I know the way by heart, and I don't want to draw the MPs' attention." She turned it off.

Five minutes later they were at the fence and began walking single file. Suze was glad Charlie was wearing a white T-shirt. It made him easy to follow in the dark. After another five minutes he whispered, "Give me the light." She handed it to him and he turned it on, covering it with his hand, letting thin slats of light through his splayed fingers.

"Slide under," he said, shining the light on the hole under the fence. "On your butt's easiest. I'll pass the light when you're through."

Suze lay on her back on the cool ground. Pine needles poked through the thin cotton of her shirt, but she wiggled under the fence, feet first. She brushed the leaves and dirt off her legs and reached for the light. Charlie was big, but he wriggled quickly through the opening with the ease of long practice.

"How far is it?" Suze whispered as they stepped through the underbrush.

"Five minutes in daytime. Maybe ten now, 'cause we're moving slower."

Suze saw the ladder before anything else, its regular horizontal rungs distinct against the vertical jumble of the forest. "Wow," she whispered. "This is swell."

"Yeah," Charlie said. "You should see it in the day-time." He was whispering too, but she could hear the pride in his voice. "I'll go up first, see if she's there."

Suze shook her head. "No. Let me." She paused, then added, "Please?"

"Yeah, okay." He didn't sound happy about it, but he handed her the flashlight, which she tucked into the back of her shorts. The metal cylinder was cold on her skin. Suze climbed the ladder. When her head was level with the opening, she said, "Hey. Dewey?"

There was no reply.

Suze pulled herself up onto the smooth linoleum floor of the tree house and sat against one wall, pulling the flashlight out from her back and putting it in her lap. Her eyes had adjusted to the dark and she could see shapes— the angles of shelves and the windowpanes, a pile of blan-kets in a corner.

The blankets moved.

"Dewey?"

"What do *you* want?" Dewey said.

Suze was startled. She'd never heard Dewey that angry.
"I went to the Sandovals' house," she said. "They moved
back to Albuquerque last week."

Silence.

"I thought maybe you lied because you were doing
something secret for my birthday. But then I found your
Shazam stone on my pillow."

"Keep it." Dewey's voice was cold.

"But *why*?" Suze asked, and to her complete surprise,
she felt like she was going to cry.

"I thought we were friends. I was wrong," Dewey
said. Her tone didn't change.

Suze sat silent for a moment, and then said quietly,
"We are."

"Yeah, right," said Dewey. "That's why you didn't tell
me? That's why your mom just left a paper *sack* on my
bed?"

Suze rubbed her eyes with her knuckles. "I was going
to tell you after dinner. But you didn't come home."

"Home?" There was a long silence, then Dewey
sighed, a long, achy-sounding sigh. "Look, I knew it was
only for the duration. I did. But when I heard your mom
say it, I just couldn't stick around and watch."

"Watch what?" Now Suze was confused. She wished she could see Dewey's face, get some kind of clue.

"Watch you all drive away. Watch you leave, like everyone else." Dewey sighed again. "I figured I'd stay up here until you were gone, and then, I don't know. Turn myself in."

"Jeez Louise," Suze said. "It's only a two-day vacation."

"What?" It was Dewey's turn to sound startled.

Suze scooted over until she was a foot away from Dewey. "We're going on a vacation," she said slowly, as if she were talking to someone who didn't speak much English. "For my birthday. Daddy won't tell me where."

"Oh." Dewey was silent for a few seconds, then added, "Well, I hope you have a nice time."

"Goofus." Suze punched Dewey on the part of the blanket where she hoped her arm was. "You're coming too. *That's* what the sack was for."

"I am?"

"Sure. I asked, and Daddy said the whole family's going."

"Family?" Dewey made a funny sound in her throat but didn't say anything.

They sat in silence for a minute, then two.

"I did make you a birthday present," Dewey said finally. She dropped the blanket and reached into the paper sack, producing a small, lumpish package, about the size and shape of a box of Velveeta.

Suze turned on the flashlight. The package was wrapped in newspaper and tied with rough orange twine. She opened it. Inside was a metal contraption about five inches tall. It had four wire legs, each ending in a small cork, and a brass key poking out of its boxy top. Surrounding the key were six small metal discs with white letters:

SHAZAM

"Wow. It's . . . It's, well—" Suze turned the piece around in her hands. "It's nifty," she concluded. "What is it?"

"Just a gizmo," Dewey said. After the morning in July, she had stopped calling them gadgets. "The letters are typewriter keys. And watch." She reached over and held the gizmo steady with one hand while she wound the key with the other, three clinking winds around. When she let go, the figure began to move, bobbling and dancing on its cork feet, skittering across the linoleum like a tipsy windmill.

Suze started to giggle, then laugh, a full belly laugh. The gizmo was too funny, dancing across the floor of the tree house. After a few seconds, she heard Dewey chuckle too.

When it had finally wound down, Suze looked over at Dewey. "Thanks."

"You like it?"

"Yeah. A lot." She reached into her pocket. "I've got something for you too. If you want it back." She put the dark stone into Dewey's hand. "Shazam."

"Shazam," said Dewey, her fingers closing around the stone.

"Hey," Charlie yelled. "Are you okay up there? I'm getting bit up by bugs."

"Are you okay?" Suze asked.

"I guess so," Dewey said. "Kind of hungry. I didn't have any dinner, and the cookies in the tin up here were *really* stale."

"Maybe the PX is still open and you can get a hamburger on the way back." Suze moved to the door of the tree house. "We'll be right down," she yelled.

Dewey stood up. "What *are* your parents going to do when the war ends?"

Suze sighed. "I don't know. I figured we'd just go back to our old house. You could have your own room there."

"Really?"

"Sure. It's plenty big. Except now Daddy's talking about staying around here. I guess we'll find out when they tell us." She tucked the flashlight back into her pants. "It feels weird not to know."

"Yeah. It does," Dewey said. But she sounded kind of happy.

August 5-6

THE GREEN GLASS SEA

SUNDAY MORNING, August fifth. Suze's birthday. Mrs. Gordon was up early, making stacks of ham-and-cheese sandwiches that she wrapped in waxed paper. Dewey and Suze put their paper sacks onto the floor of the backseat of the big black Chevy and just before 11:00 they showed their passes to the guard at the East Gate and set off down the long twisting road that led from the mesa to the highway several thousand feet below. The temperature climbed as they descended.

Dewey and Suze sat in middle of the backseat, the road map spread out across their laps. Los Alamos wasn't on the map, of course, but a thin blue line trickled down from the mesa through Pojoaque. When it became a fatter red line, Highway 285, in Santa Fe, Dr. Gordon turned right and they headed south.

Dewey stared out the window. It was the first time

she'd been down from the Hill since she and Papa arrived. The land was flat and endless, bounded by craggy brown mountain canyons on one side and distant dusky blue ridges on the far horizons. Close up, everything that went by the window was brown. Brown dirt, brown fences, brown tumbleweeds, brown adobe houses. But all the distances were blue. Crystal blue, huge sky that covered everything for as far as she could see until the earth curved. Faraway slate blue, hazy blue mountains and mesas, ledges of blue land stretching away from the road, blurring into the sky at the edges. Blue land. She had never seen anything like that before.

Dr. Gordon had gotten gas coupons, and he filled up the tank in Albuquerque. They stopped for a late lunch on the banks of a trickle of river a few miles farther south, eating their sandwiches and drinking cold bottles of Orange NEHI in the shade of a piñon pine. The summer sun was bright and the air smelled like dust and resin.

"How much farther are we going?" Suze asked, putting the bottle cap into her pocket.

"Another three, maybe four hours. We'll spend the night in a little town called Carrizozo," Dr. Gordon said.

Dewey and Suze bent over the map and Suze's finger found Carrizozo. It was a very small dot, and other than being a place where two roads crossed, there didn't seem to be anything interesting nearby.

Suze looked puzzled. "Why are we going *there*?"

"We're not. It's just the closest place to spend the night, unless you want to sleep in the car. I certainly don't." He lit his pipe, leaned back against the tree, and closed his eyes, smiling mysteriously.

After Albuquerque, the land stayed very flat and the mountains stayed far away. There was nothing much to see. Beyond the asphalt the land was parched brown by the heat, and there were no trees, just stubby greasewood bushes and low grass, with an occasional spiky yucca or flat cactus.

Dewey's eyes closed and she slept, almost, just aware enough to hear the noise of the car wheels and the wind. When the car slowed and bumped over a set of railroad tracks, she opened her eyes again. They were in Carrizozo, and it was dusk. The distant blues had turned to purples and the sky was pale and looked as if it had been smeared with bright orange sherbet. Dr. Gordon pulled off onto the gravel of the Crossroads Motor Court.

They walked two blocks into town for dinner. Mrs. Gordon carried a large bundle wrapped in white paper. Carrizozo was not much more than the place where the north-south highway headed toward El Paso crossed the east-west road that led to Roswell. There was a bar called the White Sands, a Texaco station, and some scattered stores and houses between the railroad tracks and the one main street.

Through the blue-checked curtains of the café Dewey could see mountains to the east. "Are we going into the mountains in the morning?"

"Nope," said Dr. Gordon, spearing a piece of meat loaf. "The other direction."

Dewey frowned. She had spent most of the day looking at the map. There wasn't anything in the other direction. It was an almost perfectly blank place on the map. White Sands was a little bit west, but almost a hundred miles to the south. If they'd been going there, Dewey thought, it would have made more sense to stay in Alamogordo, near where—

"Oh—" Dewey said.

Mrs. Gordon smiled. "I thought you might figure it out. Of course, it isn't *on* the map. Not yet, anyway."

Dewey nodded. "Because it's secret."

"Exactly. And speaking of secrets . . ." Mrs. Gordon signaled to the waitress, then opened the bundle from the seat next to her and lifted out a pink bakery box. "Anyone for birthday cake?"

Suze grinned and opened the box. Inside was a cake with dark chocolate frosting and silver dragees that spelled out S U Z E.

"My favorite," she said. "Is it chocolate on the inside too?"

"Well, let's just see," said Dr. Gordon. "I think I can

handle cutting a cake. I've done a fair amount of preci-
sion work lately." He sliced a generous wedge out of the
cake and laid it next to the scoop of vanilla ice cream on
the plate the waitress had brought. "Yep. Chocolate in
and out." He pushed the plate across the table to Suze.

She took a bite and groaned with pleasure. "Real cake.
Thanks, Mom. And Daddy," she added.

Mrs. Gordon set a smaller, cloth-wrapped bundle
on the table. "Happy birthday, sweetie." Suze undid the
string tying the neck, and the cloth fell open to reveal a
small, round pot, about five inches across, tapering to a
narrower opening. The surface was a deep, shiny black,
like the shell of a beetle. Around the rim was a two-inch
border of gray lines that outlined the black, creating a
crisp geometric design.

"We got it at San Ildefonso on Saturday. Carmelita's
aunt made it," Mrs. Gordon said.

"Maria Martinez," said Suze, nodding. She was some
kind of famous potter. So famous that she'd made pots at
the World's Fair and had met Mrs. Roosevelt. Suze traced
the band of designs with a fingertip. "It's really nifty."

"I thought that since you've become such an artist
yourself, you might appreciate it." Mrs. Gordon smiled.
"And the other part of your present is that she'll give you
a lesson in making them, when we get back."

"Wow," Suze said.

"Can I see it?" Dewey asked.

Suze picked up the little pot and put it into Dewey's outstretched hands.

It was heavier than she thought it would be, and felt cool on her skin. It was the perfect shape for two cupped hands, smooth as glass. Dewey held it for a minute, then very gently put it down on the table. "What's it made out of?"

"Just clay," said Mrs. Gordon. "That's how powerful fire is. It can turn batter into cake, and mud into art. Amazing when you think about it."

They sat in contented silence, eating cake and looking at the little pot.

It was barely light when Mrs. Gordon woke them the next morning. Dr. Gordon had gotten two cups of coffee in paper cups from the café, and Cokes for the girls, even though it was breakfast. The air was still and already warm, and everything was very quiet.

They drove south, and then west for an hour, the rising sun making a long dark shadow in front of the car. For about a mile there was nothing on either side of the car but burnt, crumbly-looking rock. An old lava flow, Dr. Gordon said. *Malpais*. The bad country. Then the road wound up and down hills dotted with cactus and sagebrush silvery green against the brick-red dirt. There were no houses or landmarks, nothing much to see out the window or on the map. At an unmarked dirt road, Dr. Gordon turned left.

The car raised plumes of dust so thick that Dewey could see where they were going, but no longer where they'd been. Thin wire ran between wooden fence posts, separating the red dirt of the road from the pale pink-beige of the desert sand and the bright yellow flowers of spiky yucca plants.

After half an hour, they came to a gate with an MP. He seemed to be guarding more empty desert. They showed their passes and the Gordons' Los Alamos badges. The man nodded and waved the car through, then closed the gate behind them.

Dr. Gordon pulled the car off to the side of the road a mile later and turned off the engine. It ticked slowly in the hot, still air.

"Daddy? Where *are* we?" Suze asked after a minute.

They didn't seem to be anywhere. They had stopped in the middle of a flat, featureless desert, scattered with construction debris—pieces of wooden crates, lengths of wire and cable, flattened sheets of metal. Low mountains loomed to the east, and the far western horizon was broken by the soft shapes of another, distant range.

Dr. Gordon smiled. "This is Trinity," he said. "I thought you'd want to see it. Let's walk."

They started across the dirt. There were no plants, none at all, not even grass or yucca. Just reddish beige, sandy dirt. Every few yards there was a charred greasewood bush. Each bush was twisted at the same odd angle, like a little black skeleton that had been pushed aside by a big wind.

They kept walking. The skeletons disappeared, and then there was nothing at all. It was the emptiest place Dewey had ever seen.

After about five minutes, Dewey looked down and saw burned spots that looked like little animals, like a bird or a desert mouse had been stenciled black against the hard, flat ground. She looked over at Mrs. Gordon. Mrs. Gordon had stopped walking.

She stood a few yards back from the others, her lips pressed tight together, staring down at one of the black animal shapes. "Christ," she said. "What *have* we done?" She lit a Chesterfield and stood there for almost a minute, then looked up at Dr. Gordon. He walked back to her.

"Phil? Is this safe?" She looked around, holding her arms tight across her chest, as if she were cold, although the temperature was already in the eighties.

He nodded. "Ground zero's still pretty hot. But Oppie said the rest is okay, as long as we don't stay out too long. Ten minutes. We'll be fine."

Dewey wasn't sure what he was talking about. Maybe

sunburn. There wasn't any shade. There wasn't any anything. Mrs. Gordon nodded without smiling. A few minutes later Dewey saw her reach down and take Suze's hand, holding it tight.

They kept walking through the empty place.

And then, just ahead of them, the ground sloped gently downward into a huge green sea. Dewey took a few more steps and saw that it wasn't water. It was glass. Translucent jade-green glass, everywhere, coloring the bare, empty desert as far ahead as she could see. It wasn't smooth, like a Pyrex bowl, or sharp like a broken bottle, but more like a giant candle had dripped and splattered green wax everywhere.

Dr. Gordon reached down and broke off a piece about as big as his hand. It looked like a green, twisted root. He gave it to Suze.

"Happy birthday, kiddo," he said. "This is what I really wanted you to see. The boys call it Trinitite."

Suze turned the glass over and over in her hand. It was shiny on the top, with some little bubbles in places, like a piece of dark green peanut brittle. The bottom was pitted and rough and dirty where it had been lying in the sand. "Is it very old?" she asked.

He shook his head. "Very, very new. Three weeks today. It's the first new mineral created on this planet in millions of years." He sounded very proud.

Dewey counted back in her head. Today was August

sixth. Three weeks ago was when they got up early and saw the bright light. "The gadget made this?" she asked.

"Yes, it was so hot that it melted the ground. Over one hundred million degrees. Hotter than the sun itself. It fused seventy-five acres of this desert sand into glass."

"How is that going to win the war?" Dewey asked.

"It'll melt all the Japs," Suze said. "Right, Daddy?"

Mrs. Gordon winced. "Well, if cooler heads prevail," she said, "we'll never have to find out, will we, Philip?" She gave Dr. Gordon a look, then took a few steps away and stared out toward the mountains.

"You girls go on, take a walk around," he said, glancing back at his wife. "But when I call, you scamper back pronto, okay?"

Dewey and Suze both nodded and stepped out onto the green glass sea. The strange twisted surface crunched and crackled beneath their feet as if they were walking on braided ice. They walked in from the edge until all they could see was green: splattered at their feet, merging into solid color at the edges of their vision.

"I didn't know war stuff could make anything like this," Suze said. "It looks like kryptonite. Or what they'd build the Emerald City out of." Suze reached down and picked up a long, flat piece. "The Wicked Witch of the West's powerful magic glass." She held it out at arm's length. "It's a nifty green," she said. "It changes when you turn it in the light."

She watched the sun play on its surface for a minute, then pulled the bottom of her seersucker blouse out to make a pouch and dropped it in. "I'm going to take some home."

Dewey stood still, then turned slowly around, trying to take it all in. This place was more wonderful than anything she could have imagined. Sometimes, when Papa had talked about how beautiful math and science were, his voice had sounded just the way she felt now. She knelt down and put her hand flat on the green surface. "Papa helped make this," she whispered. She wasn't sure who she was talking to, but it felt right to say it out loud.

After a minute she stood up and walked carefully across the jade-colored ground, looking for one perfect piece to take back with her. The glassy surface was only about half an inch thick, and many of the pieces she picked up were so brittle they crumbled and cracked apart in her hands. One odd, rounded lump had a thin glass casing on the outside that shattered under her fingers like an eggshell, revealing a lump of plain dirt inside. She finally chose a flat piece about the size of her hand spread out.

Dewey was looking closely at a big patch infused with streaks of reddish brown when Dr. Gordon whistled. "Come on back. Now," he called.

She caught up with Suze, who had filled her shirttails with pieces of the green glass in all sizes and shapes, and was holding the fabric in both hands.

"It's a good thing you're here too," Suze said, gesturing with her head. "No one else would believe this."

Dewey didn't say anything, but put her hand on Suze's elbow. They walked back in silence, holding their fragile treasure. At the edge, Dewey stopped and turned around, trying to fold the image into her memory like a photograph. Then she stepped back onto the bare, scorched dirt.

When they got to the car, Dr. Gordon was squatting back on his heels, holding a black box with a round lens like a camera. "Good," he said, squinting up at them. "Now hand me each of the pieces you picked up, one by one."

Suze pulled a flat piece of pebbled glass out of her shirt pouch. When her father put it in front of the black box, a needle moved over a bit, and the box made a few clicking sounds. He put that piece down by his foot and reached for the next one. It was one of the round eggshell ones, and it made the needle go all the way over. The box clicked like a cicada.

He put it down by his other foot. "That one's too hot to take home," he said.

Suze pulled out her next piece. "This one's not so hot," she said, laying her hand flat on top of it.

Her mother patted Suze's shoulder. "It's not temperature, sweetie. It's radiation. That's a Geiger counter."

"Oh. Right." Suze handed the piece to her father.

"You've only got the one?" Dr. Gordon asked Dewey when Suze had emptied her shirttails.

She nodded. "Can I do it?" She pointed to the Geiger counter.

When he agreed, she held the glass in front of the black box. The needle didn't swing too far, or make too many clicks, and to her relief, he said, "That one's fine."

Dr. Gordon made Suze leave behind all the eggshell pieces and two with long reddish streaks. He wrapped the rest in newspaper and put them into a shoebox, padded with some more newspaper crumpled up, then put out his hand for Dewey's.

Dewey shook her head. "Can I just hold mine?" She didn't want it to get mixed up with Suze's.

After a glance at Mrs. Gordon, he nodded and tied the shoebox shut with string. He put it in the trunk. Then they took off their shoes and socks and brushed all the dust off.

"Shotgun," Suze said.

Her mother made a face. "All right. Because it's your birthday," she said. "And only back to Carrizozo." She got into the backseat with Dewey.

Suze nodded. She climbed into the front seat and kissed her father on the cheek. "Thanks, Daddy. I bet this is the best birthday party I'll ever have."

Dewey thought that was probably true. As they drove east, she watched the green shimmer in the desert fade away through the back window. When it had disappeared, Mrs. Gordon curled an arm around her shoulder, and she snuggled into it, closing her eyes and listening to the rhythmic rumble of the car wheels. The comforting weight of her talisman rested in her lap. One last present from Papa, a piece of the beautiful green glass sea.

———

Back on the paved road again, Suze said, "Can I turn on the radio?"

Dr. Gordon nodded. "Go ahead. I don't think you'll get anything way out here. Maybe El Paso, if you want Mexican music." He turned and looked over his shoulder. "But not too loud. I think your mother and Dewey are sleeping."

Suze nodded. "Any music would be good." The radio popped and crackled with muted static. She was almost to the end of the dial when a man's voice came through, soft but clear: ". . . onto the Japanese city of Hiroshima this morning . . ." She turned past it to more static and shook her head. "Nothing but war news," she said, clicking the radio off. "We can always get that later."

AUTHOR'S NOTE

IN THE MID-1940s, neither Los Alamos nor the site known as "Trinity" appeared on any maps. But they were—and are—very real places. And while Dewey and Suze and their families are fictional characters that I've placed into this historic setting, Dorothy McKibbin, Robert Oppenheimer, and Richard Feynman—among many others—were real people, working on what was known as "the Manhattan Project," the development of the atomic bomb.

In the sixty years since the end of World War Two, countless books have been written about them and their work. To find out more about the history of nuclear physics, the development of the bomb, or life on "the Hill," the following sources are a good place to start.

Broder, Bernice. *Tales of Los Alamos: Life on the Mesa 1943–1945.* Los Alamos Historical Society, 1997.

Conant, Jennet. *109 East Palace: Robert Oppenheimer and the Secret City of Los Alamos.* Simon & Schuster, 2005.

Critical Mass: America's Race to Build the Atomic Bomb. Corbis, 1995. (CD-ROM)

Fat Man and Little Boy. Paramount Pictures, 1989. (Film; DVD release: 2004)

Mason, Katrina. *Children of Los Alamos: An Oral History of the Town Where the Atomic Age Began.* Twayne Publishers, 1995.

Michnovicz, Toni, and Jon Michnovicz. *Los Alamos 1944–1947.* Images of America series, Arcadia Publishing, 2005.

Ottaviani, Jim et al. *Fallout. G.T. Labs, 2001.* (Graphic Novel)

Rhodes, Richard. *The Making of the Atomic Bomb.* Simon & Schuster, 1995.

ACKNOWLEDGMENTS

NO ONE WRITES a book in a vacuum. *The Green Glass Sea* was born at a meeting of my Cleveland writing group, the Cajun Sushi Hamsters, where Maureen McHugh, Mary Turzillo, and Geoff Landis (et al.) gave me comments and critiques on the short story that became its last chapter. My virtual sister, Delia Sherman, read draft after draft as the story turned slowly into a book, and gave me pep talks and sound advice every step of the way. My biological sister, Professor Mary Klages, was very patient on a road trip to New Mexico, driving two hundred miles out of the way so that I could visit the Trinity site in person. Erich Draeger of the University of Arizona very kindly sent me a sample of trinitite, my very own piece of the green glass sea. During the two years I was writing this novel, Karen Joy Fowler, Nalo Hopkinson, Pat Murphy, Eileen Gunn, Michael Swanwick, and Ursula Le Guin gave me comments, encouraging words, and bits of wisdom that continue to help me be a better writer. And I am indebted to dozens of eBay sellers who provided vintage period material—*LIFE* magazines, New Mexico postcards, out-of-print books—that helped bring the 1940s alive for me.

This book would not have been possible without the knowledge and invaluable assistance of the librarians and curators of the Los Alamos Historical Museum, the New Mexico State Library, the Tularosa Basin Historical Society in Alamogordo, and the Cleveland Public Library system. My agent, Michael Bourret helped it find a home, and my favorite redhead, my editor, Sharyn November, gave it the polished form it has today. I am forever grateful.

ELLEN KLAGES lives in San Francisco, California. Her story "Basement Magic" won the Nebula Award for Best Novelette in 2005. She is the coauthor of four children's science books written for the Exploratorium Museum, which was founded by Frank Oppenheimer. Her short fiction has appeared in *The Magazine of Fantasy & Science Fiction* and SCI FICTION, and has been on the final ballot for the Hugo and Spectrum Awards. She was also a finalist for the John W. Campbell Award, and is a graduate of the Clarion South writing workshop.

Ellen also serves on the Motherboard of the James Tiptree, Jr. Award (www.tiptree.org). When she's not writing fiction, she sells old toys on eBay and collects lead civilians.

She is currently working on the sequel to *The Green Glass Sea*, tentatively titled *White Sands, Red Menace*.

Her Web site is www.ellenklages.com.

Literature Circle Questions

Use these questions and the activities that follow to get more out of the experience of reading *The Green Glass Sea* by Ellen Klages.

1. At the beginning of the book, Dewey is sitting on the front steps of Mrs. Kovack's house in St. Louis. Who is she hoping will appear?

2. According to the book, what is a "fizzler"? A "stinker"?

3. What sort of terrain surrounds the Hill? Why is this important, given the work the scientists are doing there?

4. It is now 1944. Several months have passed since Dewey arrived from St. Louis. Based on what you read beginning in the chapter titled "Jumping Rope," how has she adjusted to life on the Hill?

5. On page 224, Suze and Dewey come home to find a man they know as "Oppie" sitting on the couch. Who is Oppie? What do the girls think is the reason he has come to the house?

6. Patriotism is very important to the residents of the Hill. Choose a character in the story and list two things he or she does that are patriotic. Then briefly explain why each action you have described is patriotic.

7. Suze tells Dewey that the rock with Shazam painted on it will give them secret powers, like wisdom or strength. If you had a Shazam rock, what secret power would you want it to give you, and why?

8. Using examples from the text, show how Dewey uses numbers and patterns to comfort herself during difficult situations. Why do you think numbers are so important to her?

9. On page 280, the residents of the Hill have learned that "the gadget" works. Dr. Gordon says, "The genie's out of the bottle, Terry. No way to put it back now." What do you think he means by this? Choose two characters from the story and briefly describe how each character reacts to the successful test of the gadget.

10. Late in the story, Dewey uses the word "kinship" to describe her relationship with Mrs. Gordon. Why do you think these two characters get along so well? Do you think Dewey considers any other adult besides her father a friend?

11. On page 290, Dewey thinks to herself, "People don't change." Do you agree with this statement? In your opinion, does Suze change during the story? Use evidence from the text to support your answer.

12. At the very end of the story, Dewey and the Gordons are driving through

the desert when they hear the beginning of a radio broadcast. Reread the portion of the broadcast printed in the book. Then make a prediction. What do you think the passengers in the car would have heard if Suze had not changed the station?

13. Reread the first few sentences of the first chapter and the first few sentences of the chapter beginning on page 41. What is different about the way the author is using language? Why do you think the author chose to do this?

14. On page 231, Mrs. Gordon says to Suze, "Dewey's a pretty private person, you know." In your opinion, is this an accurate description of Dewey? Support your answer using examples from the text.

15. Secrecy and rules are a part of life for the residents of the Hill. There are off-limits areas, no phones, and the government censors mail. In your own words, explain how you would feel if you were a resident of Los Alamos. Would these restrictions frustrate you or would you view them as a way to contribute to the war effort?

Note: These questions are keyed to Bloom's Taxonomy as follows: Knowledge: 1–3; Comprehension: 4–6; Application: 7–8; Analysis: 9–10; Synthesis: 11–12; Evaluation: 13–15.

Activities

1. Reread the letter on page 190 that Jimmy Kerrigan writes to Dewey from Washington, D.C. Then reread the passage on page 199 in which Dewey explains to Suze what the letter really says. Exchange letters with a classmate, using a code like the one Jimmy Kerrigan used. See if you can break your classmate's code. What information did you try to pass along in secret?

2. Using descriptions from the text, draw a map of the Hill. Include as many places as you can remember from the book. Possible locations to plot on your map might be the Tech PX, the dump, Morganville, and the tree house. Make sure to include a legend for your map. Then, compare your map with a classmate's map. How are the maps similar? How are they different?

3. Dewey and Suze like to read comic books. Some of their favorite characters are Wonder Woman, Captain Marvel, and Captain America. Use a blank sheet of paper and colored pencils or crayons to create your own comic book hero or heroine. Give your character a name. What special powers does he or she have?

Author Web Site

http://www.ellenklages.com